The acolytes had divided their forces, half hanging back to hold the torches and prevent her escape, the others moving in to engage her directly

One of them had already [...] dead. He screamed and flailed [...] flopping around like a rag with [...]

The woman stood in the mid[...] fiant, blood—whose he coul[...] her face and body. She held her [...] next acolyte to step within range.

But seeing their fallen fellow, the others were in no hurry. They could wait for weakness or inattention. Perhaps they would even wait for reinforcements to be attracted by the noise. With a little patience, they probably could have killed her easily enough, but they wanted to take her alive.

They wanted a living sacrifice.

Then Anok struck, and everything changed in a second . . .

*Coming soon, the continuing adventures
of Anok, Heretic of Stygia . . .*

HERETIC OF SET
THE VENOM OF LUXUR

And don't miss the Legends of Kern . . .

BLOOD OF WOLVES
CIMMERIAN RAGE
SONGS OF VICTORY

Millions of readers have enjoyed Robert E. Howard's stories about Conan. Twelve thousand years ago, after the sinking of Atlantis, there was an age undreamed of when shining kingdoms lay spread across the world. This was an age of magic, wars, and adventure, but above all this was an age of heroes! The Age of Conan series features the tales of other legendary heroes in Hyboria.

AGE OF CONAN™
HYBORIAN ADVENTURES

ANOK, HERETIC OF STYGIA
Volume I

SCION OF THE SERPENT

J. Steven York

ACE BOOKS, NEW YORK

THE BERKLEY PUBLISHING GROUP
Published by the Penguin Group
Penguin Group (USA) Inc.
375 Hudson Street, New York, New York 10014, USA
Penguin Group (Canada), 90 Eglinton Avenue East, Suite 700, Toronto, Ontario M4P 2Y3, Canada
(a division of Pearson Penguin Canada Inc.)
Penguin Books Ltd., 80 Strand, London WC2R 0RL, England
Penguin Group Ireland, 25 St. Stephen's Green, Dublin 2, Ireland (a division of Penguin Books Ltd.)
Penguin Group (Australia), 250 Camberwell Road, Camberwell, Victoria 3124, Australia
(a division of Pearson Australia Group Pty. Ltd.)
Penguin Books India Pvt. Ltd., 11 Community Centre, Panchsheel Park, New Delhi—110 017, India
Penguin Group (NZ), Cnr. Airborne and Rosedale Roads, Albany, Auckland 1310, New Zealand
(a division of Pearson New Zealand Ltd.)
Penguin Books (South Africa) (Pty.) Ltd., 24 Sturdee Avenue, Rosebank, Johannesburg 2196,
South Africa

Penguin Books Ltd., Registered Offices: 80 Strand, London WC2R 0RL, England

SCION OF THE SERPENT

An Ace Book / published by arrangement with Conan Properties International, LLC.

PRINTING HISTORY
Ace edition / October 2005

Copyright © 2005 by Conan Properties International, LLC.
Cover art by Justin Sweet.
Interior text design by Stacy Irwin.

ISBN: 0-441-01336-8

ACE
Ace Books are published by The Berkley Publishing Group,
a division of Penguin Group (USA) Inc.,
375 Hudson Street, New York, New York 10014.
ACE and the "A" design are trademarks belonging to Penguin Group (USA) Inc.

PRINTED IN THE UNITED STATES OF AMERICA

10 9 8 7 6 5 4 3 2 1

Acknowledgments

This trilogy is the most massive undertaking I've ever been involved with, and it could not have happened without the assistance, support, and occasionally the patience of many wonderful people.

First I'd like to thank my agent, Jodi Reamer, for her able support and council.

As always, my deepest thanks to my wife, Chris, whose huge assistance proved not merely to be invaluable, but indispensable. Also for her eternal understanding and support. I hope I'm up to returning the favor as she faces her own deadlines.

My thanks to all the great folks at Conan Properties International who have participated in this project and guided it through its various stages, including Fredrik Malmberg, Matt Forbeck (with special thanks to Matt for tolerating my frazzled nerves, all the way to the end), Theo Bergquist, and Jeff Conner.

Special thanks to Ginjer Buchanan at Ace, who has stood with me through five novels now.

My thanks to all the friends who have offered encouragement, support, advice and offered feedback through the project, including Sean Prescott, Dean Wesley Smith (yes, Dean, you told me so), Kristine Kathryn Rusch, Loren Coleman, Rose Prescott, the entire Sunday Lunch Gang, and my buds from the Sandbox who helped keep me sane when I ceased to have a life.

Thanks to my family, especially my father, Jim York, my mother, Martha York (secret sleuth of the Internet), and my brother Tim, who help keep me anchored through all the rough spots. Thanks to my kids, Shane and Lynette, for actually thinking something I do is cool.

Finally my gratitude to Justin Sweet for some of the most breathtaking covers I've ever seen.

And of course my appreciation to Robert E. Howard. Without him, we are nothing.

Though I have traveled across the known world, there is one land I have never visited, never been allowed to visit. Few civilized outsiders have ever penetrated the feared borders of ancient Stygia and lived to tell the tale. Of those that have, they speak of it only in whispers, if they speak at all.

Of all the lands of the Thurian continent, it is the one most shrouded in mystery and legend. All that is certain is that it was once a great power, holding dominion over much of the world, and this power faded, not by war or conquest, but by some calamity or corruption from within. This once-great and fertile land is now but a dusty shadow of its former glory.

Some say great evil was unleashed here, liberated from the sumptuous depths, or called down from the dark ether, or simply released from a forbidden box. Some say there was a war between gods here, where men chose sides, and all lost in the end. Some say that all evil in the world, and of that I have found a great deal, originated within its trackless deserts. They say it poisoned the lands to the south forever with dark magic, turned its own forests into deserts, and released countless demons and monsters that will trouble mankind until the end of time.

As for me, I cannot say. For how does one find truth in a land forged from evil and lies?

Yet, I believe this: The land of Stygia cannot be, as many say, a land that is entirely evil, for such a place would consume itself in a single night. For this black ember of a place to have smoldered so long, there must be good there as well, holding back evil from its final conflagration.

There must be love, courage, honor, loyalty, and all the noble inclinations of the heart.

And I wonder if, for all that, we would be better off if it were not so, and the foul place would simply burn, before it can produce more evil to plague the affairs of men.

— THE SIXTH SCROLL OF VAGOBIS, THE TRAVELER

PROLOGUE

The Port of Khemi, Stygia

THE BOY, SEKHEMAR, stood in the small garden, sandaled feet planted apart, sword clutched in his sweaty right hand, a shield of hammered brass over his left arm. His heart pounded, every sense alert, his eyes studying the dark corners behind the shrubberies and trees. He sniffed the air, smelled the night-blooming desert flowers. It seemed peaceful and serene, but he knew attack would come.

He heard a slight rustling in the high, decorative grass behind his right shoulder but gave no sign. He struggled to keep his breathing slow and even, but his body tensed, like a trap, waiting for the right sound to put him in motion.

There!

Time slowed.

He took one long step forward, then spun. He threw his shield up to intercept the sword, which he heard slicing air long before he saw it.

He planted both feet, bracing for the impact. The sword clanged against his shield, nearly knocking him backward. His attacker was a head taller than he, half again his weight.

The sword slid off his shield to the left, and as it did, he shifted his left arm, pushing against the sword to throw the attacker off-balance.

He jabbed with his sword, but the attacker jumped back, and the point of his sword only grazed the attacker's chest plate. He couldn't match his attacker's reach any more than he could his size or power. What he did have was speed and agility.

He prayed they would be enough.

The attacker replied, sword slicing through the air in front of him. The move was more defense than attack, and Sekhemar sensed a momentary weakness. He lunged forward with the shield, taking the offensive. He feigned a high jab with the sword, pulling back just as his adversary moved to counter.

Sekhemar used his shield to push the attacker's sword aside, making an opening. He swung the sword at his attacker's exposed right side. Once again, the man was too fast for him, stepping to one side, quickly recovering his stance. He made two quick slashes at Sekhemar, back and forth, pushing the boy back off the garden path.

Sekhemar stumbled in the loose gravel, lost his stance. The attacker pressed forward rapidly, his footwork sure and aggressive. The sword swung down toward Sekhemar's head, and he raised his sword defensively.

Blade clanged against blade, and pain seared down Sekhemar's arm as though he had been stuck by lightning, nearly causing him to lose the sword. His hand went numb from the impact, and he struggled for breath. Desperately, he swung the shield, striking his attacker's left arm edge on.

The blow landed solidly, but the man took advantage of the opening to grab the strap of the shield, using it to hold Sekhemar defenseless. He stood eye to eye with the man for a fraction of a second, close enough to smell his scented hair oil.

The man's sword jabbed, and Sekhemar was barely able to direct the point past his body using his own sword.

Sekhemar yanked his arm free of the shield, and it

clattered to the stone walkway. The attacker pressed his advantage.

Sekhemar turned and ran toward a wooden table covered with weapons. His eye fell on another sword, a twin to the one in his still-tingling right hand. He scooped it up in his left hand and turned to face his attacker just as the sword fell toward his head.

The boy bent his knees to absorb the impact, the swords crossed above his head. One sword met two, the twin blades slid across each other in response to the impact, until their guards locked together, stopping the blade with a loud report. Using both arms, he was better able to withstand the blow, and he straightened his legs suddenly, pushing the man back.

Sekhemar followed him onto the path. Disengaging the lower sword, held in his left hand, he pushed the attacker's sword away with the sword in his right.

Unused to the left-handed attack, the man was slow and clumsy in his defense. The sword struck chest armor hard enough to knock the wind from the man's lungs.

Sekhemar pressed again, slicing both swords back and forth in front of him. He changed his footing and attacked with the right arm again, using the left sword defensively. The sword struck the man's left shoulder solidly, causing him to gasp in pain.

The boy shifted his feet again, feinting right, striking left, then left again. *Shift.* Then right.

The blades danced in front of him, and the boy's confidence grew. His attacker was confused, off-balance. Sekhemar struck with his left sword at his attacker's sword arm, forcing an awkward defense that left the man totally open to the right sword, the point of which struck out, viper quick to find the man's throat.

It stopped there, poised just in front of the man's bobbing Adam's apple.

"No," said the man, "this is wrong."

Sekhemar smiled a twisted smile. "You say this only because you are losing."

"I say this is because it is wrong. Put down the sword, my son."

The boy's smile faded, and he drew back, lowering his swords. "I was winning."

The man pulled off the bronze helmet covering his curly black hair and sighed. "How many times have I told you, Sekhemar? This is not a contest. This is so you can *learn.*" He put the helmet and his own sword on the table. "You are too impatient. You have certain natural gifts that give you an advantage, yes. You are young and fast. You can fight with your left hand just as easily as your right, but this is only a trick, not true skill." He reached out, and Sekhemar handed him the swords, hilt first. He placed them on the table alongside the others.

As he unstrapped the leather practice armor that covered most of his upper body, Sekhemar's father turned back to study his son. "You must learn to fight with one sword in your right hand, like any other boy. *Then* you can fight with one sword in your left. When you have mastered that, then you can learn to fight with both. That is the way it should be done."

The boy stood as tall as he could, squaring his shoulders. "I was winning." His voice cracked as he said it.

His father smiled sadly and shook his head. "Your impatience will be your downfall, Sekhemar. You must learn to wait. All things have their appointed time."

"I was winning," he insisted.

Sekhemar's father laughed and reached out to tousle the boy's hair. "You were. But I am only an old merchant with some small skills, not a true warrior. Your tricks might work on me, but they would fail against a true warrior."

"You've said yourself that most men who wield a sword, even soldiers, are clumsy louts."

The expression on his father's face turned serious. "So most are, Sekhemar, but you must not let that fool you." He gestured toward a carved stone bench, near the high wall that separated the compound from the city beyond. "Sit with me."

Sekhemar sat down next to his father. As he did, he noticed that the difference in their height was not so great as when they were standing. He was growing by the day. Soon he would be as tall and broad as his father. Perhaps even taller.

"Son, you must understand the limitations of what small skills I have impressed upon you. In any group of fighting men, be they soldiers, pirates, or bandits, most are unskilled and unseasoned and man to man, easy pickings for a true warrior of skill. Few ever truly have those skills tested. They survive battles though luck, surprise, number, tactical advantage, and the aid of more seasoned warriors. When the fateful day comes that their mettle is challenged, few survive.

"If they do somehow survive that first real battle, they have learned enough to become at least a little dangerous, though even this only occasionally stays with them through the second day. But if they survive a third true test, then they are to be respected and feared. Few men live to fight a dozen battles. Not one in a hundred, or perhaps one in a thousand, but those men are almost unstoppable.

"Wars are lost by the unseasoned many, but they are won by the practiced few. Before such men, the likes of you or I would stand no chance."

"I am skilled, father. I am quick, and I grow stronger by the day."

"You are the son of a merchant, Sekhemar. A trader, not a warrior. Pray these skills I have given you are never tested. I teach you only so you can defend yourself. Perhaps, if I have taught you well, you have almost the skill of a soldier on the second day of battle. But you have never known true fear, never known true pain, never experienced the horrors of the battlefield. To steel yourself against those things is also part of the seasoning of a warrior.

"Do not fool yourself, Sekhemar. When you turned and ran from me, that was the correct course for such as we. Run if you can and let others fight the battles."

At these words, Sekhemar felt an unexpected anger

growing in his heart. He was no coward! "Did you run, father, when the bandits came for mother and me?"

Immediately Sekhemar regretted the words. He had been but a toddler when their trading caravan was set upon by bandits. He remembered the events of his mother's death only in flashes of sense memory, and his father had rarely spoken of it. Even now, long years later, it caused him great pain.

His father's head sagged, his hands clasped tightly together. He took a deep breath, and let it escape slowly through his barely parted lips. "You are old enough to know, Sekhemar, that there was little love between your mother and me. Ours was a marriage of convenience, a business alliance as much as a marriage. I would never otherwise have taken a bride of pure Stygian blood, even a noblewoman. Still, she was the mother of my son, and I would have died to save her, and you, that day. I did not run. I fought with all my heart and soul, but it was not enough."

"I'm sorry, father. I should never have mentioned it."

His father looked up at the full moon just climbing above the towers of the city, and Sekhemar was shocked to see that his eyes were wet.

"No, it is well past time we talked of this, Sekhemar. You should know what happened that day. I did not have the skills to save you both, and she pushed you into my arms. 'Save him,' she said to me. 'Leave me and save him.'" He nodded. "In that final moment, I knew your mother's true heart, and in that last moment, I came to love her. But then it was too late. She took up a sword from a fallen camel driver and covered our flight into the desert. I heard her cry as she fell. She called your name."

There was silence for a time. "I am sorry this pains you so, father. But don't you see? This is all the more reason I must be a skilled fighter."

His father turned and looked at him, his eyes moist, but filled with hot rage. "That is all the more reason you must avoid battle. I did not save you in the desert, your mother did not pay for your life with her blood, so that you could die fighting some fool in an alley.

"You've lived most of your life in this compound. You cannot truly appreciate what lies beyond this wall. Stygia is a cursed land, its soil and its people tainted by ancient evil. We have lived here because, for now, we must. But a day will come when we will return to my father's land of Aquilonia. Only then will you be safe. Only then may you live the quiet and happy life that you were meant to live, a life that I have denied myself and that I wish for you instead."

He stood and placed his hand on Sekhemar's shoulder. "Come. It's late, and the night grows chill. Leave the armor for the servants. But bring the blades."

Sekhemar gathered up the weapons from the table and followed his father through an arched doorway into his library. It had been daylight when they left the house to begin their practice, but before their return the servants had lit the ornate oil lamps that hung from the walls. At either end of the room, wooden shelves ran from floor to ceiling stacked with scrolls and parchments. In the center, a scribe's desk, with its own work lamp, stood, its surface covered with half-filled sheets of parchment, records of his father's trade business.

The far wall of the room was covered with weapons: swords, knives, axes, spears—some utilitarian, some ornate and exotic. The weapons were not just for display. They hung from metal hooks, easily taken down for use at a moment's notice, in the unlikely event the compound was ever attacked by bandits or invaders. Several sets of hooks hung empty, until Sekhemar replaced the weapons, one by one, in their rightful places.

Lastly, he replaced the practice swords that he and his father had been fighting with. Each practice blade, dull of edge and point, hung next to a deadly twin, having the same dimensions, heft, and balance, but honed to a razor edge. Sekhemar lingered for a moment, his fingers brushing over the scabbards holding the twins to his practice swords. He longed for the day he would be trusted to wear them.

He turned back to his father. "If this place troubles you so, why do we not leave? I would prefer anyplace where I could walk the streets freely and not be trapped behind these walls."

"I would wish no less for you, my son, but I have obligations that you cannot yet understand. Promises made by my father, and my father's father, and on back a dozen generations. I have hopes that those obligations will soon be met, that we can be free of this place, and that I will never need to pass this family burden to you. That is my fondest hope. But not today, and perhaps not tomorrow."

His father slid onto the stool in front of the desk, uncorked a clay bottle of ink, and picked up a quill. He repositioned the desk lamp to better illuminate the sheet of parchment in front of him, then set to work as he did every night.

Sekhemar turned away from his father so only the shadows could see the look of unhappiness on his face. The scrolls and maps in the room, tales told by his father and the household staff, what he could see of the city from the compound's protective towers, these were virtually all he knew of the world beyond the walls.

Often he had removed the map of Khemi from the shelf and imagined walking the streets beyond the walls of the compound, even beyond the walls of Akhet, the city within a city where non-Stygians such as his father and their servants were grudgingly allowed to live.

He imagined strolling the Great Marketplace, where vegetables and meat were sold side by side with mystic artifacts of ancient power. He imagined walking the narrow alleys that separated the great black palaces and temples of the inner city, where sunlight barely penetrated on the brightest of days. He even imagined visiting Odji, the waterfront slums where freed slaves and other Stygians of impure blood were allowed to live, where allegedly every pleasure and vice was available for the right price.

He longed to see all those things with his own eyes, and even more. To travel beyond the city to the great desert, or to the River Styx and the northern lands beyond Stygia, or to the vast Western Ocean just beyond the city's harbor. But for now, they were only dreams, and he wondered if the day would ever come when that would change.

In later days, he would come to curse this moment, as if his wish had somehow brought about everything that happened next.

From the front of the house, the door gong, a hanging cylinder of forged iron, sounded its long, deep note.

His father looked up from his desk. "Who would be calling this late? It's a full moon. Only a fool travels the streets on the night of the full moon." He put down the quill and capped his ink. He watched the doorway to the rest of the house expectantly.

After several minutes, the gaunt figure of Hericus, the chief house servant, appeared in the door, a scrap of folded parchment in his hand. "Master, there are visitors. They asked me to give you this."

He passed over the parchment, which Sekhemar's father promptly unfolded and read. His brow furrowed, but Sekhemar was sure he was hiding some stronger emotion.

"I have unexpected business to attend to. It is late. Retire to your room, and we will speak again in the morning." He glanced at the wall of weapons and seemed to hesitate. He reached for the deadlier counterpart to Sekhemar's first practice sword and took it down from the wall, passing it to Sekhemar. "You are old enough now to keep this in your room."

Then he hesitated only a moment more, before reaching for the twin of Sekhemar's second sword. He pressed it into his Sekhemar's hand without another word.

Sekhemar blinked in surprise, but his father was already hurrying to his business. "Go to your room. Good night, my son."

He climbed the curved stairs to the house's second floor, but paused halfway down the hallway leading to his room and looked at the swords he carried in his hands. On another day, under other circumstances, he would have been pleased, even honored, at this gift, but not tonight. He had no sense that his father had given him the weapons because he deserved them.

No, his father suspected their late-night visitors represented a threat, and Sekhemar intended to find out who those visitors were. He looked around carefully and, seeing none of the servants or guards in sight, slid behind a tapestry hanging from the west wall. He slid his fingers under the edge of a decorative column and pushed against a hidden metal bar until he heard a soft click. The false column swung out smoothly on cunningly designed hinges, and he slipped into the dark passageway beyond, pulling the column shut behind him.

The passage was dark. Engraved grooves ran along the walls, marked with carved patterns that could be identified by feel. They allowed him to navigate with complete confidence. He slid his finger down the wall until he found a groove carved in a spiral pattern, like the coils of a rope, and followed it into the darkness.

The house was one of the oldest in Akhet, only a little newer than some of the ancient castles and temples that towered in the center of Khemi. Built by the ancients, its design possessed both a sinister beauty and great cunning. A series of ducts in the walls and ceilings connected to open towers above and cool underground chambers dug below the foundations. During the day, the natural flow of air would bring cool air from below and exhaust hot air through the towers, keeping the house comfortable.

But just as importantly, a series of hidden doors, discovered by his father and later shown only to Sekhemar, allowed entry to those passages from many locations in the house. Through the same panels of marble grillwork that allowed passage of air, it was possible to spy on the common rooms without being observed. In addition, a bolted door in the chambers far below connected to the sewers, providing an emergency escape route from the compound.

The large central passage Sekhemar was traveling reached a junction with several smaller air shafts spreading out through the house. To avoid unintentionally making noise, he stashed his swords in a corner of the junction room, where he could easily find them again, even in darkness.

The air passage leading to the entry hall was much smaller than the central passage, enough so that Sekhemar had to travel on hands and knees. The floor was covered with a fine, powdery dust that felt like talc beneath his hands and bare knees.

In the darkness he felt the hard, dry touch of a house scorpion as it scrambled across his fingers. Other than remaining still for a moment until it passed, he ignored it. Though the species was fairly venomous, he was less sensitive to their poison, like most people of even mixed Stygian blood. In addition, he had been stung so many times climbing up the secret ways as a child, that he had developed some immunity.

There was occasional light here, shining up from the rooms below through the ornate air grills, casting strange patterns on the roof of the passage. He was careful to crawl around the grills, not only to avoid being seen, but because he questioned whether they would support even his boyish weight.

Finally, he reached the entry hall. He heard male voices below and crawled stealthily to the edge of the grill, where he lay on his chest. Careful not to push dust through the grill, he peered through the hand-sized openings to the room below.

Three men in dark silk robes stood talking with his father just inside the bolted door. He did not recognize the visitor's voices, and the robes had hoods that hid the men's faces from view. Through there were no raised voices or threatening gestures, even from his hiding place Sekhemar could feel the tension in the air. His father's expression was grave, his skin pallid in the lamplight.

In a way, he would have preferred yelling, as they spoke in low voices that made it impossible for him to pick out more than a word or two. He heard one of the hooded men, one who seemed to be the leader, say "Ibis," the name of an outland god rarely spoken of in Stygia, and "heretic," but not much more.

Then there was a moment of silence. Sekhemar thought that perhaps the conversation was over, the men would leave.

Nothing could have been farther from the truth.

The leader's hand moved, a small gesture. Only on later reflection would Sekhemar recognize it as a silent command to his companions. After that, things moved quickly.

One of the men stepped behind his father. He was very fast.

Before Sekhemar realized what was going on, before he could draw breath to shout a warning, the man's hand was over his father's mouth.

The leader produced an ornate dagger from under his robe, and plunged it into Sekhemar's father's chest with practiced skill. At once, his father's legs buckled, and the man holding him let him slide into a heap on the entry rug.

Sekhemar watched in helpless horror. He wanted to cry out in rage and grief, but his instincts kept him quiet, pushed his emotions into some dark side passage of his mind, distant from his pounding heart. He felt his body become as cold as the stone on which he lay.

At the edge of his field of vision, another figure entered the room, Hericus. He gasped at the sight of his fallen master, but that was all he had time for. One of the hooded men grabbed him from behind and twisted his neck violently until there was a snap of parting bone.

Hericus fell to the floor with a heavy thud.

One of the men rushed to the door, lifting the bolt and throwing it open.

Immediately, a dozen men, also hidden by robes, dashed into the house.

The leader spoke, his voice now distinct. "Search the house. Kill everyone you find, servants, slaves, wives, children, livestock, dogs—anything that lives. They all carry the taint of Ibis! Then fill your satchels with anything of value and return. Quickly!"

The men vanished, and he could hear them moving all around him, through the corridors below, up the stairs, into the rooms around him, and on the roof above. He heard some fighting, the clashing of blades and the breaking of household objects, and one by one he heard the cries of the household staff as they fell.

He counted them, recognizing some of the voices. The cook, the baker, one of the chambermaids, the gardener, the scribe. The two house guards fought the longest and hardest, but they were outnumbered and overwhelmed.

All too quickly, the sounds of combat and death were replaced by those of hurried looting and vandalism.

The commotion below covered the sounds of Sekhe-mar's movements as he scrambled through the hidden passages. He watched as his father's treasured scrolls were thrown on the floor and trod beneath heavy feet. The men grabbed the finest of the weapons from the study wall. One of them cried in triumph as he noticed a loose tapestry, pulling it back to uncover a hidden door. Unable to find the secret latch, the largest of the men set in upon it with a war axe, slamming it down again and again until the heavy wood splintered and cracked. They ripped the rest of the shattered door aside, exposing his father's cache of gold and trade-gems.

With hoots of delight, the men rushed in like hungry dogs to meat, sweeping the gleaming treasure into their bags. In moments, a lifetime's accumulation of wealth was gone.

He could hear the men moving back to the front of the house, and he followed, back to the grill over the entryway, where the leader and a lone underling stood waiting over his father's body.

The men assembled in front of their master.

He addressed them, "Are they all dead?"

The men shouted in the affirmative.

"Then burn this place! Let nothing remain!"

Again, the men fanned out, taking lamps from the wall and pouring the oil onto anything burnable: tapestries, rugs, pillows, furniture, scrolls. The house below dimmed as, one by one, the lamps were extinguished.

Sekhemar remained above the entry, staying as close as he could to his father. He chewed his lip until he could taste his own blood. It was all he could do to contain his rage. Again and again he pushed it off to that distant place, and each time more welled up to take its place.

Then, a miracle.

His father moved.

Just a twitch, a slight movement of his limbs, but he still lived!

Sekhemar was not the only one to notice the movement. As his father's foot had moved, the edge of his sandal had scraped slightly against stone, making a small, dry, sound.

The underling turned. "I heard something. Are you sure this one is dead?"

The leader made a sound of annoyance. "I've killed a hundred or more on the altar, fool. My blade is sure."

Sekhemar felt something crawl across his bare arm. *Scorpion!*

He quickly grabbed the creature by the tail, ignoring the pain as the stinger punctured his finger and began to pump its poison into his hand. He dropped the animal through a grate opening to the floor below, where it landed with a dry crack, and began to scamper across the rug.

The leader watched the scorpion as it scuttled toward a dark corner of the room. He reached out with his foot and crushed the thing, laughing contemptuously. "There's your noise. Even the scorpions serve Ibis in this house. Even the scorpions will pay the price."

The men were returning, filing out the front door burdened with pilfered loot.

The leader watched them pass. Then he took a last lamp from a table near the door. He stepped to the threshold and paused, looking back into the house.

"For Set," he said, and flung the lamp across the room, where it struck a hanging tapestry, which burst into flame.

Sekhemar could feel the heat, and black smoke began to roll up through every opening. If he stayed here, he would cook in minutes.

Sekhemar scrambled back to the central chamber, guided by touch, trying not to cough, lest his presence be detected by any straggler. He recovered his weapons, useless though they now seemed, and found his way to a vertical shaft leading down to the first level.

He climbed down a hidden ladder, no longer able to control his coughing. The heat coming up the shaft was almost unbearable. Reaching the bottom, he found a hidden latch, and a panel in the entry wall popped open, allowing him to clamber out on hands and knees, keeping low to stay under the layer of black smoke.

All around the room, the tapestries were burning, as was the edge of the very rug on which his father's upper body lay. Sekhemar reached his side, grabbed his arms, and tapping some hidden reserve of strength, pulled his father away from the spreading flames.

He lifted his father's head, looking down on his face, orange in the flickering light of the flames. His father's eyes fluttered, the lids parting slightly. "Sekhemar, my son. This day has come too soon."

"I will save you, father. I'll pull you outside."

Sekhemar started to move, but his father's hand grabbed the front of his tunic with surprising strength. "No! I am already dead. The blade only nicked my heart, because I have been told by healers that it is on the wrong side of my body, but I am still dead. I save my last breath for you, my son."

"No, father, it isn't true."

"Listen to me, Sekhemar. There is an amulet around my neck. Other than you, it is the only thing of value I can lay claim to. Take it. Care for it." He gasped, and coughed. Blood spattered around his lips. "Find your sister. She will know what to do with it."

He parted his father's robe and found a thick, base-metal medallion hanging there from a simple chain of iron. Sekhemar knew the medallion well, for his father had always worn it, as long as he could remember. But it was a plain and worthless-looking thing, and he had never understood its value. He still did not.

He looked back at his father's face. Could he be delirious? "This is nothing of value, father, and I have no sister."

His father's eyes glared at him, serious and alert. "I know of what I speak, Sekhemar. I sired her by another mother, before you were born. Find her—"

"But father, how will I find her?"

He looked back into his father's eyes, just in time to see the light fading from them.

He was gone.

A single sob shook Sekhemar's body, and he looked up at the room. The heat seared his bare skin, and his father's hair was beginning to smolder. "This will be your funeral pyre, father. It is all I can give you."

He gently lowered his father's head to the floor, then crawled back to the hidden door.

Inside the passage, he was momentarily shielded from the worst of the heat, but that would not last. Feeling his way through the darkness, he found another opening and pulled open the wooden lid sealing it.

A powerful stench emerged from the downward passage, its walls lined with still-cool stone. Iron rungs projected from the stone, forming a ladder down into the inky darkness. Sekhemar found them by touch and climbed down into the limitless darkness, into the safety of the sewers.

He had never taken this path, but his father had described it to him, and he was sure he could find the way. He would follow the sewers, under the compound wall, out into the city that he had thus far seen only from a distance.

Now he would have to find a way to survive there, on its streets, in its slums. He had nothing but his swords, the medallion, and the clothing on his back. Not a single coin of silver or crumb of bread.

But somehow he would survive.

He would find his unknown half sister and give her the medallion.

Then he would find those responsible for his father's death and make them all pay.

But first he had to survive, and that would start with the next rise of the sun . . .

1

The Port of Khemi, Stygia—six years later

THE MAN NOW known only as Anok Wati stood on the roof of the Paradise brothel, looking out across the great waterfront slum of Odji, which he called home. From here he could see the vast sweep of low buildings, most walled with mud and brick, many roofed only with awnings of hide, woven straw, or, for those who could afford it, colorful silks.

The streets were crowded with people as well as many animals: horses, goats, pigs, camels, dogs. Everywhere there were cats, perched on windowsills, walking the tops of walls, prowling the garbage-strewn alleys among the feasting pigs. They protected the city's granaries from rats and vermin.

In one place, a broad boulevard down the hill, he could see the crowds part and the animals turn aside, moving warily around a spot as though parted by some hidden force.

He knew there in the street, hidden from his view, lay one of the great constrictor snakes, warming itself on the sun-drenched cobblestone. The great serpents were sacred to the followers of Set, and it was forbidden, under penalty of death, to harm them. They roamed unmolested in the streets, feeding on whatever livestock or unwary humans fell within the grasp of their crushing coils. Fortunately, the number of the largest ones was small, and they were rarely ravenous enough to attack an adult human. Mainly their hunger was sated with goats, pigs, dogs, and the occasional sleeping child.

Beyond all this lay the dark, towering skyline of the inner city, surrounded by a huge wall of ancient stone turned black as coal by some unknown growth. Ornate spikes and carvings covered the parapets, and great guard towers, topped with statuary of demons and long-forgotten gods, stood to warn away attackers.

The walls were dwarfed by the towers within, great palaces and temples that rose up to meet the cloudless sky. They were tall only for the sake of intimidation and pride, some decorated with gold and carved marble, others hung with silks printed in magical and religious signs, and still others black as a kraken's ink even in the full light of day. Tallest of all, was the Great Temple of Set, whose central tower rose black and perfect above the entire city, topped with a carved head, half-snake, half-human, its golden eyes terrible to behold.

The city was a dark and fearful place, where only those of Stygian blood remained after dark, and during the day only servants and those on business were allowed. Guards checked all who entered, and only Stygians of noble blood were allowed to carry weapons.

Beyond the slums, nestled at the base of the walls of the inner city, he could see the much lower, white-marble walls of Akhet, the enclave of foreigners. Within those walls, merchants, diplomats, and other welcomed foreigners of status lived. Within the enclave he could see the houses, small palaces, and rooming houses where short-term visitors of wealth stayed.

The very sight of the place stung him, a persistent pain, like sand in his eye. Except on business, he had been back there only once in the last six years, to stand before the burned-out hulk of his former home. It still stood empty, its stone walls crumbling and bleached by the sun, its gardens turned to sand, its empty windows staring out like the eyes of a skull.

Yet that day, years earlier, only he had dared look on the ruined compound. Everyone else averted their eyes from the place as though, on that night six years before, it had simply ceased to exist.

Perhaps it had, just as Sekhemar, son of Brocas the trader, had ceased to exist that night.

He shifted his stance on the roof so he could look down at the entrance to the brothel. A group of sailors, loud, drunk, and probably fresh from the boat, were strolling in the front door, beckoned from within its walls. He could see only the arms waving at the men from every window, slender and graceful, skin of every color from ivory to deepest black, long nails painted, decorated with bracelets and rings.

Though he could not see them, he knew the women in the windows were brazenly naked, as was the custom among the whores of Stygia. He had bedded a few of them, but that was not the reason he knew them all by name. He was protector to this place, for which service he was given humble quarters in the building's basement, a place he and his friends called "the Nest."

Time, he thought, is like the shifting desert sands. Nothing can resist it, and it changes everything. That which it cannot wear away it simply covers. It had once swallowed up Sekhemar and Brocas. Now it threatened to swallow Anok Wati.

"Anok, it's been too long." The voice that addressed him was sweet as bells, but no longer the voice of the boyish girl who had found him living on the streets and brought him to this place. It was the full-blooded voice of a woman. As he watched her step off the ladder to join him on the roof, there was no longer any question of boyishness.

"It's barely been a cycle of the moon, Sheriti, but even that is too long without seeing your beauty."

Indeed, she was beautiful, and it was hard to imagine there was a time he hadn't noticed. Had she changed so much, or had he? He took her in, as though for the first time. Sheriti's hair was the color of honey and sunshine, her fair skin lightly browned by the unrelenting Stygian sun. Her movements were supple, graceful, her body lean but curved in the right places, curves accentuated by the colorful silks tied around her body. As she looked at him and smiled, her sapphire blue eyes twinkled with mischief. He knew that any of the sailors in the brothel below would have given a full voyage's pay for one night in this exotic flower's bed. And he knew, by her mother's oath, that such a thing would never happen.

She stepped up and put her hands softly on his shoulders. "How have you been, brother Raven?" Then, unable to restrain herself, she embraced him tightly.

He could smell the spicy, complex scent of galbanum in her hair, so different from the flowery fragrances preferred by the whores downstairs—and her mother.

She held the embrace for a moment, and he returned it, reluctant to show too much enthusiasm lest it be taken the wrong way. Or so he told himself. Her embrace was more sisterly than passionate, but there were times Anok wished it was more. *She's meant for better things than the likes of street trash like me.*

She gave him a peck on the cheek and stepped back to regard him. "Every time I see you, Anok, I wonder if it will be the last. Times are changing, and I don't know what's happening to us."

His skin burned where her lips had touched, and he was glad the dark complexion he had inherited from his Stygian mother would hide his blush.

"Step away, defiler! Lay not another hand on that innocent flesh!" The voice boomed, as a tall, dark figure vaulted the edge of the roof, sandaled feet landing heavily.

He was a gaunt giant of a man, no bigger in girth than Anok but two heads taller, his skin nearly dark as charcoal. In his hand, he carried a mighty bow of Stygian design, and a leather quiver of arrows was slug across his naked back. He wore only a loincloth and a klaft—headcloth—over his long, black, curls.

Anok reached down, putting a hand on the hilt of each of his two swords. His eyes narrowed, and he growled, "What business is it of yours, Kushite?"

The man's dangerous scowl dissolved into laughter. "I was talking to her, not you, fool!"

Anok returned his grin. "I'm glad you came, Teferi, old friend. I need you like I need my right arm."

He chuckled, and it rumbled like thunder. "Half as much as other men, you mean, 'two-bladed devil'?"

"It's just a saying, Teferi." He patted the hilts of his twin swords, "Coined by lesser fighters than me."

Teferi only laughed.

Sheriti stretched up to put a hand on Teferi's shoulder and pulled him down to place a kiss on his cheek. "Welcome, brother Raven. I was afraid you would already be gone."

Teferi frowned at her words. "I would be, if I could secure passage north from this cursed land, but all my efforts have failed me. The lords of Stygia frown upon us of low birth leaving this place for better lands. They know that if one could do it, all would, and who would tend their fields, clean their houses, and fight their wars? But on my father's tribe, I will find a way to leave here and see the world."

Anok nodded sympathetically. "Your misfortune is our gain, old friend."

Teferi's smile returned as he looked down at Sheriti. "What of you, sister? How is the Temple of Scribes treating you?"

She shrugged. "It's hard. Anok taught me so much, and without it I would never have been accepted as an apprentice. But at the temple, I feel like a simpleton."

Anok laughed. "I warned you, Sheriti. You were a fine student, but I'm a poor teacher. Though I have read and studied much on my own since, I never completed my education, and I was never meant to learn the skills of a scribe."

She squeezed his arm. "I was blessed to have any teacher at all in this place, Anok, much less one as good and patient as you. My mother always wished I would be able to leave this place for something better, but only you could make that hope real."

He smiled sadly. Sheriti's success was both his triumph and his heartbreak. Stygia was a land tightly bound by matters of class and blood. There were few ways that a commoner, much less one from Odji, could cross into the upper classes. But scribes were highly valued in Stygian society, and a scribe's skills were valued over any concerns about birth or upbringing.

Anok had passed to her all his skills in reading, writing, and numbers, and it had been enough for her to be accepted as an apprentice scribe. But it also took her away from the Ravens, and put her on a path that would hopefully leave them and Odji behind.

"Each time I call the Ravens," said Anok, "I fear it will be the last. The day you two fail to return is the day I know the time of the Ravens is truly done."

An uncomfortable moment of silence passed between them. Finally, it was Sheriti who spoke. "Have you heard from Dejal?"

Anok looked away, at the dark towers of the inner city. "Word was sent, but I've heard nothing. I haven't seen him since before the last time the Styx flooded its banks. I fear he's lost to his father's cursed cult, one more loss for which Set owes me."

"Be careful, Anok," said Teferi, his deep voice lowered nearly to a whisper, "in Stygia, even serpents have ears, and they're everywhere."

"I don't care who hears me, Teferi. If I have abandoned

my thirst for revenge against the cult as suicidal foolish-ness, then I can at least speak my mind. Let them do to me what they will."

They both looked at him silently, and he knew the ques-tion they wished to ask. But they knew, from long experi-ence, he would not tell them why he hated the cult so, or why he wanted vengeance. He'd never told any of them, even Sheriti, his true name, or how he'd found himself or-phaned and lost on the streets of Odji.

At first, he had withheld it for their safety. They had both helped him, saved his life really, in those early days, and he couldn't be sure whether those who killed his father were still looking for him. If they were, they might well kill him and anyone who knew him.

Later, when those concerns had passed, it seemed just as well to let the name of Sekhemar stay buried. His grief had never left him, and his anger against the Cult of Set re-mained eternal, but it no longer flowed as hot in his blood as it once had. Any plan for revenge would be suicide, and he kept telling himself that wasn't what his father would have wanted.

So why did it still trouble him so? Why did it still haunt his dreams and turn his stomach to knots every time he saw one of the robed priests of Set?

Sheriti reached out and brushed his forearm softly with her fingers. "Poor Anok. Is your anger at the cult, or at Dejal?"

"He's chosen his path, and it's no longer with us, Sher-iti. Yes, I'm angry at him. The day he told us he was joining his father's cult was the day the Ravens began to wither."

"You speak of me as though I'm dead, brother."

Shocked, Anok turned to see Dejal climbing the ladder.

Beneath the hood of Dejal's bloodred cult robes, his face was a white as chalk, the mark of a full-blooded white Stygian, and his eyes were black as onyx. He threw back the hood, revealing that his head was shaved, but for a black, braided ponytail that started at the crown of his head and hung to his thick neck. He stood on the edge of the roof and spread his hands. "As you can see, I'm right here."

Anok blinked. "Dejal" was all he could manage to say.

Dejal smiled, but the warmth there seemed false. "Here we are, brothers—and sister—the last of the true Ravens, together again, for one last time. All others are but pretenders and hangers-on, and once we are gone, there will be none."

Sheriti broke the uncomfortable silence that followed. She smiled, stepped forward, took his hands, and looked him over. "These robes look strange on you, brother. Still, it's good to see you."

But Anok's voice was still chilly as he spoke. "You speak of the Ravens as though they're already dead, Dejal. If that's so, why did you come?"

"For no other reason than to see old friends before my duties at the temple leave me no time." He stepped closer to Anok and stood before him, arms crossed. "The Ravens are part of our past now, Anok. Accept it. We're not children stealing on the streets anymore. Sheriti and Teferi have turned onto their own paths not because of me but because we've outgrown such pursuits."

"I never approved of stealing, Dejal, except to survive."

He laughed. "Nobel Anok. If not for your scruples, the Ravens would all be a good deal richer now, and perhaps we could be something more than a gang of street children whose small days of glory are past them. But to follow that path to adulthood we would have to learn to steal without hesitation, act without conscience, and kill without mercy, something *you* could never do."

"Leave then, Dejal. We don't need you."

Dejal tilted his head and raised his open palms toward Anok. "You misunderstand me, brother. I come only out of concern, for you most of all. The rest of us have found some pursuit in life beyond the Ravens. You must as well, Anok." He extended his right hand. "Until then, let us share one last adventure together, like old times."

Anok stared at the hand and considered. Dejal had saved his life, too. Not once, but many times. Though their relationship was often troubled, there had been a time when they were as close as any two real brothers could be. He finally took Dejal's hand in his own and shook it. "For old times, then."

He turned to Teferi. "Did you speak with Rami?"

Dejal wrinkled his nose. "You asked that cowardly little weasel to help? Recall what I said about hangers-on."

Anok frowned at him. "Rami has his talents. He may not be dependable, but he's occasionally useful, and his face is less well known on the streets of Odji than any of ours. I thought it might be useful to send him ahead as a scout."

Teferi nodded. "He should already be at the Great Marketplace, looking for our pirates."

Sheriti frowned at Anok. "Pirates? Then we have a job? As it's Festival night, I'd thought you'd invited us back to party the night through, for old times."

Anok considered the sun's position in the sky; "There's still time for both, sister. We've been hired to meet with a crew of pirates just landed and negotiate the purchase of an ancient artifact, some object of supposed mystic power, which I doubt."

Sheriti looked suspicious. "Hired by whom?"

"I don't know. I was contacted by an intermediary, but,"—he reached into his pouch and came out with his hand full—"there was a down payment." He tossed each of them a shiny red bauble. They all examined them.

"Blood rubies," said Teferi, clearly impressed.

"Cut," said Anok, "and perfect." He patted the pouch, which rattled. "There are more to purchase our prize, and if I can keep the price down, the rest are ours, plus a bounty when the object is delivered."

"It seems," said Sheriti, "a high price for such a simple task."

Anok grinned. "You know, lovely sister, that such things are *never* as simple as they sound. We'll earn our trinkets this day, I'll wager. And then we'll come back here to the Nest and party away the night."

Sheriti grinned back. Even now, danger was like candy to them. "Well then," she said, "to the Great Marketplace."

2

AS ANOK AND his companions made their way to the Great Marketplace, they were like fish swimming upstream—the flow of traffic against them—burdened with supplies to see them through the long night to come. There was a festive yet nervous energy in the air, smiles and laughter all around. There was also a stink of fear, noticeable even under the usual smells of the street, of cooking food, strange spices, woodsmoke, and the ever-present stench of livestock.

The sun sank low in the western sky, casting long shadows inland from the sea and placing many of the narrow streets of Odji in premature twilight. Nervous, almost giddy, anticipation of Festival night gripped the slums. Already many of the shops were shuttered, and the taverns were doing a brisk business, as a constant stream of men emerged loaded down with wax-sealed jars of beer and bottles of wine.

Women and children carried home such edible delicacies as their humble lot could afford: baskets of dates, jars of olives, fragrant flatbreads fresh from the ovens, salted fish, roasted ducks, or greasy tied bags containing seasoned and fried silkworms, a prized luxury.

Others worked at rounding up animals, ducks, geese, goats, donkeys, even camels and horses, and locking them indoors. The streets would be empty tonight but for the serpents, the followers of Set, and those unfortunates who, having no place else to go, would be their sacrificial victims.

In order to remain inconspicuous, the Ravens had spread themselves through the crowd, with Anok bringing up the rear and keeping an eye out for the others. He was surprised when, halfway to the market, Dejal fell back to join him. "Good Festival to you, brother Anok."

At the sight of his robes, the people fell back, and the usual jostling of the crowd stopped. Anok saw, with some disgust, that Dejal seemed to enjoy the fear his station generated. "Couldn't you have left your robes back at the Nest, just this once?"

Dejal pushed back the hood and grinned at Anok. "This is who I am now, old friend. See how they fear me? *That* is power and only the barest taste of what awaits me on my new path."

Anok snorted. "What is power? Can you eat it? Can you drink it? Can you spend it in the market? Will it warm your bed at night? Power is the narcotic of fools, Dejal."

Dejal only laughed. "Spoken by one who has none. But that could change, Anok. My father has influence, and you would have my recommendation. Despite your mixed Stygian blood, there might be a place for you at the temple."

It was Anok's turn to laugh. He waved at the others, walking a few yards ahead. "And them as well?"

"They do not have Stygian blood in their veins, Anok. The true blood of Set. I say this to you only, out of friendship."

"Friendship crosses all lines, including those of blood. He who fights at my side stays at my side. As did you once, Dejal. What happened to you? You came to the streets of Odji seeking to rebel against the inner city and your father. Now you walk in his footsteps."

He smiled knowingly. "As far as they will take me, but my father has wasted opportunities, and true power has always eluded him. I'll go farther in the temple than he ever did, and I could take you with me."

Anok quickened his pace to distance himself from Dejal. "Then, 'old friend,' walk your new path, but walk it alone."

As he pulled away from Dejal, he noticed Sheriti looking back at him. She waited and took his arm, leaning her cheek against his shoulder. She glanced up at him with a smile. "Blending in," was all she said.

He was still angry at Dejal. Sheriti made him feel better, and he didn't want to feel better.

"I hate to see my brother Ravens like this," she finally said.

"Dejal is right. The Ravens have all but ceased to exist. You've seen it. Teferi has seen it. I should have, too."

"We will always be Ravens, Anok, even if we don't roam the streets in search of adventure together. We'll always be what our time together has made us."

He said nothing. His gaze and attention were well ahead of them, on a familiar face moving toward them, bobbing in and out of the crowd.

Rami was a Shemite, a small-framed example of those famous horsemen. Dark-skinned, and hook-nosed, his blue-black hair fell about his shoulders in greasy curls. His large eyes were shifty, and his perpetual half smile never seemed sincere on the best of days. He brushed past Teferi, acknowledging him only with a slight glance and a nod, and moved casually toward Anok and Sheriti.

Anok couldn't help but smile slightly as Teferi, out of long habit, checked his purse, patting it to make sure it was still tied to his belt and the contents were intact. Rami's skills as a pickpocket were legendary, and he was not above using them on his friends, if only as a prank.

Rami fell in next to them without making eye contact, pretending his proximity to them was merely a coincidence.

Anok didn't look at Rami either as he spoke. "Our pirates?"

"Fresh off the boat, eager for food, drink, and anything female. Most of them anyway."

"Most of them?"

"There's a barbarian among them."

Teferi frowned. "This isn't the start of another barbarian joke, is it?" Though he had lived his entire life in cities, Teferi still took barbarian jokes personally, and Rami knew it.

"A barbarian *woman*. Probably from a northern land somewhere. Maybe even the same place as that barbarian king in Aquilonia one hears tales of—Kutaman."

"It's *Conan*," corrected Anok, "King Conan."

"That's the one. Anyway, she's tall, dark hair, dusky skin, and a sword as long as I am tall. By the way she carries herself, she knows how to use it, too. I'd watch out for her."

Anok glanced at Sheriti and nodded.

Rami stroked the little tuft of beard on his chin. "They're at the Duck and Olive Tavern. About a dozen. A mixed lot, Argosseans and Zingarans. The captain's Argossean, and bears watching. The rest are a motley bunch. Maybe not much good in a fight, but surly and unpredictable. They won't need a reason to cause trouble; they might do it just for fun."

Anok nodded again. "Then we make it quick. In and out before they get jumpy. Go tell the others."

Rami glanced at him, his grin twisting slightly. "You have something for me?"

Anok grunted in annoyance. He hated to trade payments right out in the open. He reached into his tunic, pulled one gem from the bag hidden there, and pressed it quickly into Rami's palm. "Inspect it later," he hissed quietly. "Now tell the others."

Rami glanced back at Dejal and curled his lip in disgust. There was no love lost between the two. Never had been. "Him, too?"

"Him, too."

Rami pocketed the gem and moved off to pass the word to Teferi.

But Rami had barely vanished into the crowd when a trio of men stepped into Anok's path, an older, bearded man, about Anok's height, with long gray hair and dusky skin, and a pair of identical twins, dark-skinned, muscular, bald, half-naked, and towering over their companion. The twins each wore a greatsword in a scabbard slug over his back, and they both looked fully capable of using the massive weapon one-handed.

The twin giants were new, but Anok knew their elder companion too well and greeted him without enthusiasm. "Lord Wosret, good Festival to you." Wosret wasn't a true lord, or anything like it. He was a seasoned street rat with at least a little Stygian blood in his varied ancestry, and, for many years, the leader of the powerful White Scorpion gang.

As with all the gang lords in Odji, Anok and the Ravens had worked for the man many times in many capacities, as runners, messengers, negotiators, collection agents, guards, and laborers to name a few. Anok had no love of the gangs, but they were a fact of life in Odji, and among the most reliable employers of the Ravens' services over the years. Only recently had the street lords failed to call on them, another contributing factor to the decline of the Ravens.

Anok had a feeling he knew why Wosret had stopped him, and he didn't want to discuss the matter, especially right now. "I'd like to talk, but I've got other pressing business before sunset." He started to slip past them, but Wosret put a surprisingly powerful hand against his chest and gently pushed him back.

"Your old friend and benefactor asks a minute of your time, and you refuse him? I thought you were better than that, Anok Wati."

Anok frowned but held his tongue. There was no way he

was escaping the confrontation, and he hoped the others had noticed his plight and were waiting for him.

"I made you an offer recently, Anok. Have you considered it?"

He tried to answer as diplomatically as possible. "It would be an honor, of course, to join the White Scorpions, my lord. But I've always prided myself on my neutrality in gang affairs. If I were to join any gang, it would be yours, but I don't . . ."

Wosret's expression turned to anger, and his dark eyes flashed. "It's the River Rats, isn't it? They've been trying to edge into my territories lately, and they'd love a chance to wrest the Paradise from me. What did they offer you?"

"Nothing, lord. I haven't even talked—"

"Lies! One of my minions saw you talking with Nakhti down near the poisoners' district last week!"

Anok groaned inwardly. He had indeed had a chance encounter with Nakhti, leader of the River Rats, much like the one he was currently entangled in. "Nakhti approached me, it's true, and I refused him without even hearing his terms."

Wosret laughed. "You look remarkably unbruised for someone who rejected Lord Nakhti so harshly. Did you tell him you'd think about his offer? Perhaps you play one of us against the other to obtain better terms of employment." He waved his hand, and the two giants stepped forward, looming over Anok. "Let me make it simple for you, Anok. Accept Nakhti's terms, whatever they are, and you'll never live to collect. I have the power to protect you from any threats he's made. He can't make the same claim."

"You're quite powerful, lord, but I don't wish to join any gang."

He laughed again, louder this time. "You speak as though you have a choice. We've no interest in most of your little band, the Kushite, or the whore's daughter. We need true men of skill and breeding, not women or inferior stock. Dejal, yes, but he's pledged to the Temple of Set and beyond our reach. But you, Anok. You have skills, talents, and great potential. Like me, you have Stygian blood in your veins. One day, I could even see you becoming one of my chief lieutenants. Or even my chosen successor."

"I'm flattered, Lord Wosret, and I will think on it. But the sun is low, and I've business to attend to."

Rami appeared out of the crowed and casually stepped in next to Anok. He cheerfully greeted Wosret, who grunted without taking his eyes off Anok. Rami turned to Anok. "Hey Anok, we're late—for that"—he hesitated, thinking—"that thing. You know, that thing we're late to."

Wosret continued to ignore Rami. "You will join me, Anok. You'll join me, or you'll die."

"I'll join you," said Rami. "Sign me up."

Wosret turned quickly and walked away, his giant body-guards moving out ahead of him to push aside the crowd.

"I'll join you," said Rami, shouting after them, but he was completely ignored.

He sighed, and his shoulders slumped. "If the Ravens break up, I'm just going to have to go back to picking pockets full-time."

"When did you ever stop?" Anok looked around. "Are the others waiting?"

Rami nodded. "I saw what happened and got the word to everybody. They're around here somewhere."

"Then let's get moving. We've lost valuable time."

The crowd thinned rapidly as they entered the Great Marketplace. Most of the stalls were closed or closing, merchants loading their remaining wares onto carts, rolling up their colorful tents and awnings, and preparing to leave. What little business was still being done took place mostly around the edge of the open market, where permanent businesses, mostly taverns, bakeries, smiths, and merchants in luxury goods kept their shops.

The Duck and Olive was located on the far side of the market, and with the sun as low as it was, each step farther away from the Nest made Anok more uneasy. To make matters worse, a bank of yellow, sulfurous-looking clouds was rolling in from the ocean, and bringing with it the first traces of fog. It was as though the night was rushing up to meet them.

The marketplace was rapidly emptying, and there was little point trying to disguise their movements, so the Ravens closed ranks and walked the rest of the way to the tavern as a group. Anok heard a crunching sound, and looked over to see Rami munching from a clay cup filled with fried silkworms. He frowned. "Did you pay for those?"

Rami looked indignant. "Yes!" After a moment. "Maybe." Then, "No! But he wasn't going to sell any more this late in the day anyhow."

Anok looked over his shoulder for any sign of pursuit, and seeing none, grunted. "It would be fine if you lost us our prize because you had thieved something to satisfy your belly."

Rami shrugged and held out the cup. "You want some?"

Anok pushed the cup away. "We're here."

The Duck and Olive was a small tavern at the edge of the market. The old glyphs for "duck" and "olive" were carved into the masonry above the open door, but the green-painted shutters were always closed and locked tight. A wiry, bald-headed man stood at the door, arms crossed over his chest, a mixture of anger and alarm on his face. Anok would have bet his father's amulet that the fellow wasn't a pirate. He would have been surprised if the man had ever been to the waterfront. "We're closed," he said.

But Anok heard male voices and laughter from inside. "Sounds like you still have customers."

"Pirates, fresh off the boat. The fools won't leave, and I have to get home to my wife and children. They either don't know that it's Festival, or don't care."

Anok grinned slightly. "We'll get them out for you—for two pieces of gold each."

"That's robbery!"

"If it was robbery, you'd know. We're the Ravens. You've heard of us."

The man's eyes widened slightly with recognition. "I may have." He looked nervously over his shoulder at the men sitting at the bar inside, then back at Anok. "Don't break anything."

"Two pieces of gold each—in advance."

The man grumbled and dug into a purse hidden behind his leather apron. "Robbery. I was right the first time."

Anok took the coins and passed them to Sheriti for distribution to the others. Then he leaned his head inside the door. Most of the pirates were at the bar. A barrel of a man stood on the bar, pierced silver coins braided into his long hair, one ring-encrusted hand holding down a wild salt-and-pepper beard while he poured a jar of beer down his throat. Anok took him for the captain.

The barbarian woman Rami had mentioned sat alone at a table, feet up, leaning back on her bench with her shoulders against the wall, a bottle of wine clutched in her hand. Anok had somehow expected a brutish hag, but she was quite striking, long dark hair pulled back in a ponytail, a leather skirt and top showing much of her dusky skin and amply curved body. Her limbs, especially her arms, were lean and well muscled. Her dark eyes twinkled in the gloom of the shuttered tavern, and her angular features were hard but attractive. Though she made a great show of relaxation, she was alert and aware. Anok became aware that she was looking at him, and her free hand slid casually over to rest on the hilt of her oversized cutlass.

"Hey!" Anok turned his attention back to the captain. "I'm looking for Captain Danyo, of the *Seahawk.*"

The man on the bar looked at him blankly, dropped his now-empty jar to shatter on the floor, and reached for his own cutlass. "Who seeks him?"

"Anok Wati and his Ravens."

"I don't know the name."

"You wouldn't. We were hired to purchase an item from you and told you'd be expecting us."

The tavern keeper glared at Anok, seeing he'd been

taken, but said nothing. Doubtless it would be worth the gold to him if they'd simply leave.

The captain let his half-drawn cutlass slide back into the scabbard. "Aye, we have a thing for sale. A rare thing of great value."

"We'll see," said Anok.

"Come inside. Drink with us. We'll talk."

"I prefer to talk outside."

"Inside."

Anok shrugged and held up a crimson bauble. "If you've no need of these blood rubies, then we'll be on our way. It's getting late."

The captain's eyes widened slightly, and he licked his lips like a hungry dog spying meat. "Lads," he said, "and lass. Let's outside with us."

Anok and his fellow Ravens stepped back from the door as the pirates emerged into the twilight gloom. Already the fog was thick enough they couldn't see the far side of the deserted market.

The tavern keeper watched the last pirate emerge, then slipped in the door and slammed it behind him. The sound of a heavy bolt falling could be heard. The last pirate turned and pounded on the now-locked door. "Hey!"

Captain Danyo gestured him away from the door. "There are other taverns."

Anok nodded. "There are some open all night, but you'll have a hard time finding one that will open the door this late on Festival night."

Danyo snorted. "Festival! The barkeep tried to spook us with his wild stories of Festival. Old woman's tales! We're not afraid."

Teferi stepped in close behind Anok's right shoulder, bow in hand. "You should be. How can you be pirates on this coast and not know?"

Danyo laughed. "Giant snakes. Sacrificial altars. By morning, they say, the sewers run red with blood, and the plume of scarlet can be seen well out into the open sea. Foolishness!"

"Nobody stays on the streets at night and lives, friend," Anok jerked his thumb over his shoulder at Dejal's red robes, "except for his lot."

Dejal flashed an evil-looking grin, and Anok had to hide his amusement. For a moment, it was as though his mischievous childhood companion were back.

"Once we've made this transaction, we'll help you find a safe place to wait out the night. No additional charge."

The captain looked skeptical. "You said something about rubies."

"You said something about an item." Anok hadn't been told what the item was, only that it was small, mystical, and of great value, but only to one who knew what it was and how to use it.

The captain reached under his chest plate and brought out a folded piece of oilcloth about the size of his spread hand. He unwrapped it, and Anok saw the glitter of gold. The object was flat and inscribed with ornate designs, but Anok couldn't see it well from where he was.

He reached under his tunic and pulled out the bag of gems. It was considerably less full than when they'd begun their journey. While they'd been walking, he'd transferred many of the gems to several hidden pockets inside his clothing, giving him more room to negotiate the price. He rattled the bag. "Twenty blood rubies, each perfect and big as the one you saw. Each worth a hundred gold pieces."

The pirate captain's eyes narrowed, and he rubbed his beard. "Lost two good men in gaining this trinket." He pretended to consider for a minute, but Anok knew he already had a figure in mind. "I couldn't take less than fifty."

Men died getting this small thing? Anok didn't like the sound of that, or what it said about who else might be looking for it. The sooner he handed it over to their mysterious employer, the better. But to do that, he'd have to close the deal.

Anok studied the captain's face carefully in the gloom. He was about to take a calculated chance that could well cause offense. But there was always a great deal of

turnover in pirate crews, and often enough hands were con-
veniently "lost" when they had overstayed their welcome.
"A high price, even for two men, captain. Well then, the
question is, did you like them—and did they eat much?"

The captain's bushy eyebrows went up, and his expression was grave. Then his belly convulsed, and a chuckled
escaped his lips, turning into laughter. "Well, I suppose
you have me there, Anok of the Ravens. I don't miss them
that much. But I will have to seek replacements before
leaving port. Cost of doing business, eh?"

"Twenty-five," he returned.

"I've come a long way just to be insulted. Forty, and
don't test me farther than that."

"Thirty, and that's my final offer. That's all I've got in
fact." It was a lie of course, but the negotiating was eating
all his profit. He reached into two of the hidden pockets,
removing five gems from each, and dropped them into the
bag with the others. Two other pockets were untouched.

"I don't know why I'm even considering this, but
thirty-five."

Anok's eyes narrowed, and he tightened his jaw. "I *said,*
thirty."

The tension in the air was thick as the fog. Around
Anok, friend and foe slowly reached for their weapons.

"Thirty," said the captain. It wasn't a reply. It was like
he was hefting the word to test its weight. "Thirty." He
growled softly, then sighed. "Then it be—"

His words were cut off by a sound from behind Anok, a
deep note played on the strings, melding into an angry-
hornet buzz that ripped past his ear and ended in a wet *thok*
as the arrowhead passed completely through the captain's
throat and emerged through the back of his spine. He
flailed, eyes wide, gasped once, and dropped like a broken
toy onto the dusty street, twitching in a growing pool of
black blood.

Everyone was too surprised to act immediately. It took a
moment for Anok to look behind him to see who had taken
the shot. That day, he and Sheriti were the only ones who

had not brought their bows, but as he turned back, the other three all had theirs slung over their shoulders. Had someone moved quickly to hide their actions, or had the shot come from elsewhere behind them? He was suddenly alert for ambush.

A tall Zingaran, whom Anok had pegged as the first mate, finally stepped forward and pulled his cutlass, the curved blade glinting blue against the fog. "Treachery! Kill them all!"

Anok pulled his right sword and engaged the Zingaran. The arming swords he carried didn't have either the reach or power of a pirate's cutlass, but he had confidence in his skill and speed, as well as the power of his right arm. He'd hold the second sword in reserve until he'd seen what the pirates were made of.

Past the first mate's shoulder, he noticed that one of the most formidable pirates had taken Sheriti prisoner, a fact that caused him little alarm. She squealed and kicked her feet in the air as he held his arm around her throat, but he saw her right hand slip into the slit at the side of her skirt.

Anok was quickly on the defensive, as the pirate proved to be a powerful, if not swift, foe. As he fended off blow after pounding blow, he allowed himself to be maneuvered in with his right arm close to the wall of the tavern, a position that should have put him at a disadvantage.

Anok made a momentary show of looking weak, then tossed his sword from his right hand to his left and went on the offensive.

The pirate was taken by surprise. Off-balance and uncertain how to respond, he stepped back. Anok followed, pressing in close so his shorter sword worked to his advantage. Then he reached across with his right hand and drew the other sword, underhand, from its scabbard.

The heavy bronze pommel smashed into the pirate's sword hand. He heard bones crack, and the cutlass went flying.

He plunged the left sword forward, feeling the meaty crunch as it plunged deep into the pirate's belly. The man's eyes went wide with shock, then wider as Anok jerked the blade upward to finish the kill.

Anok kicked the man backward off his sword before it could become entangled in the dead mate's fall.

He looked up in time to see Sheriti, still held by the same pirate, swing her body wide to her left side, depending on the grip around her neck to support her weight. The stiletto held in her right fist plunged down behind her to bury itself nearly to the hilt in the unfortunate man's groin.

He dropped her and staggered back, wailing, but Sheriti spun and pulled a second stiletto from the hidden scabbard strapped to her left hip under her skirt. She dashed forward, plunged it deep through the pirate's left eye, into his brain, and pulled it back just as quickly. The man was dead before he hit the ground.

She dashed back in to recover the first weapon, and stood, a bloody blade in each hand, a streak of blood across the front of her silk dress, a snarl of defiance on her red lips.

He saw Teferi fighting off two of the pirates, and was going to help, when arrows began to sprout from the men's shoulders. He glanced over to see Rami firing from atop a nearby fountain; a dead pirate slumped headfirst into the pool at his feet, slowly turning the water dark with his blood.

Nearby, Dejal was more than holding his own against another pirate.

Five down.

He heard a noise behind him and spun, bringing up both swords as he stepped inside a clumsy swing by a pirate who had hoped to surprise him.

The move was lightning fast and instinctive as he pushed the twin swords, crossed at the hilt, against the pirate's throat.

With an animal roar, Anok yanked them apart in a powerful slashing motion, slicing through muscle, tendon, and finally slipping between neck bones to slice the head off cleanly.

The head spun in the air for a moment, and hot blood splattered Anok like summer rain.

Another movement behind him.

Heart pounding from the fresh kill, he spun, right arm raised, barely in time to deflect the cutlass flashing for his head.

The barbarian woman bore down on him fearlessly, a look of grim determination on her angular features.

She was fast, and nearly as strong of arm as the first mate had been. Even with two blades for defense, he found himself stepping back, again and again. Her blade slashed through the air, never striking from the same angle twice. Anok had fought better, but not many.

Then, to his surprise, she began to talk. "The arrow—was that your plan all along?"

"I neither want nor beg favor, barbarian!"

Blades flashed, and the ringing of steel was constant.

"Nor do I offer, *townsman!*" Her Stygian came with a strong accent. "If you have honor, say it!"

Still he was pushed back, her attacks had not let up at all. Steel clashed angrily against steel, like temple chimes in a gale wind. "I came to buy a thing—at a fair price." Another step back, but not so far this time. "That's all."

Her advance stopped. She seemed to make a decision.

He responded to her hesitation with a counterattack, but she ducked under his sword, which plunged into the chest of a surprised pirate who charged in behind her. The pirate gasped, managing a flailing swing of his cutlass.

Anok easily struck it aside with his remaining sword, and seeing that the wound was not immediately fatal, slit the man's throat with his counterstroke, yanked the embedded sword free, and quickly disarmed him as a precaution.

Unnecessary, as it turned out. The man fell, and Anok looked for the barbarian woman. It took him a moment, as his eye was drawn to those still fighting.

She was kneeling next to the captain's corpse, not out of concern. She clutched the scrap of oilcloth containing the artifact. As she did, the oilcloth fell away, revealing its contents: a simple, iron medallion that bore an outline of a crescent moon and two stars.

Anok gasped as he recognized the thing, his hand swinging up to clutch at his chest. He had seen such a medallion before—he owned it—and he knew that he could not let this twin escape his grasp.

The barbarian met his eyes for a moment and, grinning, shoved the parcel between her ample bosoms. A wave of her sword, and she was gone, heading across the market at a fast trot.

It was, he noticed suddenly, very dark.

Then he heard the horns, from every tower of the inner city, the deep and eerie notes that sounded the beginning of Festival.

"Get to safety," he yelled to the others. "I'm going after the woman! I'll find you, by morning if I must!"

Then he was after her, running swiftly into the darkness.

3

HE MOVED QUICKLY across the empty marketplace, barely able to see the walls of the nearest buildings. Though he didn't see which way the woman had gone, he had seen her general direction, and though she probably didn't know it, that direction offered few outlets. He had a good chance of finding her.

The sound of echoing footsteps and voices caused him to turn. Down a street to his right, he saw moving torches, and in their light, a group of robed and hooded figures.

Acolytes of Set!

He quickly moved past the street, so that he could no longer see the acolytes, and with luck, they had not seen him. Still, there would be many more on the streets, and they could lie in wait around any turn. He wondered if the woman had any more understanding of the current danger than her captain had.

Festival was a night of sacrifice to Set, when the cult offered blood to their evil serpent god. That blood could come from any source: slaves, imprisoned criminals, convicted heretics, prisoners of war, the rare virgin (and there were naturally precious few of those in Stygia), and anyone ignorant enough, foolish enough, or unfortunate enough to be caught on the streets after dark.

The locals knew to lock and shutter themselves away, to drink and sing and party, and to deny the horrors going on outside. But foreign visitors sometimes didn't know, or didn't believe the warnings they were given, and made ripe pickings for the acolytes.

The woman was a strong fighter, true, but the acolytes would simply overwhelm her with numbers, or stand off at a distance and disable her with a well-placed arrow.

When he had last seen the barbarian woman, she had been moving fast, but she might not be expecting pursuit this far into her flight. Doubtless she was several streets ahead, well lost in the thickening fog and gloom.

But she didn't know the streets like Anok did. Even in the fog, he knew every turn, doorway, and alley, and though the path ahead of her seemed open, all the streets for some distance either dead-ended, or fed back into this one. He could count on her getting lost and doubling back at least once, so he might be able to catch up with her at his leisure. The trick was not to miss her entirely in the fog and not run headlong into a band of bloodthirsty acolytes.

He slowed. He could barely see now, but for those that knew where to find them, hidden but distinct markings were carved in the stones at the corner of each building. Years before, a blind beggar had shown him the secret in return for two pieces of silver, perhaps the best coins he'd ever spent.

His soft sandals allowed him to move along the bricks and cobbles in near silence, but the barbarian woman was wearing worn boots of heavy leather. He paused periodically, straining his ears into the darkness, rather than his eyes.

There!

At the third major turn, he heard a few muffled footsteps. The street was home to bakers, and he could smell the lingering yeast, flour, and woodsmoke of the day's work. It was also a dead end.

He stepped back into a doorway, looked into the gloom to his left, waiting for some sound or sight of her inevitable passage.

When the sound came, it was to his right, not one set of footsteps, but many.

Then the light of torches.

Followers of Set!

He was no coward, but only a fool would fight such numbers unnecessarily. He stepped as far back into the shadows of the doorway as he could, sliding down into a tight crouch to hide even his shape.

The fog seemed to brighten, then glow with flickering light.

He saw the torches, the dark, rippling shapes of their robes, right in front of him, at least half a dozen large men. They passed so close in front of his hiding place that he could smell the temple incense on their clothing, the perfumed ceremonial oils in their hair. If one so much as turned a head in his direction, he was doomed.

But none did. He listened as their footsteps became more distant.

Then the shouts.

The feminine cry of defiance.

The echoing clash of blades in the narrow street.

They had found her.

He took a deep, long-delayed, breath. *I should leave her to her fate.*

She fought well, that one, but against so many, she wouldn't last long.

Without help.

She has our prize. I can't let it fall to the temple.

With an annoyed grunt, he sprang from his hiding place, running toward the sounds of battle. *When had the thing become worth dying for?*

It was a foolish question. The moment he recognized the artifact, he would have given any price to have it.

As he saw the light of the torches, he pulled his swords and plunged into the fray.

The acolytes had divided their forces, half hanging back to hold the torches and prevent her escape, the others moving in to engage her directly.

One of them had already fallen, though he wasn't dead. He screamed and flailed on the ground, his robes flopping around like a rag with mouse trapped inside.

The woman stood in the middle of them, fierce and defiant, blood—whose he couldn't tell—splattered across her face and body. She held her sword at the ready for the next acolyte to step within range.

But seeing their fallen fellow, the others were in no hurry. They could wait for weakness or inattention. Perhaps they would even wait for reinforcements to be attracted by the noise. With a little patience, they probably could have killed her easily enough, but they wanted to take her alive.

They wanted a living sacrifice.

Then Anok struck, and everything changed in a second.

They weren't expecting an attack from behind. He stepped in behind one of the torchbearers, slitting his throat, then shoving him forward into the shocked swordsmen.

Seeing an opening, the woman stabbed her sword into the back of one of the distracted men, then jumped back out of range of a counterattack by another.

In fear and confusion, the acolytes' organized circle dissolved. Torches were dropped as priests struggled to draw swords from under their robes, and Anok saw a large opening in the line behind the woman.

He feigned a charging attack on the men, but slipped through their ranks while barely touching blades with them. He slipped one sword back into its scabbard and grabbed the woman's arm. They were both running before he had time to speak. "Come with me, and we both may live out the night!"

She grunted in agreement, and he released her arm, trusting her to keep up with him on her own. Confusion had bought them precious seconds but not much more. In a matter of yards, the light of the torches began to fade into the fog behind them, and soon they were gone.

Looking back, he could barely see the woman, but he'd heard tales that some of the barbarian northmen had unusually keen senses. Perhaps she could see better, but if not, she would simply have to follow him by sound as much as sight.

He rounded a corner into an alley, then stopped, his back against the cool brick of the wall. His fingers brushed the glyphs pressed into the clay of one brick just below waist level, the crane, the scarab, and the ankh. They were leaving the street of bakers, and headed for the district favored by smiths, potters, and brickmakers. Like the bakers, they depended on large ovens and kilns and drew on the same scarce supply of burnable fuel.

He leaned close to the woman. She smelled of sweat, leather, and—surprisingly—flowers. "Quiet," he said.

He tried to quiet his own ragged breathing and still his heart pounding in his ears, straining to hear any sign of pursuit.

"They are coming," the woman said, matter-of-factly.

"You're sure."

"They move slowly in the name of stealth, but they are coming. By Crom's name I swear it."

Crom? Who was Crom? It didn't matter. "Up ahead," he said, "there are iron gates, used to close off part of the alley to pen the mules that haul wood for the ovens and kilns. We can bar them behind us and escape through the other end of the alley. If they catch us, it will only be after a long detour."

"Then lead on, Anok of the Ravens."

He trotted down the narrow alley, hearing her right behind. "Just Anok," he said. "You have a name?"

"Fallon of Clan Murrogh."

"Fallon," he said, slowing his pace.

Ahead, a wall with a narrow archway cut across the alley. He could barely see the wall, and had to find the arched opening by touch. "Through here," he said.

Once again by feel, he found the iron bars of the hinged door. It swung shut with a screech of metal and a loud clang, which would doubtless be heard by their pursuers. If all went well, it wouldn't matter.

He found the heavy iron bar he knew would be leaning against the alley wall and jammed it through a pair of iron rings in the door. A metal pin hanging from a chain on the wall locked the bar in place, and, for good measure, he grabbed the top of the pin with both hands and threw his weight against it. The thin metal bent, then snapped off at the top, leaving the end of the pin stuck inside the catch.

"Come on. There's another gate, then we'll be away."

He ran another fifty paces down the alley to where he knew the second wall and archway awaited. His fingers found the edge of the masonry arch, but the barred door was not where it should have been.

For a moment, he was confused, until he stuck his hand into the archway and jammed his fingers painfully into a metal bar. *The door was closed!* He grabbed the bars with both hands and pulled. *Locked!*

Fallon came up beside him, tested the door with both hands, then threw her weight against it, hard. The door simply rattled. "You've trapped us!"

"This door should be open! It's always left open at night!"

"Indeed, it was this night as well," a familiar voice came from the far side of the gate, "until I came along."

"Dejal! Let us though."

Anok could see nothing in the darkness, not even a silhouette.

The answer was only smug laughter.

"Open the gate! I hear them up the alley!"

A soft blue light made Dejal's chiseled features visible to him, and Anok noticed the full moon peeking out from behind a ragged veil of black clouds.

"Perhaps, brother Raven, we can come to an arrangement."

"Open the gate, Dejal!"

"Give me the Scale."

"The what?"

"The Scale of Set. The gold medallion you collected from the pirates. It is mine."

"This—Scale is paid for."

He laughed softly. "Paid for by me. I'm your mysterious employer, Anok. A gift of one last adventure for the fabulous Ravens."

"That, and an arrow into the captain's neck?"

"As I said, Anok, one last adventure . . ."

Anok heard voices up the alley behind them.

"Let us through, Dejal. They're coming!"

"Indeed, and there are more at the end of the street behind me. Give me the Scale. I'll show you a hiding place and lead the others away."

Anok turned and boldly reached down between the barbarian woman's breasts, grabbing the Scale. She gasped, but he was too fast. He turned back to Dejal, the cool metal of the Scale against his hand, and hesitated.

He'd known Dejal for years, since his first days as an orphan on the streets. They had faced death back-to-back dozens of times. And he was strangely shocked to realize that Dejal didn't trust him and equally aware that he no longer trusted Dejal.

What was this Scale? Why was it so valuable? And who would Dejal be willing to kill for it? Anok did not know why it would be so important to anyone but him. His own reasons were purely personal—on so he'd thought.

He gripped the medallion tightly in his hand until its thin edges cut into his fingers. He felt a tingle, like the warning shock just before lightning strikes. There could be no doubt that this was an object of mystic power, a fact that made him even less eager to be rid of it.

"I don't have a choice, do I?"

"No, you don't."

Although it galled Anok, he handed the medallion through to Dejal, who slid it inside his robe. There was a thoughtful pause, before Dejal stepped out of view. Anok heard him fumbling with the lock, then the metal bolt was pulled back. He hesitated before fully withdrawing the bolt, looking past Anok. "Should we kill the barbarian woman? It would be easier to cover your escape if I could produce at least one fresh corpse."

Behind him, Anok heard Fallon smoothly draw her sword.

"Fallon and I have an arrangement. And if I were you, I'd favor watching how you use say 'barbarian,' if you value your extremities. You'll show us both the hiding place."

Dejal sighed and pulled the bolt the rest of the way. "Very well, then. Follow me."

Fallon glanced at Dejal as she passed him, her sword high between them. "Say it," she said, "but say it with *respect!*"

Dejal led them to the end of what Anok knew was a dead-end street and down a narrow alleyway. After a dozen steps, it widened into a courtyard surrounded by low, arched, doorways almost too small for a man. "Bread ovens," Dejal explained. "Climb inside this one."

Anok hesitated.

Dejal chuckled. "What? You think I'd bake you for my breakfast? Get in."

Anok practically had to crawl to pass through the low archway, and the interior was nearly dark, except for a circle of sky he could see through the chimney above. The floor of the oven was thick stone, still the slightest bit warm from the day's baking and covered with a residue of some kind of coarsely ground meal. At the back of the oven it became slightly warmer, and he felt for the stone grate leading down to the firebox under the oven.

Fallon crawled in behind him.

He saw Dejal's face dimly as he leaned down and peered through the door. "I'm going to roll the cover stone in place, then I'll lead the others away from here. If you value your lives, you won't try to follow me or leave here before dawn."

Anok didn't like the sound of any of it, but they had little choice. Any attempt to fight their way out would be suicide. He could only hope that Dejal had no hidden reason not to keep his word.

The round cover stone, set in a slot in the stone just out-side the door, began to roll into place. It was quite heavy. Just as the light from the door had almost disappeared, the stone stopped. Dejal's face appeared just for a moment, then he tossed something inside. It landed on the floor with a muffled rattle. "Payment as agreed, and more," he said. "I recovered the gems the pirate dropped. They're yours. This Scale of Set will secure my position in the temple and is worth far more than the price paid"—he chuckled—"in my father's money." He hesitated. "That thing I mentioned ear-lier? Last chance."

"You have my answer."

He frowned. "Farewell then, Anok. I am Raven no more."

Then the stone rolled the rest of the way. Anok put his back against the wall of the oven and slid down it to sit on the floor. He heard Fallon sit down next to him.

They said nothing for a long time, quietly listening for sounds of pursuit or discovery. They heard a group of acolytes, perhaps the ones who had originally pursued them, their voices growing closer. Then they moved away, and the two fugitives heard nothing, save the sniffing and whine of wild dogs searching the streets for scraps, and the distant screams of those wretched souls captured for tem-ple sacrifice.

Even as his eyes adjusted, it was too dark to see Fallon sitting next to him, except for a vague impression of move-ment when she shifted position. He could smell her, though, her sweat, the coppery smell of the fresh blood that covered them both. The hearth was cooling in the night chill, and he could even feel the heat of her body where it was close to his. Despite the danger, his blood raced, and not at all from fear.

He heard her unstrap her sword and put it on the floor near at hand, and after a moment's hesitation, removed his as well. It did little to ease the distrust between them. Sit-ting, their weapons were actually easier to draw.

Fallon finally broke the silence. "I have heard tales, that

the morning after Festival in Khemi the sewers are so gorged with blood it streams far out to sea. But I never believed such foolishness. There isn't that much blood in a body, or that many bodies in all the city."

"I have seen it, with my own eyes. I don't know how it can be, but it is. Some say there is dark magic at work. Some say vast caravans of virgins are brought in across the desert on moonless nights to be sacrificed at Festival. Some say the followers of Set have a magic potion that can make people bleed like fountains and prolong their deaths, or to turn the entire body, flesh and bone, into blood. I can only say that many die. If you'd stayed on the streets, your captain and crew would have been dead anyway."

She sniffed in contempt. "As if I care for their fates. They were bad pirates and worse companions. I'm well rid of them."

"Your loyalty is touching."

"A pirate's loyalty is earned, not given by duty. They did nothing to earn mine. I was going to take my share of the booty and go my own way. There are many wild tales of Stygia, why not see if any of them are true?"

"Too many are, I fear, as you'd soon have discovered."

She laughed. "A Cimmerian fears no man, devil or monster. We live for battle."

"Is that so? Because you'll find all three are common enough here, sometimes all in one body. If you have any sense at all, you'll sign with the first crew that will have you and never come back."

"Then why do you stay? You have Stygian blood, but I sense you are no Stygian."

He hesitated to answer. Or did he even have an answer? "I am my father's son, and he was an Aquilonian trader. But this cursed place is the only home I have ever known, and it is where he died. I can say only that I have unfinished business here, though even I am not sure what it is."

"Revenge?"

"Once I would have relished it, but my father preached against it."

"A wise man, then. Unless there is treasure in it, what good is revenge?"

"I'd feel safer then, if we didn't have these jewels here."

She laughed. "I've been thinking about those."

Unconsciously, his right hand moved toward one of his swords. "Thinking what?"

"That they are mine by right. The trinket was delivered, and the rest of the crew is dead or run away."

"It was delivered because I hunted you down and found it."

"Your fellow, the acolyte, double-crossed us and killed our captain." There was anger in her voice. Not desperate, but the dire, warning anger of a growling animal. "What was I to do then?"

He hesitated. "I would have done the same."

"The jewels are mine, then."

He considered. He would have paid those jewels for the Scale anyway, and she did not know of the others jewels hidden in his tunic or those he had already distributed among his fellows. Anok's reputation for fairness, often at his own expense, was legend on the streets of Odji, and part of the reason the Ravens' services had always been in demand.

But neither was he known as a fool. Hadn't the woman forsaken any right to the payment when she had deserted her crewmates? And would she cut his throat anyway the moment he nodded off, no matter what he offered her?

"You can have half."

She laughed derisively. "Half? Why should I settle for half?"

"Because it's more than nothing, which is what I should give you."

She was silent for a while. "That was a fair bag of gems, enough to keep me in drink and luxury for some time. Any more, and I might go soft and lose my fighting edge. Where would I be then?"

"Half."

"I'll consider it."

Again, she was silent for a while. Outside, he could hear the dogs fighting over some scrap, or at least, he hoped that was all it was.

He heard Fallon making a noise. She seemed to be adjusting her garments. "The night will be long," she said, "and cold."

He was startled as some thrown object slapped into his chest. Leather. It took him a moment to figure out that it was her tunic. By then, another piece of leather hit him, and he more quickly guessed it was her loincloth. He wondered if it was a trick. If so, it was an interesting one. "This is a curious action for one who claims to be cold."

He heard her move in the darkness, but nothing that indicated she had picked up her sword. That didn't mean she hadn't taken a knife or dagger from her clothing as she undressed. He casually reached back and pulled his own dagger from where it was tucked in his belt, and held it behind his back.

Then she moved closer, straddling his legs. He reached forward with his free hand, and encountered only bare, soft, flesh, slightly sticky with partially dried blood. Her nipple pressed hard against his palm, and, despite his caution, his body did not hesitate to respond.

Her hands, both of them he noted, rubbed across his chest, pulling open his jerkin to find naked skin. "There are better ways to stay warm," she said.

"I thought we were still trying to decide if we were going to have to kill each other over these jewels."

"There's time for that in the morning. As for now, can you tell me that all this danger and battle has not stirred your blood as it has mine?" She reached back until her right hand rested on his bare thigh, then slid upward, under his kilt. She laughed, huskily. "I see that it has." She reached down to fumble with the belt holding his kilt.

He softly laid down his dagger next to his sword and used the freed hand to help her. He could feel her breath

against his ear, quick and ragged. "We've crossed swords
in battle, and I found you a worthy adversary. Now I would
test your mettle once again."

"And I yours," he said, as she lifted herself enough to
pull his kilt down around his knees, then settled back down
on him.

She took a deep breath, and let it out in a shuddering
gasp.

He hooked one arm around the back of her head, and
pulled her lips hard against his as her hips began to move.

The night might be long, but it was certainly no longer
cold.

4

THE LIGHT OF a clear blue sky shining through the open chimney woke Anok, and he blinked against the glare.

His first thought was to curse himself for having fallen asleep. His second was to wonder that he was still alive. His third was of the warm barbarian flesh pressed tightly against his own. Fallon spooned against his side, her dark hair soft against his chest. Without thinking he reached down and stroked it.

Her eyes snapped open, wide and instantly searching for danger. She probably regretted falling asleep as much as he did. He wondered if she regretted anything else. She sat up, and he realized that, despite their night of passion, he was seeing her naked for the first time. She brushed a coating of meal, picked up from the floor, off her dusky skin. The powder had acted as a dry bath, removing most of the blood and sweat from the previous evening's adventures.

He was mesmerized by the sight of her, the graceful blending of hard and soft, angular and curved, those places no longer secret to him but until now unseen. He found himself wanting her again and knew it was not likely to be.

She noticed him watching her and seemed slightly disapproving. But she picked up her clothing and dressed casually, making no special effort to hide herself in the process. She clearly had no more modesty than a wild animal, but an all-too-human awareness of what power her nakedness had over others. Doubtless, in certain circumstances, she treated it as just another weapon, like a knife or a spear. The fact that he was still alive suggested that it would not be used so on this occasion.

Beyond the cover stone, he could hear sounds from outside. Not screams, or chants, or packs of hungry dogs, but the mundane sounds of the street, people talking, carts and livestock, the sounds of tradesmen working.

She looked at him as she strapped on her sword. "Half, you said? You've earned my respect, Anok of Ravens. For that reason alone, I'll settle for your offer."

Anok recovered his tunic and kilt. His unsheathed dagger still sat in a corner near the wall. If she had noticed it, and he suspected that very little escaped her attention, she gave no sign.

He dressed in silence, finally recovering his dagger and strapping on his two swords. Trying not to be too obvious about it, he checked his purse and hidden pockets. If anything was missing, he could not detect it. He dumped out the bag of gems out on the floor, counting out two even shares where she could see. She watched him intently, her eyes never leaving the gems. *She trusts me, but only so far.*

Finally, he scooped up half and deposited them in his own purse. He tossed her the empty bag so she could collect the rest.

She had just finished gathering her bounty when the cover stone rolled back.

Anok turned and looked into the wide eyes of a Shemite baker-woman. Before he could speak, he reached into his purse and tossed her a silver coin. "Rent, for use of your oven for the night." He glanced back at Fallon and grinned. "You might want to clean it out before baking your bread today."

The market was already bustling with business, though many looked tired and bleary-eyed from the traditional Festival-night parties. There was little sign of the horrors of the previous night, and all shared in the lie that it had never happened.

Anok knew otherwise.

He stopped at a stand to buy an assortment of dates and dried fish for their breakfast, then led Fallon to the bell tower at the western corner of the market. It had been built by the ancients as part of some great temple. The main part of the building had long ago fallen in on itself, its floor forming the greater part of the market, but the tower still stood.

She followed him up the circular stairway, turn after turn, until they were the height of twenty men above the ground. A small balcony surrounded the tower just below the highest level, and it was here that Anok emerged. From this vantage point they had a sweeping view down across Odji to the waterfront and the mouth of the River Styx with its delta of low islands, and to the Western Ocean beyond.

Fallon stepped onto the balcony, momentarily stunned with the view. Then she gasped in surprise. "I did not believe it could be true."

Anok leaned both hands against the hip-high stone wall that surrounded the balcony. "Now you know."

The sewers of the city emptied through a culvert inside the great seawall that jutted out to the north of the harbor, and beyond the end of that wall, a ribbon of scarlet flowed out into the ocean, fanning out and becoming more diffuse as it reached for the horizon.

"Welcome to Stygia," he said. "May your visit be a pleasant one."

THEY ATE THEIR breakfast on the tower. As they were finishing, Fallon happened to glance west to the harbor. "Our ship is gone," she said with little emotion. "We left a skeleton crew aboard. Either they double-crossed the cap-

tain and sailed during the night or, more likely, some of my
former fellows survived and returned to them with news of
our troubles."

"You almost sound relieved."

"I'm just as happy I'll not have to kill any more of them
over the matter of these jewels or our lost cargo. With them
gone, there will be no false claims against my bounty. If
the ship remained, we might have taken it for our own, but
I have little use for a ship now and none at all for the crew
that remained."

"I might have had a use for a ship," Anok said. He
thought wistfully of the Ravens' long-ago talk of gaining a
ship and forming a pirate crew. The dream opened for him
again painfully, like an old wound ripping apart. It might
have been one way the Ravens could have stayed together.
Instead, it was, once again, nothing more than a foolish and
impossible dream. "Let's get going," he said.

They climbed back down the long, winding stairs to
the market. He was eager to ensure that the rest of the
Ravens were safe. It turned out they were just as eager for
news of him.

They had barely left the market, heading west toward
the Paradise brothel and the Nest, when he spotted Teferi
across the crowded street. He put two fingers to his lips and
whistled.

Teferi turned and smiled widely. He bent down for a
moment and effortlessly hosted Sheriti up onto the crook
of his arm, where she waved furiously, even as Teferi
started walking toward them. He dropped Sheriti back to
the cobblestones, and, a few moments later, Teferi, Sheriti,
and Rami emerged from the throngs crowding the street.

Sheriti leapt upon him with a whoop, throwing her arms
around his neck, her legs around his waist, and planted a
big kiss squarely on his lips. There was an awkward moment as, still clinging to him, she noticed Fallon standing
at his side. Sheriti slid down off him, still holding on to his
hand, but said nothing.

It was too loud and crowded to talk anyway, so Anok

jerked his thumb toward a nearby tavern, and they slipped inside.

The place was clean and orderly, all the furniture upright, a sure sign that it had closed rather than hosted a Festival party the night before. They pulled up benches around a barrel set up as a makeshift table, and Anok ordered thick beers for everyone. The tavern keeper returned quickly with five large mugs. Anok grabbed his and tossed back a gulp. The beer was thick, yeasty, sweetened with mashed dates and honey. As much food as beverage, it was traditionally served in the morning. Anok wiped his upper lip with his fist and noticed that nobody else was drinking.

In particular, Teferi's suspicious gaze never left Fallon, and his hand never left the hilt of his sword. Rami sat back a ways from the table, seemingly ready to bolt, while Sheriti leaned across the table, her eyes wandering from Anok to Fallon and back again, as though studying a particularly vexing problem.

"This is Fallon, of Cimmeria. She and I fought back-to-back last night, and I vouch for her character. She has forsaken her crew, those that might have survived yesterday."

Teferi had relaxed somewhat, but he still looked suspiciously at Fallon. "What of the medallion? Do you have it?"

"Dejal has it. We were pursued by acolytes, and he trapped us behind a locked gate until we surrendered the prize to him. Just as well, as it was he who hired us to claim it."

Teferi raised his eyebrows. "That doesn't make sense."

Anok shrugged. "Dejal has finally and truly left us now. He has been seduced by Set and his father's cult. Who can say what his reasons were. But I suspect it was a way of squandering his father's money, a petty act of revenge upon him. As for us, in his twisted way he may have been trying to give us a gift. One last trip into danger for the Ravens. Never mind that he manufactured the danger himself."

"He fired the arrow that killed the captain," said Rami. "I saw him."

Anok nodded. "He admitted as much. Idiot."

"He was," said Fallon, in a tone that some might use for discussing the weather, "wiser than you think. The captain had planned to take both the medallion and the payment and slit all your throats."

Teferi rose for his stool, reaching for his sword. "What! You were planning to kill us then?"

Fallon put her hand on her sword casually, but did not draw steel. "Not knowing you all, I wasn't sure how I felt about his plan. I held back taking blood until I saw the nature of your character. Then, when it seemed you had double-crossed us, Anok would not let his blood be taken. My doubts returned, and it was clear that my crewmates would not prevail in the battle. So I decided to claim the prize and go my own way."

"You mean," said Teferi, sarcasm in his voice, "you stole the medallion and ran."

She did not seem insulted. "If you prefer."

"Seems sensible to me," said Rami, holding his mug in two hands, a bit of foam stuck to his upper lip.

Teferi shot the little pickpocket an annoyed glance.

Rami just rolled his eyes and shrugged. Then he seemed to remember something, and his eyes narrowed. "What about the jewels?"

"Dejal returned them to me. In turn, I have given half to Fallon."

The outrage from the others was immediate.

Anok stood trying to calm them. "She acted in good faith, and it was Dejal who first broke the truce. Later, their cargo was delivered to our employer as planned. She felt she deserved the entire payment, but I convinced her otherwise."

"Your mind is clouded by this woman," said Teferi. "She deserves nothing."

Rami's expression turned into a leering grin. "You say you fought back-to-back with her. Did you joust front to front as well?"

Sheriti looked at him, seemingly waiting for a denial, but none was forthcoming.

Teferi rolled his eyes and groaned. "I should have known it."

"So," said Rami, "barbarian women. Are they good?"

Sheriti glared it him. "Shut up, Rami." Then she looked at Fallon, and her expression changed. It said something, but in some woman's language that Anok couldn't grasp.

Was Sheriti jealous? Angry? Disappointed? Simply upset about the jewels? He couldn't be sure, yet he was puzzled. He was no virgin, and she knew it. Why should she be upset that he'd been with Fallon? In any case, he had more immediate concerns. "What may or may not have happened between Fallon and me is no concern of yours, and no influence on my decision. I have always been fair, you know this, and I judge her to be a person of honor. She is worthy of our respect, and we must deal fairly with her. It's always been the way of the Ravens, has it not?"

Teferi and Rami looked at each other.

"It has," said Teferi.

"To my frequent regret," said Rami.

Sheriti said nothing for a while. Then finally, "Give her the gems. She's earned her share."

Fallon took a swig from her cup, then put it down solidly on the table. "Indeed I have," she said, without irony. Her eyes scanned the four of them. "And know this, I am fair with you as well. I could have taken what I wanted last night, all the gems and more, but I did not. Better I should settle for less. I'll only squander the gems on soft beds, fine food, and drink, and a barbarian can only stand so much of such fineries. Better I should pay generously"—and here, she grinned slightly at Anok—"for services rendered, so that if I one day should need friends or allies in this foul land, the Ravens might look upon me with favor."

She raised the cup high, gulped the last of the beer, then slammed it down on the table. "I take leave of you now, Ravens. I have money to spend and places to see. We will meet again if the winds will it. If so, let it be with open hands and not drawn swords."

Anok watched as she marched purposefully out of the tavern.

"Everybody," said Rami urgently, patting his tunic and purse, "check your pockets."

"Why," said Teferi, looking after Fallon and considering whether to give chase, "is something missing?"

"No," said Rami, "but I'd have picked everyone's pocket if I were her."

"Then," said Anok, "we're fortunate that she isn't you. Sit down, Teferi."

He sat, and there was silence for a while. Anok noticed that they all looked tired. He doubted any of them had slept. "Did you make it back to the Nest last night?"

"We waited as long as we could," said Teferi, "but the acolytes were thick on the streets last night. We did as you said and returned to the Nest."

"Where," said Anok with a slight grin, "you celebrated well? I hope the refreshments I laid in were adequate for the night."

The look Sheriti gave him was surprisingly tender. "There was no party without you, Anok. We held vigil, hoping you would return, but you never did. So we waited until dawn and returned to the market to search."

He nodded. "You're good friends, but if what you say is true, the refreshments sit wasting, and we've all been deprived the Festival party that is our due." He tossed several coins on the table that would more than cover their beers. "Come then. Time is short!"

5

THEY RETURNED TO the Nest, a large room with several stall-like sleeping areas, located under the Paradise brothel. Actually, the smaller rooms had been built as stalls for horses and mules, though it had been decades since animals had been kept there.

The furnishings were mostly brothel castoffs, ornately carved chairs covered in faded but elaborately woven fabrics, worn and patched silk pillows decorated with tassels and gold thread, mismatched curtains and tapestries, some bearing nude figures, depictions of lovemaking, or vast and elaborate orgies. They all seemed far too fancy and garish for the simple rooms constructed of crudely fashioned boards and undressed stone.

But the place was comfortable and familiar, and it seemed to Anok that he had lived here forever, sometimes alone, often with guests or companions. Teferi had lived there for several years before securing his own room over a tavern a few blocks away, and Dejal had frequently come to stay for days at a time, avoiding the oppressive home of his father.

Sheriti's room was upstairs, in the private area in back of the brothel where the customers were never allowed, and men, even those as closely associated with the brothel as Anok, were rarely permitted. Though she didn't sleep here, she had been a daily visitor, often bringing meals or wine left over from parties upstairs, or crusts of bread and fruit pilfered from the kitchen when there was nothing else to be had.

Anok had always looked forward to seeing her smiling face as she descended the narrow stairs to the Nest. It meant more to him than all the naked flesh wantonly displayed by the whores who lived and worked just above his head. Not that he objected to that sight either. He was only human after all, and he had even, on occasion, taken his payment for some special service, to the brothel or one of the whores, in trade.

Kifi, Sheriti's mother, had once told him that the whores believed lust and love were separate, if related, matters, and that only simple people allowed them to become indiscriminately entangled. The whores had many such beliefs, their own code of honor, and their own secret goddess they worshiped at a private shrine that even Anok had never been allowed to see. Some people—not Anok of course—looked down upon whores. It was only appropriate that they, in their own way, looked down on almost everyone else.

Or so they said. Yet whores rarely had children, despite ample opportunity, and despite her pride, Kifi's greatest wish was that her daughter have almost any life other than the one she had taken for herself.

As they entered the Nest, Anok pulled back a tapestry covering a low, round table covered with jars and baskets: strong, amber-colored evening beer, sweet Argosian wine, likely pirated from some passing ship, flatbreads sweetened with honey, all manner of dried fruits, dried squid marinated in exotic spices, pickled duck eggs, and other exotic treats.

Anok tried to put on a good face for his companions, but

his heart wasn't in it, and in the end, neither were theirs. They were bone-tired from fighting and sleep-deprived. The four of them ate their fill, and the wine and beer began to do their work. Teferi eventually wandered off, and they soon heard him snoring softly in one of the little side rooms.

Rami curled up on a pillow with a large jar of beer, which he scooped out by the mugful until he finally passed out, spilling his last cup onto the floor.

That left Anok and Sheriti. He watched her, eyes closed, sitting with her back against the wall, a cup of wine still cradled in her two hands. Thinking her asleep, he quietly slid off the pillow where he'd been sitting the last hour and withdrew to the farthest sleeping chamber from the door, the one he considered his personal space.

There was no door, only a curtain that he slipped through. Inside there was a small but ornately carved bed held off the floor by what seemed to be lion's legs, a chair, a few large baskets for his clothing and other belongings, and an oil lamp. A small window, high in the wall, permitted a single shaft of light to enter.

He sat on the bed, but he did not feel like sleeping, despite his fatigue. His arms ached from battle, and a dozen bruises and cuts nagged him with their small pains despite the numbing glow of his recent drink.

He put his hand against his chest and felt the lump there under his tunic, the cool circle of metal against his breastbone. He reached up with both hands to grasp the simple chain and lift it over his head. He held the medallion in his hand. It was large, the span of it such that it completely covered his outspread fingers. The metal was iron, and not very well forged. A simple outline of a crescent moon and two stars was carved into its surface.

It was a simple thing. Some might even say ugly, hardly even worth stealing, but Anok was now sure its crudity was intentional. He'd had the thing for years, the only reminder he had of his murdered father, and the only clue to a sister he had never known. He'd looked at it hundreds of times,

never suspecting that it was anything other than a solid
piece of iron. But the medallion had hidden secrets.

He was not sure how he had accidentally discovered the
trick, but discover it he had. He pressed the medallion between the palms of both hands, with the chain attachments
pointing upward, the carved side against the left hand, and
twisted his hands in different directions, left hand twisting
away from his body, right hand toward it. What seemed to
be a solid piece of metal was actually two, connected by a
joint along its edge so fine, so cunning, that even close inspection by eye could not detect it. He twisted the two
pieces against each other, just a certain distance, far
enough, but not too far. There was a barely perceptible
click, then the left half pushed upward, again, just the right
distance, not too far or too little. Only then did the two
halves hinge apart and reveal the hidden space within.

It was empty now of course, but it hadn't been the first
time he'd opened it. He stared into the empty recess for a
moment, then pushed the halves back together. It closed
with an audible snap, and again appeared to be a solid
piece of metal. He tossed the medallion on the silk sheets
and turned to reach down behind the bed. His fingers found
a particular stone with a broken corner. He grasped the
edges of it with his fingertips and pulled. The stone pulled
outward and came free. He put the stone down on the floor
behind the bed and reached into the recess, finding the cool
metal within.

The object shimmered as he pulled it out into the light.
It tingled in his fingers as it always had, but he'd never understood that until the previous night. Like its twin, which
was now in Dejal's possession, it was an object of mystic
power. He'd long suspected that this sole legacy that his father had passed to him was a kind of a curse. Now he was
certain of it.

He looked at it. It was flat, oblong, cut straight across
the top, and slightly thickened, forming a tube through
which a cord or thin chain could be threaded. The sides

were curved, tapering to a rounded point. The shape was like some kind of seashell, shield, or even leaf.

But Dejal had called it a "Scale of Set." That made sense, based on the fine relief carving on the front side. Running down the middle was a stout-looking sword, hilt up. Running down either side of the sword were twin serpents, their bodies undulating upward, until the heads curved back toward the blade and down, almost as though bowing to the sword.

The back was engraved with a kind of writing Anok had never seen. Though he'd never shown the object to anyone else, he had taken a rubbing of the symbols, using papyrus and charcoal, and taken that to the Temple of Scribes. There, after offering a suitable tribute of gold coins, he'd been referred from one puzzled scribe to another until finally he'd been led to a high tower, where an ancient scribe sat hunched over his sloped desk, reed pen in hand.

The old man had taken the papyrus and squinted at it for a moment. Then his eyes widened, and a look of alarm came over his face. He quickly held the papyrus over his lamp and burned it before Anok could stop him. "It is an ancient language, written by the giants who ruled Stygia long before true-men came. A lost tongue should remain so. No good can come of it." Then he'd ordered that Anok's gold be returned and had him removed from the temple under guard, with instructions never to return.

Anok recalled the day well. It was when he'd finally given up hope of ever finding his lost sister and fulfilling whatever mission his father had set him upon. He'd sealed the medallion—Scale—into its hiding place and tried not to think about it.

Until now. Had his father been killed over this—trinket? A mystic trinket to be sure, but to Anok's mind that only made it worse. Everything he had ever learned from his father, everything he had seen in his years on the streets of Odji, had taught him that nothing good ever came of sorcery. What were power and riches if they came at the cost of madness and corruption of the body and spirit?

Angrily he threw the Scale back into its hiding place. He was just pushing the stone back into position when he was startled by her voice.

"Anok?"

He turned to see Sheriti holding open the curtain, a look of concern on her beautiful face. "I worried when you failed to return. You seemed troubled, brother. Would you speak of it with me?"

"I thought you were sleeping," he said, casually sliding back on the bed so that his body blocked any view of the Scale's hiding place. "Or that you were angry at me and simply wished me gone."

She smiled slightly. "Because you had a lustful dalliance with a wild woman? I have no claim on you, Anok. Your petty adventures are your own business."

"You don't like her much, do you?"

"I don't know her well enough to dislike her, Anok. But I don't trust her either, and men are such fools to allow themselves to be led around by their nether parts. You're lucky she didn't put a knife in your back the moment you had your kilt down."

He smiled just a little in return. "How do you know I didn't have it up, instead?"

She grabbed a pillow from the end of the bed and threw it at him. By the time he'd ducked it and looked back, she had slipped past him and was sitting in the room's lone chair. She leaned forward, bracing her elbows on her thighs, fingers knitted together, her expression suddenly serious again.

"I worry about you, Anok. I was worried about you before this adventure, and I worry more about you since."

He felt his face harden, and he turned away from her. "Leave. I don't want to talk about this."

"You *do,* Anok, admit it or not. You *need* to talk of it, but your misplaced pride won't let you." She looked at him thoughtfully for a moment. "Your love of us won't let you speak of it, will it?"

"That's foolishness."

She put her hand softly on his knee. "Time is like sand, Anok. If you don't move with it, it will bury you. We have had amazing years together. Wonderful adventures. Shared a bond of trust and blood that few will ever understand. But we're no longer bold children who can be useful to those more powerful than we. For a time, we played as kings and queens of our tiny realm, but those days are gone."

She stood and paced the short length of the room. "We are adults now, Anok, and the rules have changed. The street gangs and warlords who once found our services convenient now see us as threats, potential competitors to their enterprises. They can't stand still for that. Very soon now, one of them is going to give us a choice. Join them, or die."

"What do you care? You'll be well away from here, as will Teferi. Dejal is already gone."

"I care about you, brother Raven."

"Then care not. I'll join them willingly. I'll live by the strength of my arms, and the cut of my sword, just as I do now."

She shook her head sadly. "You will for a time. You're a dangerous man, Anok Wati, but you have qualities that would never let you survive that life. There is still in your heart a capacity for mercy, for kindness, for honor. Soon, very soon, you would have to cross blades with those you claim to serve. Your blades are swift and sure, but you're one, and they are many." She looked away into a dark corner of the room. "I would not care to mourn over your funeral pyre, Anok. But that is the only place where this future leads."

"Then what would you have me do? I have no place but this one, no life but this one."

"Come with me to the Temple of Scribes. If I can gain admittance simply from what you've taught me, you should be able to—"

He thought of his long-ago visit to the temple and the warning not to return. Perhaps the old scribe was dead, but that was the problem with scribes. It wasn't that they had long memories. It was that they wrote everything down.

"That way was closed to me long ago, Sheriti. I wish you well there, but it isn't for me."

"Then go with Teferi on his adventures."

"Teferi tells great tales, but the only adventure he truly seeks is a plot of land, a cow, and a fat wife to pop out babies. It's just that he wants that plot to be anywhere but Stygia. I would only be a hindrance to him in his quest."

She sat next to him on the bed and took his hands in hers.

"There must be a future for you, Anok. A destiny. You simply have to find it."

"I had a destiny once. My father passed it to me. But I lost my way. I am off the path, and I'll never find my way back."

"You dwell on the past, Anok. We were talking of the future."

He threw her hands away in anger, stood, and turned his back on her. "You don't know what's in my past, Sheriti. You don't know anything about me."

She was silent for a time. Then said, "No, I don't. I know you're an orphan, that your father was Aquilonian, and that your mother was Stygian. But beyond that, you have been very private about such matters, and I've respected that. I know your heart, Anok. I don't need to know your past if you don't wish to tell it."

He stared at the blank wall. He'd always kept his secrets, not for lack of trust in his companions but out of concern that the knowledge might endanger them. It was still true. Evidently the acolytes of Set still sought the golden Scales for some purpose of their own, and they would not hesitate to kill to get them.

Yet the secrets weighed heavy on his shoulders like a yoke. After these long years, could he finally share his burden with another?

She was silent for a long time. Then he spoke a single word. "Sekhemar."

"What?"

"Sekhemar. It's my name. My *real* name. The one my

father gave me. Strange, because I don't even think of myself any more as anything other than Anok Wati."

"You don't have to tell me this."

"It's time I did." He recounted for her that terrible night when his father had been killed. How many times had he relived those events in his head? Thousands? More? But he had never spoken of it, not even once, but somehow this was different. It was like picking back an itchy scab. It was a great relief to do it, but what it exposed was raw, painful, and ugly. Sometimes it bled.

The words poured out, but he left his little room behind. He was back in the walled enclave of Akhet, in the compound of his father; the pain, the fear, the anger, were fresher than they had been in years. It seemed as though he were exhuming his own grave, pulling out his dried corpse and somehow shaking it awake.

He ended the tale with him stumbling through the sewers, fleeing unknown and unseen pursuers, plunging into a darkness from which, he now realized, Sekhemar had never emerged. Something else had crawled from the sewers and struggled to survive on the streets of Odji, something that was not Sekhemar. Sekhemar was only a memory, one that had faded with time.

Finally, he pulled the Scale of Set from its hiding place and showed it to her.

"It's beautiful," she said. "May I hold it?"

Her admiration surprised him. He'd thought of the object in many ways, but never as beautiful. Absently he handed it to her.

She cried out and dropped the Scale on the bedding. "It burns!"

Cautiously, he touched the Scale. It was cool, and he picked it up, feeling only the familiar tingle. "It must be the magic," he said, quickly returning the Scale to its hiding place. "I've always thought it was evil."

He was puzzled. Why did it burn her and not him? He'd never let anyone else touch it. He'd never even seen his father touch it directly, and the iron of his father's medallion seemed to contain its effects.

He held her hand, examining the palm. There were red marks, as though she'd held something hot from the fire. "I'm sorry," he said. "I should have thrown it away years ago. I'd melt it down, but perhaps the gold itself is cursed. I don't want to risk that."

"It's all you have from your father, Anok."

"I don't think it was my father's possession, it was his burden. Now it's mine, and I don't even know why. I want to be rid of it. I'm lost, Sheriti, and I'll never find my path until I'm properly free of the thing."

"What do you mean to do?"

"Teferi once told me his tribe has a ritual they call 'Usafiri.' It means something like 'journey.' A young warrior, taking no food, water, or weapons, walks into the wilderness until he can go no farther or until a vision tells him to return."

Sheriti frowned. "That doesn't sound like you, Anok. Do you believe in such things?"

"Visions?" He shrugged. "But if I walk far enough into the sand, and throw this damned thing as far as I can, I will be rid of it forever. They say the sand swallows all things, and that I can believe."

6

ANOK FLINCHED AS Teferi rubbed foul-smelling white paint on Anok's face. "What's in this stuff?"

"The fat of a new calf, herbs, galeha, bat guano—"

Anok pushed his hand away.

Teferi grinned. "I was only kidding about the bat guano."

Through the Nest's small windows, Anok could see the orange light of sunrise. Teferi insisted that Usafiri must begin at dawn, and only after ritual preparations. He'd seemed delighted when Anok had asked him about Usafiri. "Usafiri is just what you need to put you on your proper path, Anok. By rights, you should have had yours years ago, when you first reached manhood, as I did."

But along with that delight came all these rituals and preparations. Anok went along with them to humor his friend, but he didn't have to like them.

Anok frowned and let him continue with the painting. "Is this necessary?"

"You want to go on Usafiri? You must have the face

paint, or Jangwa, wise god of the empty places, will not speak to you. What good would that be?"

"I don't believe in your god, Teferi."

Teferi laughed. "It doesn't matter if you believe in a god. What matters is, does he believe in you?" He stopped for a minute and critically inspected his work, then dipped his fingers back into the shallow dish filled with paint. "Worse, without the face markings, false gods and evil spirits may seek you out and steal your soul. I paint your face to look like a skull. This frightens the false gods and evil spirits, but Jangwa is wise and not afraid. He knows you by your bones as well as your flesh, and he respects the seeker who shows his inner self."

"I will keep an eye out for evil spirits just the same."

Teferi gave him a disapproving glance. "You scoff, and yet your Usafiri takes you toward the Black Pyramid. You may not believe in my gods and devils, but all who live in Khemi fear the Black Pyramid."

Anok had never seen the Black Pyramid, though it was said to be not far east into the desert. Some said it was a day's ride by camel. Others said it was just out of sight of the band of hills, groves, and farmlands that separated the city from the desert. He'd even heard it suggested that the Pyramid moved, or that it appeared out of nowhere, like a mirage. It was said to be ancient beyond measure, built by the Giant Kings who ruled Stygia before the coming of true-men. It was said that it contained treasure beyond reckoning but that no man had ever entered it and returned.

"I have no business at the Black Pyramid. I'd like to see it, yes, but I promise to steer well clear of its walls."

"There," said Teferi, dabbing at Anok's forehead, "it is done."

A basin of water sat on the table next to them, and Anok bent down to look at himself. White covered his forehead and surrounded his blackened eyelids. His nose, too, had been blacked out, and a band of white extended from the corner of each eye, down across his cheekbones, to his chin. Narrow black lines drawn outward from his lips suggested exposed teeth. It was indeed fearsome, and he won-dered what people would think as he walked through the streets.

Teferi looked him over one last time and nodded. "Are you ready to depart?"

Anok patted the front of his tunic, feeling the medallion hanging there, the Scale of Set safely sealed inside. "I'm ready, I suppose." He looked around the Nest one last time, his eyes drawn to the narrow stairs leading up to the brothel and the closed trapdoor at the top. "Where is Sheriti? She said she'd come to see me off."

Teferi grunted. "I told her not to come. Only males must attend to a male going on Usafiri. It would be bad luck for her to be here. I asked Rami to come, but he couldn't be bothered to awake before noon unless there was gold in it."

Anok chuckled as they stepped out the door, and he closed it after them. Hidden latches clicked shut, so only one who knew their secrets could open the door. He patted his palm against the solid wood of the door, as though test-ing its strength. He hesitated for just a moment, telling himself that he'd likely be back before sunset, minus his father's burden. Yet he felt strangely as though he were leaving forever, as though it was the last time he would ever see the place. It made his stomach knot.

Teferi stared at him, concern on his face. "Are you all right?"

Anok nodded. *I don't believe in this.* He started walking.

Teferi walked alongside him. "I will walk with you to the edge of the city, but from there, you must travel alone. I'll wait at the Nest until you return."

As they proceeded down the street, he glanced back over his shoulder at the brothel. It was too early for the whores to be plying their wares, and the curtains were drawn across the large windows where naked women often lounged, beckoning passers-by. He thought for a moment that one of those curtains fluttered back and that he saw someone looking through at him. *Sheriti.*

But then the curtain fluttered closed, and he couldn't be

sure. Perhaps it had only been the wind and his overactive imagination.

His face paint drew stares and strange looks from the people they passed. Small children hid behind their mothers, shopkeepers closed their doors as he passed, and strangers gave him wide passage on the street. That didn't bother him, but he felt exposed and naked without his swords and knife.

Unconsciously he must have been reaching for his missing swords, and Teferi noticed. "You must trust," he insisted, "that Jangwa will provide what you need in your travels."

"I told you, I don't believe in Jangwa."

"Then believe in yourself, that you will find or make what you need."

They traveled east through Odji, past the white walls of Akhet and the black walls of the inner city, until the buildings became lower and were spaced farther apart. There were fewer people, and more livestock, and he could smell growing things. Looming over them, the inland hills were covered with groves of olive trees, dates, black mulberries to feed the silkworms, and carefully tended patches of tilled and irrigated land.

Only a narrow strip of land between desert and sea was suitable for agriculture, so every square foot of arable land was put to use producing food, fuel, wood, or silk. It was true of all of Stygia. Only on a little land along the coast, and along the fertile banks of the Styx and its tributaries, could food grow. Without extensive trade, via ocean, river, and desert caravan, Stygia would starve, which was why traders such as his father were tolerated within the otherwise closed and reclusive state.

Several times before reaching the outskirts of the city, he was passed by camel caravans bound across the desert for points unknown, possibly as distant as Iranistan, or the banks of the Vilayet Sea. A few of the drivers were known to Anok from his years working around the Great Market, and he waved as they passed. When one of them stopped on the road just ahead of him to readjust a camel's load, he approached a familiar driver and asked for a drink of water. The man passed over his water bag and allowed Anok to drink his fill, but the expression on his face told the story. He was staring at Anok's face markings and wondering what sort of fool would head out into the desert without water.

Anok thanked him and continued on his way without explanation. He wasn't sure he could explain what he was doing even if he had wanted to. He wasn't sure he knew himself. But he was formulating a plan.

He would walk into the desert, to where the great and shifting sand dunes began. Then he would walk a bit farther into the sand, to the point where he could just see solid land behind them. There, he would take the Scale of Set and throw it as far as he could. Then he would return to the city. He doubted it could be done before nightfall, but with luck, he would be able to find another friendly caravan and secure water. Perhaps he could even share their encampment for the night. He would return to the city in the morning, rested, free of his burden, and possibly with a new clarity of purpose.

He had dressed for the desert, a full headcloth, and loose and layered clothing like the caravan drivers wore. Even so, it was hot, and his thirst soon returned. He cursed Teferi for his insane rituals, but still he continued. The way climbed, winding up the steep hills that separated the city from the desert. As he crossed the ridge, the last of the greenery disappeared. Ahead grew only scrubby brown brush, cactus, and the occasional deep-rooted tree, dwarfed by lack of water and nearly devoid of leaves.

The houses and buildings became farther and farther apart, until finally there were none. He could look in any direction, and other than the clear trail of the caravan route, there was no sign at all of human habitation. The realization made Anok stop. He scanned the entire horizon to verify that it was true. No house, no buildings, no streets, no walls. All he could see was reddish-brown dirt, rocks, scrubby brush, and jagged, rocky hills.

Anok was, he realized, as alone as he'd ever been in his entire life. He'd been born in Khemi and only knew life on its streets. He'd heard countless tales of the desert and places beyond, from merchants, travelers, and caravan drivers, but he hadn't been there himself since infancy—since his mother's death. He couldn't recall a thing about it, and he had never dreamed it would be like this.

He felt small. He felt alone. Yet he felt strangely powerful. There was no one to help him there, but no one to hinder him either. What he did, what he accomplished, and his very survival, were all up to his own will and resourcefulness. For the first time he began to feel that there might be something to Teferi's Usafiri, that he might be able to find something of his lost direction and purpose out here in the empty spaces.

Not far beyond, he spotted something long and dark lying next to the trail. At first he thought it might be a snake, but it turned out to be the wooden shaft of a spear. He stopped to pick it up. The shaft was some dark wood unknown to him, and the point was flaked from some glassy gray stone, also unfamiliar. Shaft and point were tied together by means of thin bindings made of some kind of leather or gut. A band of ornate carving circled the shaft just below the head, but Anok did not recognize any of the symbols. Doubtless it was a souvenir or trophy dropped by some passing caravan, possibly from Kush, Darfar, or even the Black Kingdoms beyond.

It wasn't much of a weapon, but it was far better than no weapon at all. He hefted it, tossed it gently into the dirt a few yards away. Despite its primitive construction, the balance and heft were good. It was good to have any kind of weapon again.

Eventually, the hills opened up onto a broad valley, and there he saw the Black Pyramid. It was huge, as tall as any tower in Khemi, constructed of smooth stone and as black as obsidian. No road led to the pyramid, and there was no entrance visible. He'd heard, in fact, that nobody had ever found a way to get in. Or at least, nobody had ever returned

to tell of it. Unlike some of the smaller temple pyramids in
the city, this one was not stepped. It had sloped sides, too
steep for a man to climb, forming a sharp point at the top.

He stood on an overlook, wondered what secrets the
pyramid concealed and who had built it. The Lemurians?
The Giant Kings? An even more ancient race?

He became aware of a strange sound, like the ringing
tone of a bell. But unlike a bell, the tone was constant, not
fading over time. Like the chirping of a cricket, it was hard
to locate, seeming to come from all directions at once, but
very close.

Finally, he identified the source. It was coming from his
medallion, or more specifically he suspected, the Scale of
Set itself. "It has to be the pyramid," he said to the empty
desert, startled at how dry and scratchy his voice sounded.
"Magic follows magic."

Somehow the Scale was responding to some mystic energy contained in the pyramid, as a divining rod might respond to deeply buried water. If he'd needed an additional
incentive to stay away from the Black Pyramid, that was it.
He steered a wide distance around it, even though doing so
took him off the caravan trail.

The sun was high in the sky now, beating down relentlessly. There was no shade, no place to take shelter. He
could only keep walking. Sweat streamed down his face,
and the paint began to itch and feel sticky. Finally, he gave
up and wiped the stuff off with the hem of his robe. He'd
take Teferi's superstition only so far. Let the gods and
demons look upon his own face.

As he left the Black Pyramid behind, the sound from
the Scale ceased, to his great relief. He rounded another
turn, and looked up to see something strange, perhaps a
cloud bank, in the sky behind the next hill. He stopped and
blinked.

It took his eyes a moment to make some kind of sense
of what he was seeing. It wasn't a cloud, or something in
the sky at all. It was the peak of a huge sand dune, so large
that it dwarfed the nearer hill. He'd reached the sea of sand.

He turned from his path and climbed to the top of the hill. It was a long way, and the rocks were loose and treacherous, but he needed to see. At last he staggered to the peak of the hill and looked out across the sand. The huge dune in front of him was only one of a countless number stretching toward the horizon, and perhaps not the largest. Anok had several times seen the Western Ocean during a storm, filled with towering waves that rolled with terrible slowness toward the land. What he was seeing reminded him of those waves, frozen in time and made immensely larger.

He put his hand on his chest, feeling the medallion. In this vastness, such a tiny thing could be lost for all eternity. He had only to give it over to the sand, and to do that, he wouldn't have to go very far. That nearest dune should do it. He would climb to the top, take out the Scale of Set (for he wished to keep the medallion itself as a memento of his father), and throw it as hard as he could into the desert. Very soon thereafter, it would certainly be swallowed by the shifting sand, never to be seen by the eyes of men again.

Then he could return to the road and wait for a caravan to pass. He could secure some more water and perhaps even hire a ride back into the city. It would be simple.

Many times, he had walked in the sandy beaches along the Western Ocean, and those that lined some banks of the River Styx, yet this sand was different. It was fine, smooth, and difficult to walk on. With each step, his feet sank into the hot grains, and even on level ground they seemed to swallow up the effort of each step. As he started to climb the dune, it was even harder. The sand slid out from under him as he walked, flowing in sheets like water down the side of the dune, obliterating his footprints.

He put his head down, concentrating on the effort of moving and not the destination. He trudged for what seemed like hours, until he was sure he must be a good part of the way up the dune, and fell to his knees to rest. Only then did he look up, to see the summit of the dune far above him. He'd traveled barely a third of the way up.

With a groan, he let his head hang and marshaled his strength. His lips were dry, and stung where they were beginning to crack, and he ached for the taste of water. But he had to press on or he would never be free of the curse. He struggled back to his feet and staggered up the steep side of the dune, digging the shaft of the spear into the sand and leaning heavily upon it.

Twice more he stopped to rest, each time finding himself only a little closer to his goal. On the last stop, as he let his head hang low to keep the sun out his face, he heard a strange rustling noise, almost like the fluttering of bird's wings. He looked up in time to see rivulets of sand running down the dune above him, the disturbance terminating in a curious hole in the sand, which was already filling with running sand. As he'd lifted his head, there had been just a hint of something at the corner of his eye, low, slightly darker than the sand, and moving rapidly around the curve of the dune out of his sight.

Could something be living out here, a snake or a lizard? Yet he'd never seen any reptile moving as fast as the shadow he'd seen at the edge of his vision. He considered the possibility that he was only imagining things. Then he heard the rustling noise, this time coming from around the dune above and to his right. He looked quickly, but could see nothing. Perhaps there were birds of some kind. That would explain both the sounds and the rapidly moving shape he'd seen.

He made the final press for the top of the dune. Once again, he saw a movement out of the corner of his eye, something skittering along the edge of the dune, a low, dark silhouette outlined against the blue-white glare of the sky. It was gone by the time he turned his head for a better look. He couldn't imagine what it was, but he was sure that some kind of stealthy animal lived out here in the sand.

The view from the top of the dune took his breath away. He could see the line of rocky hills curving off to his right. Beyond that, nothing but sand, seemingly to the edge of the world. For the first time in his life, he felt some small sense

of just how large the world was and how little of it he'd
seen. He'd met and talked to people from dozens of distant
lands, but from the top of the dune Stygia alone seemed
vast, almost beyond imagining. That there could be even
more to the world was staggering.

He reached under his tunic and took out the medallion,
lifting the chain over his head. It became entangled in his
headcloth, and it took a moment to extricate it. He stuck
the hilt of the spear in the sand and pressed the medallion
between his palms to open it. As he did, he saw something
skitter across the dune in front of him, partially hidden by
its downward curvature.

He hesitated, then put the unopened medallion back
around his neck. He'd just picked up the spear again when
the sand just a few yards to his right mounded up and
started to move. The sand flowed back revealing the horror
that had been hiding underneath, a monstrous spider that
eyed him with inhuman malevolence.

It looked like one of the big wind-spiders that were
common around the outskirts of the city and occasionally
could be found even in its center. They were bigger than a
man's hand and, although harmless to a human, could kill
mice and even small rats with ease.

But this thing was far larger, the size of a dog, with eight
legs, plus two thick feelers that it held out in front of its
body. Eight inky black eyes, two large ones, the others
much smaller, studied him with cold interest. The torso
was like a thick sausage and as long as his forearm, but still
small, compared to the rest of its parts. Most intimidating
were the jaws, huge, inward-curving things tipped with
needle-sharp fangs.

Wind-spiders were notoriously afraid of direct sunlight.
They came out at night or kept to the shade. But this one
seemed to have no fear of the sun at all.

It looked capable of snapping off a man's hand, but
Anok didn't care to give it a chance. He hefted the spear
defensively. He felt confident that he could kill it or at least

fend off its attack. He hoped it wouldn't come after him.
He'd back off and give it space.

He looked back down the dune, and saw another huge
spider skitter across the dune below him. Perhaps he'd
stumbled into a nest. He'd have to go forward and head
down the dune that way. Then he could double back to the
caravan road.

He started down the face of the dune, glancing back occasionally to see the huge spider, watching him from the
crest of the dune, its black eyes glinting in the sun, its hair-
covered feelers waving in the air, as though seeking some
scent of prey. So intent was he on the spider behind him
that he almost stepped on another one hidden in the sand in
front of him.

Only the hiss of moving sand alerted him to the spider's
rising up. He dug his heels in, unable to keep himself from
sliding closer to its monstrous fangs. Quickly he swung the
spear around, stabbing not directly at the thing, but under
it, the strong shaft of the spear sliding under its heavy thorax. Then, like a laborer working with a shovel, he lifted
the spider and, with a grunt, sent it flying to one side.

It only traveled a few yards but landed on its back,
where it struggled, sliding down the dune for some distance before finding purchase and flipping onto its ab-
domen. He half expected it to attack, though he hoped it
would run away. It did neither. Instead, it stood, watching
him, feelers waving.

He looked back to see the spider above him moving
cautiously down the dune, maintaining a constant distance
from him. More skittering and movement at the corner of
his eye. Two more spiders trotted down the dune many
yards to his right. Then three more on his left. They moved
in lockstep, holding a precise formation, like soldiers.

Anok felt his blood go cold as the realization struck
him. These weren't solitary animals, hunters of opportunity. *They're cooperating, stalking me like a pack of dogs!*
One spider he could fend off, or two, but not a hunting

pack, not with this spear. He cursed Teferi for convincing him to leave his swords at the Nest. With his swords, he'd have been a match for them. He was sure of it.

But he had no swords, and the spiders were driving him farther into the desert. Grimly, he looked for a defensible position. Ahead and to his left, a smaller dune had a kind of hump on the side, a shelf of sand halfway up its flanks. It wasn't much, but it was the best he could expect among the dunes.

He scrambled up the dune, once again using the spear as a walking stick. It was slow going, but he finally reached the hump. The spiders followed at a wary distance, flanking his position again, some of them going to the top of the dune above. He couldn't be sure, but there seemed to be at least eight or ten of them, assuming there were no reserves out of sight around the dunes or buried in the sand.

Three of the spiders climbed up the dune below him. The largest of them crawled just out of the range of his spearpoint, rearing up, waving its feelers aggressively. Its companions spread out slightly, skittering forward close enough that he could almost poke them with the spear, then dashing backward a few yards, only to return and repeat the performance.

Despite their constant threat, he tried to remain aware of his surroundings and the movement of the other spiders, hoping they wouldn't be able to sneak up on him. A squeal behind him made him jerk his head around. It was the spider at the top of the dune, rearing up on its rear four legs, front legs and feelers waving in the air. *The damned things can make noise, too!*

Another sound made him turn back just in time, as the big spider launched itself at him. He batted it away with the spear, but the other two were also charging him. He knocked one off-balance with the hilt of the spear, then kicked it as hard as he could down the dune. The body made a crack like a goose egg as his foot made contact, and the spider landed, twitching, on its back.

As the third spider leapt at him, he saw two more running up the dune behind it.

The thing was too close to use the spear, and he was forced to drop the weapon. He caught one of the spider's legs in each hand and, keeping his arms straight, was able to keep its jaws away from him. An amber drop of venom dripped off one of the fangs and landed on the back of his hand. He howled involuntarily as the venom began to sizzle against his skin.

He managed to fling the thing away, but the acid venom burned into his hand, and barblike hairs remained embedded in his palms. He reached down and scooped up the spear, hoping to fend off the next wave of spiders coming up the hill. Then the sand under his feet seemed to give way and drop. The hump on which he was standing collapsed into an avalanche of sand. Even as he struggled not to get caught in it, a thick wave of sand swallowed the spiders below him.

He dug in the spearpoint, anchoring himself against the slide, which was already beginning to dissipate, but the buried spiders were simply gone. Perhaps they would dig themselves free, but by then, he hoped to be long gone.

He was sizing up his escape route when the spiders above him came charging down the dune. As the first one leapt at him, he instinctively raised the spear and jabbed. The spear skewered the spider's torso, and a torrent of sticky green fluid ran down the shaft onto his hands. He tried to shake the twitching spider off the shaft, but when that didn't work, he swung the spear rapidly over his head, flinging the gored spider straight at its companions.

The spider landed on its back, and its two companions hesitated in their charge. Anok wondered for a moment if he'd frightened them off, but it wasn't that at all. Instead, the two spiders dived at their fallen companion, plunging their fangs into the soft underside of its thorax, making loud slurping sounds as they sucked out its bodily fluids.

He didn't wait to watch. He turned and started putting

as much distance between himself and the spiders as possible. Instead of climbing over the dunes, he made better time by trudging along the troughs between them. Another advantage was that at least some of the time he was in shade behind the massive mountains of sand.

The problem was it forced him onto a winding path that cost him what little sense of direction he had left. He could see little but a swath of sky and the winding sand in front of him.

Time ceased to have any conventional meaning. The world was measured in terms of his own fatigue and pain. He imagined he could feel the still, hot air sucking the water from his body, drying him like a date in the sun. His lips were dry as old parchment, cracked and bleeding. His eyes stung, and each blink seemed to drag razors across them.

The venom still burned on his hand, and in desperation, he grabbed a handful of sand and rubbed it in the wound. It made the pain momentarily worse, but the sand seemed to soak up the poison, and the pain receded.

Exhausted, he slowed, but he couldn't stop until he was sure he was safely away from the pack spiders. He also had to know where he was, and start making his way back toward the caravan road before he was hopelessly lost. He spotted the highest dune in his vicinity and started the long, and now agonizing, climb. After an interminable ordeal, he crawled the last few feet on hands and knees. Only then did he lift his head and look around.

Sand.

Sand.

He saw nothing but dunes. He was headed straight into the desert. He struggled to his feet. Slowly he turned, scanning the horizon.

Sand.

Sand!

Where were the hills? He should at least be able to see their tops. But all he saw were the rolling peaks of dunes, marching on forever.

The sun was high in the sky, offering no firm clue as to

the direction back toward the sea. He was lost. But if he waited here, the sun would start to sink. He had only to follow it out of the desert, back toward the sea.

He started to sit when a movement at the edge of his vision caught his attention.

By the time he looked, it was gone.

He did not sit.

He waited, and watched.

Then he saw them, a ragged line of low shapes, moving across the top of a dune.

Pack spiders. They were hunting him.

He couldn't wait for the sun. He had to keep moving. It was his only hope.

He turned to run, and in his fatigue, his sandal caught in the sand, one foot hooked over the other.

He tripped.

The spear flew out of his hand and from where he stood, there was nowhere to go but down.

He rolled overhead first, a human wheel on a runaway chariot to oblivion. Faster, each revolution of his body throwing him higher into the air, each landing pounding him like a mallet.

He couldn't breathe, couldn't think.

But his body could react. Instinct twisted his hips, spread his feet apart. One foot caught in the sand, twisting it painfully, and he was tossed spinning through the air. He landed roughly on one shoulder, rolling sideways.

He pushed out his arms and legs, flattened himself on his stomach, stopping his roll. Still, he slid down the huge dune, headfirst, accompanied by a river of sand. There was nothing to do but close his eyes, hold his position, and wait.

He hit the bottom of the dune so fast that the sand felt like solid rock, slamming into the side of his face so hard that he saw stars. He stopped, but the sand kept coming, warm and soft. It covered him up to the small of his back, pinning his legs.

Desperate for air, he coughed, hacking plugs of packed sand from his mouth and nose.

He looked at the world sideways, a panorama of sand starting literally right under his nose.

He was beaten.

He couldn't move. Too tired to go on.

Let the spiders have him.

Then something moved at the corner of his vision. Something big scuttling across the sand on many legs.

That was fast.

It took several moments for his befuddled mind to figure out his mistake. Not big. *Close.*

A scorpion: fat, black, its shell iridescent in the sun.

It scuttled across the sand on business of its own, uninterested in this huge interloper in its little world.

At least it will live.

He was struck by the injustice of it. A useless scorpion would live, and he would die. How was that fair?

Before he knew it, his hand was moving, his arm, flailing, uncoordinated. His hand flopped down over the suddenly alarmed creature. He felt its needle-sharp stinger jab into the ball of his thumb, the hot rush of poison, so familiar that it was almost like an old friend.

A guttural roar came from Anok's throat, whether from pain or simply as a reminder that he still lived, he wasn't sure.

The scorpion struggled under his hand, claws nipping his flesh as it tried to dig its way free.

His fingers tightened around it, and he dragged his hand back toward him. With agonizing deliberation, he reached out with his other hand, and pinched off the thing's stinger, tossing it away.

Still it struggled. He was like the spiders in that way. He couldn't just wait for it to die.

He pulled off the tail, brought the end of it to his cracked lips, and sucked out the juicy meat inside.

It was tough and bitter as he chewed, but the precious few drops of moisture made it worthwhile. He turned his attention to the rest of the thing, ripping the still-squirming body in two, sucking out every drop of its body contents. It made him retch, but he managed to swallow it all.

He tossed the shell, legs still twitching, aside and turned his attention to digging his own legs out. He could feel the scorpion venom burning its way up his arm, but that only helped him to clear his head. "Sweet poison," he said. "Save me."

At last he was free of the sand. He struggled to his feet with new resolve and looked around. Several yards away, he could see the end of his spear sticking out of the dune, and went to recover it. It took all his strength to pull the half-buried shaft from the sand, but he did it.

He stood.

He was alive.

He had a weapon.

There was a noise, a skittering, so soft that he might have imagined it.

But it was probably the spiders.

He sneered and let a hissing breath out through his teeth. "You may take me," he said, "but I won't go easy!"

7

SHERITI STOOD IN the back corridor of the Paradise brothel, the crossroads of its three worlds. Behind her were the kitchens and private quarters of the servants and whores, where Sheriti had lived most of her young life. As would be expected of a place where only women dwelled, it was a place of practical comfort and decoration. Screens of cooling vines grew down to cover the large windows, colorful pottery from distant lands lined nooks in the walls, and the spicy scent of incense permeated the air.

The decorations were simple, tasteful, and understated, almost austere in comparison to public parts of the building, as though the people living there wished to distance themselves as much as possible from that other life.

In front of her was a heavy door made of imported oak, from beyond which could be heard music, boisterous voices, laughter, and the occasional moan of passion. Beyond it was the part of the brothel that the public saw, and where Sheriti was never allowed to venture during business hours. Even through the door, one could smell the perfume, imagine the unrestrained flash of the furnishings and decorations, every sight and smell calculated to intoxicate the senses and entice the customers to hand over their purses.

It was this strange, forbidden place where her mother lived that had provided a livelihood for both of them all these years, in a world that usually did not value a good woman quite as much as a good horse or camel. It was the world that would always stand between them, for though Sheriti had never doubted her mother's love, Kifi had always held her daughter at arm's length.

More so, since Sheriti had entered into womanhood. She had long ago extracted from Sheriti a vow of chastity so that she would never fall into the life in which her mother seemed trapped. *What is this thing, mother, that you will not leave it, and cannot bear the idea of my entering it?*

Yet Kifi wished another life, any other life, for her daughter. She knew only a little of Sheriti's adventures with the Ravens, but it was enough that she often expressed her fear. Still, she had never forbidden it or even spoken against it. "Better to die on the point of a sword than live as a whore," was all she would say. And that was that.

Sheriti could never understand, could never escape the feeling that without the burden of a daughter, her mother might long ago have found some other, better, life for herself. She'd longed for the day she could leave her mother's care and cease to be a burden.

And thus the third world of the Paradise brothel, the world to which she had escaped every chance she got. The Nest.

She walked to the side of the hallway where the thick trapdoor waited, secured by iron latches yet equipped with a clever counterweight so that it could be raised with only a single finger. She opened the latches and lifted the door, looking down the narrow stair, its steps worn from years of constant use.

It was dark and quiet below, so she went back to the kitchen and lit a candle to take with her. She stepped down into the familiar gloom.

At the bottom of the stairs, she glanced around at the cast-off furnishings, thinking of the many good times they'd all shared there over the years: the long talks, the Festival parties, the long sessions planning some adventure or another, the countless hours Anok had spent teaching her to read and write.

She placed the candle on the table in the center of the room. It all seemed so empty, so lifeless, that part of her wanted to mourn.

A tiny noise made her turn. She glanced over at the sleeping cubicle, and her heart skipped a beat as she noticed that the curtain over Anok's corner cubicle was drawn. Had it been closed the last time she'd seen it? She couldn't remember.

Breathless, she stepped over and put her hand on the edge of the curtain, feeling the worn silk caress her hand. She hesitated, praying to her mother's goddesses that she would find him sleeping inside. Then she pulled back the curtain.

Her heart sank. His bed was rumpled and empty, but for a half-read scroll written in Aquilonian. A mouse nibbled at a crust of dry bread left on the table near his bed, oblivious to a stalking house snake slithering its way up the table leg. Sheriti waved her arms threateningly, and the mouse scampered away to safely, leaving the frustrated serpent to find its meal elsewhere.

Sheriti sighed, leaning against the archway, watching the confused snake, searching deliberately for its long-gone prey. Then the outside door rattled.

Somebody knocked.

Could Anok, in anticipation of a prolonged absence, have pulled the hidden latch cord inside before leaving? She rushed to the door and threw it open without even checking the peephole.

As soon as she released the latch, the door was shoved inward, making her stumble back in surprise. A matched pair of giants, swords drawn, pushed through the door, alert for danger. They found only Sheriti.

A third, much smaller, figure followed them into the room. It was Wosret, lord of the White Scorpions. He looked around the room until he was satisfied that no one was hidden there. He turned his attention back to Sheriti.

"I come looking for Anok Wati, harlot. Where is he?"

"I'm no harlot, Lord Wosret, though there are worse things I could be."

His smile was cruel. "You Ravens always had spirit. As children, it was endearing. Now, it grows—tiresome." The smile was instantly gone. "Where is he?"

"Gone."

"Then when will he be back?"

"I don't know. Perhaps never."

Wosret made a tiny gesture, hardly more than the movement of a finger. Instantly, one of his bodyguards swung his sword, so that its point hovered in the air, only a hand's width from her throat.

Wosret sneered. "Don't trifle with me, girl. I made Anok a business proposition, and I expect an answer."

"I told you, he's gone. Three days ago he walked into the desert without water or weapons." She choked on what she tried to say next. She tried to tell herself it was only a deception, a ruse to get rid of Wosret, but it gave voice to the unspoken terror that had haunted her since dawn. "I think—he's dead."

Wosret saw her emotion, and his response was to laugh. "Touching." He laughed again, seeming to consider the idea. "Anok Wati, righteous son of Odji, the two-bladed devil—dead?" He turned and paced the room. "Not what I'd planned"—he chuckled—"but it would serve my purposes almost as well. I was looking forward to taming him, though I had little hope of success. Dead now, and with far less trouble for me, that would indeed serve." He held his hand over the heat of the candle flame, watching the smoke curl through his spread fingers.

Then he looked back to Sheriti. "But I won't believe it, until I see his body with my own eyes. No more of this foolishness! I would leave him a message. Perhaps he'll see it, if I have Kyky-aa and Kyky-nedjes here carve it into your flesh."

"Let her be," a deep voice boomed from the open door. Teferi stepped inside, his sword casually drawn, as though it was more a statement than a threat. "The Paradise pays a fat tribute to you each month for its safety. You do nothing else to earn that tribute, so you could at least leave this place alone."

A look of mock surprise appeared on Wosret's face. "I *am* paid tribute, indeed, for the safety of the whores of Paradise." He made a show of looking Teferi up and down. "If you are a whore, you are indeed an ugly one." He reached for his belt. "But perhaps I should try you anyway."

The huge brothers laughed, Sheriti forgotten, their swords no longer pointed in her direction, but instead at the new threat.

Sheriti slipped closer to Wosret, and her hand casually slipped behind her back.

"Leave *him* be!"

Wosret glanced at her, and laughed. "And what would you do, little harlot? I hear you leave Odji to become a scribe. Match a pen against a sword. Which do you think would triumph?

Her fingers wrapped around the hilt of the scribe's dagger tucked into her belt. Honed to a razor's edge, it was made to sharpen quill and reed pens, but it had other uses as well.

Wosret gasped, eyes wide, as the point of the knife pressed against his groin.

The twin bodyguards were slow to recognize the threat, and while they were still figuring it out she made her position clear.

"Tell them not to move, lord, or before they can act, I will take from you your greatest treasure." It was her turn to laugh. "And whatever happens, you will not be able to take it back!"

Wosret looked desperately at Teferi. "You let this woman fight your battles for you?"

He smiled. "Are we fighting here? I'm not fighting. Sheriti is simply showing you her new blade. If I am to understand, you came to deliver a message. It is delivered. Trust that if we ever see Anok Wati again, he will quickly hear of this." His smile vanished, his face cold. "And we will see what happens then."

Furious, but outwitted, Wosret signaled the bodyguards, who sheathed their swords and marched outside under Teferi's intense scrutiny.

Teferi glanced back at Wosret. "To be clear, we Ravens do not fight each other's battles. We all fight the same battle. That is what makes us strong. You would be wise to remember it."

Sheriti withdrew her knife, holding the blade up for Wosret to see, slowly turning it so that the glint of the polished steel shone in his eyes.

He turned away with a growl and stomped toward the door. "I let you live to deliver my message. But know, this matter is not finished. We will speak again, at a time and place of my choosing, and you will not like it."

Teferi only laughed.

Then Wosret was gone.

Teferi closed the door, making sure it was not only latched, but also bolted. Then he turned to Sheriti.

She reached up to put her arms around his neck, and he bent to accommodate her embrace. Then she stepped back and frowned at him. "You shouldn't have angered him so."

Teferi smiled, just a little. "Me? You were the one who took a knife to his manhood."

She was not amused. "You know what I mean, Teferi. He's a powerful man. He *can* crush us if it suits him."

"It won't. In truth, the brothel's tribute is too important to him. In any case, he won't dare touch you in the Temple of Scribes, and I"—he grinned—"had the courage of one-who-is-about-to-be-gone."

Her eyes widened. "You found passage?"

"I'm a hand on a merchantman bound for Argos and points beyond. Though in truth, I suspect they hired me

more for my sword arm than my nonexistent sailing skills.
There are many pirates between here and the Tybor."

"When do you leave?"

"They sail with the rising tide, a few hours hence."

Her heart strained with conflicting emotions. So long
had her bother Teferi dreamed of leaving this cursed land
behind, but why did it have to be now? And she was expected back at the Temple by nightfall. What if Anok returned, and they weren't here?

What if he *didn't* return?

Sheriti sat heavily on a worn bench covered with scarlet
silk. She looked at the door and thought again of Wosret's
threats. "This," she said sadly, "is the fate to which we
abandon our brother. If he lies dead in the desert, it is because we have driven him there."

Teferi tried, not entirely successfully, to hide his own
concern. "He's fine, Sheriti. He is on Usafiri to find his
purpose. It's a poor life's journey that can be done in a single day."

"It's been three days. No weapons, no *water*. I fear the
worst. How can I not?"

"He is Anok Wati. He is my brother. I must trust that
Jangwa will answer my prayers and provide what he needs
for his journey."

"Nobody," she said sadly, as though telling some sad
truth to a child, "believes in your Kushite gods, brother.
Least of all Anok."

Teferi looked pained. He sat on the bench next to her,
his hands clasped together tightly. He was silent for a time.
"I believe," he said finally. "That will have to be enough."

They were quiet for a time.

Finally, Sheriti spoke. "What if he does return from the
desert? What then? We won't even be here. Who will be
left for him? Rami? Rami is a friend of convenience, not a
true Raven. It seems wrong that he should be the last of our
lot. What will Anok do?"

"He is Anok Wati. He will survive."

"He is our brother, and his battle is not done. Why are

we not fighting it with him? Were your words to Wosret as empty as his heart?"

Teferi had no answer to that. He looked away, as though ashamed. Then he said, "We go to do what Anok has always wanted for us. We go because it is what he wants us to do. He has always looked out for our interests. He wishes to save us from Odji, from foul Stygia itself."

"Then who will save him, Teferi? Who will save him? He says that Dejal has betrayed him, but are we any better?" She considered. "Did Anok ever tell you how we met?"

"He says you saved his life. You found him in the Great Market and brought him here. You gave him a place to live, and a purpose."

She laughed. "I know he always says that. But he saved me. My mother and I were in the Great Market, true, but we became separated, and I found myself alone in an alley with two bandits. I might never have left that alley, if Anok hadn't charged from the shadows, roaring like an angry bull." She laughed at the memory, but her eyes grew misty. "They had swords, and he had nothing. Two sticks, found on the ground somewhere, one in each hand. Two sticks against two men with swords."

Teferi smiled. "The odds were even, then?"

"A little better than that. Before they knew what was happening, he had dashed past their swords, and poked one's eye out. He smashed the other's sword hand with his stick, so hard that his fingers shattered. They dropped their weapons and fled. Anok picked up their fallen weapons and took them as his own. In that moment, the two-bladed devil was born.

"He escorted me back to my mother. She wanted to pay him, but I could see that he had no place to live. I begged her to let him stay in the old stables under the brothel. She agreed that he could stay, for one night only. But he made himself useful, and a day passed without his being asked to leave. And another. And another. Until one day, all thought of his leaving was forgotten."

"Until now," said Teferi, looking around at the empty Nest.

"Until now." She nodded. "What of you, Teferi? Anok always said you saved him."

"Like you, sister, I remember it another way. We fought together that night down on the docks, and who can say who saved whom? But in offering me his friendship and the shelter of this place, it was Anok who truly saved me. I left my family, my many brothers and sisters, and fled to this city, because I knew I was one mouth too many to feed. As the oldest, it was my duty, but I left thinking that I would likely die on these cruel streets."

"But you didn't."

"Preventing death and saving life, they are two different things. Anok may have prevented my death, and perhaps I also prevented his. But I left behind all I held dear. Without family, for me, there is no life. Anok gave me a new family. He gave me my life." He looked away, deep in thought.

"The tide will be in soon," she said.

"Indeed," he said.

"I'm expected back at the temple by nightfall. It's a long journey."

"Indeed," he said.

Neither of them moved.

Together, they waited.

8

THE HUGE SPIDER approached its motionless prey, fangs dripping in anticipation of a long-overdue meal, but still cautious. It was impossible to know if it was thinking about its pack mates that this interloper on their desert, this soft, two-legged thing-with-a-stick had already killed, or if it even possessed the capacity to remember them. But some instinct told it that this helpless-looking creature, lying facedown in the sand, might still be a danger. On the other side of the fallen prey, the only other survivor of the pack watched warily, ready to leap in should the seemingly dead creature move. They were very careful.

Sometimes instinct is wise.

This time, not wise enough.

Anok sensed their approach by sound rather than sight. His left arm was extended in front of him, half-buried, and his left hand gripped the shaft of the spear, just hidden beneath the surface of the sand. *Closer. Closer.*

He heard the thing, so near, the rustling of the hairs on

its legs, the clicking of its eager jaws, the soft hissing of its passage over the sand. Closer.

Close enough!

He scrambled into furious motion, rising to his feet and bringing the point of the spear up through the sand in an arch that intersected the soft middle of the vast spider's belly. It plunged deep, and the monster loosed its death scream, as hot juices ran down to coat Anok's hands. But still he charged forward, on his feet now, both hands on the shaft of the spear, lifting with all his strength.

Behind him, the second spider charged after him, but that was part of Anok's plan.

Still he lifted the spear, the impaled spider, over his head, turning his body as he did. The spider passed zenith, then crashed *down,* hard, on the other side of him. The skewered spider slammed down on top of its surviving companion like the head of a hammer, smashing his armored body open like an egg.

Anok let go of the spear and staggered backward, watching the twitching mass of legs and gore that had seconds ago nearly killed him. He fell back on the sand, still cool from the night's chill, arms outspread, looking at the sky—ice—blue, swept with feathery clouds—and contemplating this miracle.

These two pack spiders were the last. For three days the eight-legged demons had stalked him, and one by one, he had killed them. For three days he had lived on spider flesh, spider blood, and the occasional scorpion or cactus fruit that he had stumbled across. Every day, he thought he would surely die.

And yet, each day, he lived. The pack grew weaker, and he grew—well, if not stronger, then more resolute, more determined to make their hunt as long and costly for them as possible.

At last the business was done, and somehow, unexpectedly, he had lived to see it through.

Which left him with a problem. He had never expected to live and, therefore, hadn't thought about what he would do next. He was still hopelessly lost in the desert, still in danger of dying of exposure, or thirst, or starvation.

What now?

For the moment, he just had to live. Using the point of his spear, and being cautious of the spines, he sliced the spiders open, choking down what he could of their foul insides, sucking the bitter, thick juice from their hollow bodies. It wasn't much, but it might sustain life a little longer.

If their poison didn't kill him first.

The wind picked up, blowing sand into his face. If he continued to lie there, the sand would quickly swallow him alive. Whatever happened, he had to get up, had to move. He struggled to his feet, tying the end of his headcloth over his face to keep out the sand. He squinted and looked out across the desert. Already it was hard to see.

He considered how quickly the sand could bury something.

He'd come to this empty place for a reason. He had a mission that was still not complete. That much, at least, he could still do. His hand went to the medallion around his neck. He'd originally intended to toss it just a little ways into the shifting sand. How far into that sea of dunes had he come? Far enough. No matter what, this Scale of Set would never be seen by the eyes of man again. Even if he died out here, that would be some consolation.

He pulled the medallion from around his neck. But as he did so, he was aware of a strange, ringing sound, a sound he'd last heard near the Black Pyramid! Could he have traveled three days in the desert, only to come full circle? It seemed entirely possible. He laughed at the irony and held the medallion tightly in his hand. He could follow the sound to find the Black Pyramid, even in the blowing wind. He was saved!

The wind was howling now, and through his slitted eyelids, he could barely see through the whirling sand. But as the medallion hummed in his hand, he knew he wouldn't have to. He began to walk, letting his ears be his guide.

Occasionally the sound would grow weaker, and he

would turn until it again increased in intensity. He staggered along for some time. With each step he felt his injuries, his fatigue, his sunburn, and his thirst all the more. Each time he topped a rise, he expected to find himself back on solid ground, to see the Black Pyramid looming out of the sand ahead.

But it didn't happen, and he began to wonder if he'd been wrong. The Scale had responded to the Black Pyramid when it was relatively close, far less than the distance he was sure he'd already walked. Was it responding to something else, perhaps some even greater magic? If so, he could be following its song to his doom.

Yet he maintained hope. Perhaps it was leading him to some other refuge, some oasis, or some lost temple where he could at least find shelter.

Onward he struggled, up one dune and down the next, not daring to take a longer route for fear of losing the invisible mystic trail he followed. He walked though the day. He couldn't see the sky, or the sun, but the light grew dimmer, suggesting that it was nearly dusk.

His throat was parched and felt lined with gravel. With each step, every muscle in his body screamed, but still he pressed on.

Then something happened.

He didn't remember falling, didn't remember passing out. He simply became aware that he lay facedown in the sand, with no idea of how he'd gotten there. He lifted his head, spit sand from his cracked lips, and found himself looking straight into the razor-fanged face of a giant snake, its jaws wide enough to swallow a man whole without even trying.

He recoiled before realizing that the huge eye sockets were empty, the polished white bone of the skull exposed, the terrifying teeth and fangs dry and harmless. This was indeed a huge snake, but it had been dead a very, very long time; skin and flesh gone, even the bones petrified.

The vast skeleton lay on a shelf of rock jutting out of the sand, and though the rock appeared natural, it had been carved by human hands. A circle of inset hieroglyphs, ancient, and in writing completely unknown to Anok, surrounded the skeleton, as though meant, by some mystic means, to keep something out. Or perhaps, to keep the snake in.

Though the wind still howled, it seemed to swirl around the rock, and no sand settled on its ancient, polished, surface. Whatever it was, the rock offered a shelter of sorts from the sandstorm, and slowly, painfully, he crawled forward, over the lip. If necessary, he would gladly curl up inside the coils of the skeleton and wait for the storm to pass.

As he crawled onto the rock, his hand touched one of the hieroglyphs, a symbol that seemed to be the head of a man with a face on each side looking in different directions. As he did, his, fingers tingled. The glyph seemed to glow like an ember, and he felt an electric jolt flow up his arm, making his body convulse.

He nearly fell, but caught himself, careful not to touch the ancient writing again. He lifted his head and caught sight of the snake's skull. The eyes were on fire!

Well, not on fire precisely. In each socket floated a swirling ball of glowing green flame. He felt a strange mix of fear and fascination at the sight, but he did not withdraw.

"Sekhemar, son of Brocas!" The booming voice seemed to come from the snake, though it did not move. "Long have I waited for you to come!"

Anok tried to talk, but at first, all that came out was a dry croak. Finally, he found his voice. "I—am Anok Wati."

"You are both, young warrior, and neither. You are the traveler who walks the narrow, middle path. You are the bridge between places and things. You are many, and yet you are only one."

He coughed weakly. "Is the last thing I'm to hear before I die: a snake spouting riddles?"

The snake laughed a hissing laugh. "You have spirit. You know fear, but you do not let it control you. You will serve me well!"

"I serve no one. I am Anok Wati of the Ravens, and I

bow to no master, answer to no lord. Whoever you are, I will not serve you."

"Abandon your false pride. You *will* serve me. It is your duty by blood! Your father served me, and his father before him, and his father before him, so on, back to a time unrecorded but in my memory."

"Things change."

"Indeed, they do. You misunderstand, young warrior. I do not demand that you serve me. You will *wish* to serve me. You came to this wasteland for a purpose, did you not?"

"I came to be rid of my father's curse. I came to seek my own destiny."

"Your father's legacy, not his curse. You carry with you one of the three Scales of Set, forged before the age of man to give Set dominion over all the serpents of the world."

Anok was alarmed. He had sought to be rid of the evil thing, not to give it to this unknown power. "I carry nothing."

"You lie. I cannot see it, but I sense it. It calls to me."

He clutched at the front of his tunic, his fingers wrapped around the medallion beneath. Even in its iron prison, it rang clearly. There was no sense in denying it.

"It was given to be by my father. You will not have it. I will die first."

The snake chuckled. "You would die to protect what you so desperately sought to be rid of? I don't want the Scale, but you must not cast it into the desert. It is your burden, as it was your father's. Your destiny is already written. You have only to embrace it."

Is this an illusion? Has heat and thirst driven me mad? Anok hung his head and closed his eyes. He was too tired to argue, too tired to resist. Perhaps he would simply humor the voice for a while, and learn what he could. "If I am to serve you, what shall I call my master?"

"I am called Parath, the lost God of Stygia, forgotten by all but a few, such as your father, and now yourself, born into my cult. Hear my tale.

"Once, in the distant time before men, there were many

gods in the world. I was friend to Set, and to Ibis. But Set and Ibis were jealous of each other, and each coveted to hold dominion over the green and fertile land of Stygia.

"I tried to make a peace, to divide this land equally between them. But for my trouble, both turned on me. I was trapped in the body of one of Set's great serpents, and Ibis, fooled by Set's trickery, led me into the desert, stripped my bones of flesh, and exiled me here until the end of time. What happened next, I do not know. I slept for a thousand years, and when I awoke, the green land of Stygia was but a memory. Ibis had been driven from this land, and only the Cult of Set remained.

"We are alike in that way. Set, or his cult, have wounded us both most terribly. Like you, I thirst for revenge. But neither of us can achieve it alone. I am weak from my long exile. My followers are few and scattered. I need your eyes and your hands. I need you to be my agent against the Cult of Set."

"Then find another. I want no part of magic or intrigue. I only want a simple life for myself."

Again the snake laughed. "There is nothing *simple* about your life, Anok Wati. Does a simple man need to keep two names in his heart? Does a simple man need to keep secrets locked away, like a dragon's treasure? Does a simple man hide from his true nature? No matter what you do, the life you seek will never be yours. You will know only misfortune and discontent. The road I put ahead of you is hard, but know that all others are much worse."

"So you say, dead god, if that's what you are. Why should I believe you?"

"Look into your own heart and imagine yourself, an old man on your deathbed. Imagine never knowing who killed your father or the secrets he died to protect. Imagine knowing his death went unavenged and without meaning, that you wasted your life in denial. Will you die in peace, or will your spirit sit here on this rock with me until then end of time, wondering what might have been?"

For just a moment a gust of wind cut across the rock,

and the sand seemed to outline the unseen forms of count-less men, some in dress strange and ancient, all looking at him. Anok's eyes widened, as he desperately looked for someone familiar among those spectral faces.

"No, Sekhemar, your father is not there. He died, his task incomplete, but knowing he had done his best and that he left his son to carry on that work. His spirit rests—if your failure does not drag him back from the great beyond.

"What is your decision, Anok Wati? You see, I have waited a very long time for one such as you, ages beyond human reckoning, and I can wait a little more. If you are not my champion, then leave me to sleep and go die in the desert."

Anok sagged under the weight of his emotions. He thought back to the terrible moment when he'd looked for his father's face among the lost spirits and knew what he had to do.

"Then tell me, what must I do? I am only one man, and the Cult of Set rules all of Stygia."

"To defeat the serpent, you must use its own ways against it. The snake may kill with power, but it hunts by stealth. You must join the Cult of Set. Do whatever you must to gain their trust, learn their secrets, and strike at them from within."

"I can't do that."

"You must. Only this way can you find the other Scales of Set. Oh yes, the cult seeks them as well. Only when all three are joined together is their true power manifest. Set had them made to give him dominion over serpents, but when he had that power, he carelessly cast them aside, thinking them useless. He did not know that, through that power, he had bound himself to the scales for all time. It is written that when the three are joined, they will not only give dominion over all the serpents of the Earth, but over all Set's followers as well."

"Then if I had the Scales—"

"You could be a mighty king, Anok Wati. More than that, a god, with an army of followers willing to die in your name. You could take the Cult of Set, the *power* of Set, and make it your own. But if the cult should gain the Scales, then their power over this land will be absolute. They will crush any that will not join them, then march across the world in Set's name until his coils wrap around all the oceans and engulf the land of man forever."

"I don't want power."

"Fool. *All* want power, if only to deny it to others. Embrace your destiny, or let all you love fall to Set, if that is your wish."

His head pounded, and he felt the world swirling around him. Something, death or unconsciousness, threatened to engulf him. He barely cared which.

"I—deny Set. If I live, I will do as you say."

"*If* you live. That is the question, and I cannot answer it."

"I will not beg for help."

"And I would not grant it if I could. You must be strong if you are to serve me. The ways of Set are seductive, and must be resisted at any cost. I will help you then, if I can, but if you do not live that long, then you would have failed anyway. Go, and if you are worthy, we will meet again."

Anok groaned. He could barely move. He wasn't going anywhere.

A gust of wind slapped him in the face with sand, blinding him momentarily. Darkness swirled around him, and he fought it with all his strength. Then it passed, but when he looked, the rock, the snake, were gone. There was nothing before him but swirling sand.

He had no idea which way safety lay. He only knew it was not here. With agonizing slowness, he began to crawl.

For a thousand years he crawled, until his limbs were made of fire, and his body was as dry as the sand beneath his palms. Then, the year after that, he fell, and let the shifting sands cradle him like a blanket.

I tried.

9

"HE'S ALIVE."

The voice was very far away.

It occurred to Anok that the voice was not far from him. He was very far from the voice, at the far end of a dark tunnel.

Alive? That was good news, he supposed. Who was alive?

"I see him, Rami. Help me dig him out."

Anok wanted to help, too, but he couldn't seem to find his arms or legs.

"I found him. You dig, Teferi. I'm dying here."

"If you're going to die anyway, you might as well dig."

I'm dying, too, but I still can't find my arms and legs.

"Fine, but if I collapse, you'll have to carry both of us."

He seemed to feel something at a great distance. It seemed to be miles away, but something was touching it. Could it be his foot?

The black tunnel seemed to get longer, the sounds and sensations, such as they were, more distant.

Until they were gone.

Instantly they were back, but Anok somehow felt that time had passed during the interval. Perhaps a great deal of time.

"This bow is heavy. Why can't you carry it?"

"Because, you lazy jackal, I'm carrying Anok. It's most certainly the least you can do."

He's carrying someone with my name. That's interesting.

Then the tunnel stretched away to infinity again.

Time passed.

When he came back, somebody was coughing, and something seemed to be trying to suck him up into the sky.

"He threw up is what."

"Mercy of Bel, Teferi, what did he eat? It smells like poison."

"Those dead spiders we found. I think he had to eat them. It's a miracle he's alive. Jangwa watches over him."

"*Now* he's alive. It's still a long walk back to camp, and he doesn't look good."

Again darkness.

He returned to discover his arms and legs were back. Somebody had taken them and abused them mightily. They seemed to serve no function except to cause him pain. Thankfully the hammering in his head, and the cramping of his gut, provided a welcome distraction. It someone hadn't jammed his throat with broken pottery shards and thorns, he'd register a complaint.

He seemed to be lying on his back.

Was he dead?

He forced his eyes open, a difficult task, since someone seemed to have sewn the lids shut. Someone leaned over him.

He was dead, almost certainly, and he had been taken to some otherworldly paradise. Only that could explain the beautiful face that smiled down at him.

"Teferi! He's awake I think." The face leaned closer. "Anok, do you hear me?"

With effort, he blinked. It seemed reply enough. He was tired.

Another face leaned in next to the first. Male. Skin dark as tanned leather. Somehow familiar. "Anok. We came for you, brother. We found you at the edge of the dunes, half-dead."

Before he could think, his cracked lips were trying to form words. What came out was a dry whisper. "Which . . . half?"

The dark man blinked in surprise, then laughed. "Our brother has returned! Even the forces of death cannot defeat him."

The beautiful woman scowled at the dark man, but she was still beautiful. "Don't speak of death. He's alive." She turned back to look down at him.

Sheriti. Her name is Sheriti.

She continued, "He's going to be fine." She reached down and stroked his hair.

It made him shiver. He'd forgotten what it was like to feel anything but pain.

"Fine," he managed to croak. Then his eyes drifted back to gaze upon the dark man. "Teferi. You were . . . right. I saw . . . gods in the desert."

"I was a fool, Anok. You saw visions caused by poison. That's all."

"I know what I saw." His burning eyelids were heavy. "Sleep now."

Sheriti brushed hair. "Sleep," she said.

10

ANOK AWOKE TO the jostling of wagon wheels on cobblestones, and the fragrance of mulberry leaves. He squinted up at a strip of sky framed by colorful awnings and the stone facades of buildings. He heard voices, children playing, merchants hawking their wares, herdsmen coaxing their flocks through the narrow streets.

He was back in the city.

Khemi. It seemed like he had been gone a lifetime.

He managed to turn his head and examine the immediate surroundings. He was in a small, stake-sided wagon, lying in a bed a mulberry leaves. The leaves were doubtless bound for one of the city's many silkmakers, who would feed them to their silkworms. He could see the driver, a small woman hunched on the narrow seat at the front of the cart, reins to some unseen draft animal held tightly in her wrinkled hands.

How did I get here?

A familiar face popped into view, looking over the edge of the little wagon. *Rami!* Anok tried to talk, but before he could do much more than part his lips, Rami put a finger to his lip to signal for silence. Then drew two fingers over his eyes, as though closing the eyes of a corpse. Anok was glad to oblige.

He heard other voices nearby, arguing. Familiar voices. A female voice. "Leave him alone! He's of no use to you." *Sheriti!*

"I'll be the judge of his worth, scribe. Out of my way!" This one was harder. Familiar, but less so, and less pleasantly so. *Wosret, street lord.* That couldn't be good news.

Then the sound of scuffling.

Wosret again, "Are you going to try and stop me, Kushite?"

"No." It was Teferi. "You should see this with your own eyes."

A pause, but a dimming of the light coming through his eyelids suggested that someone was leaning over him. "Set's fangs, what happened to him?"

"We'll ask him," said Teferi, voice dripping sarcasm, "if he wakes up again. You see now, he's no use to you, or threat either."

Wosret made something like a growl. "As you say, he's not much better than a side of spoiled meat—at the moment. But I'll be keeping an eye on him."

"Careful," Teferi's voice was raised, as though talking to someone walking away from him, "that you don't get it poked out." Then he muttered under his breath, and there was silence for a bit.

"You're not dying, you know," Rami's voice was quiet, and close to his ear, as though he were leaning over the wagon, or perhaps given Rami's small stature, hanging momentarily over the side.

"He's awake?" There was excitement in Sheriti's voice.

"He is," said Rami.

Sheriti squealed with excitement, and Anok opened his eyes in time to see her leap into the wagon next to him. The whole wagon jolted, and he heard both mule and driver complain in their respective tongues, neither of which he understood. "I should really learn to speak mule," he said.

Sheriti beamed down at him, putting her hand gently next to his cheek. "Oh, Anok. I was so worried for you." She placed her hand on his sweat-covered brow. "But your fever seems to have finally broken."

"Broken," he mumbled, "along with everything else I have."

She laughed, and it was like the sound of chimes in an ocean breeze. "It only feels that way. You need rest, and food, and especially water, but you will be fine."

For a moment, he thought it might be true. Then he thought of the snake, Parath, and he knew he was not fine at all. But he didn't say so to avoid troubling Sheriti. After all she and the others had done, it was too early to give them the worrisome news, if at all.

The streets were crowded now, and bodies passed by close on either side of the cart. He caught sight of two men wearing the robes that marked them as priests of Set. One of them glanced down at him with passing interest, but they moved on by and were lost in the crowd. If the thought of what he had to do sickened him, what would his friends think?

ANOK WAS RETURNED to the Nest, where, day after day, he grew stronger. At first he took only soup and beer, but soon he was able to consume the more substantial food Sheriti brought him from the kitchen upstairs.

But while his body was stronger, his mind seemed slower to heal. He slept through the day, and that sleep rarely went untroubled by disturbing, even terrifying, dreams. Even when awake, he felt drugged, plagued by imaginary sights, sounds, and voices. Once, he pounced from his bed and took up his swords, convinced that one of the pack spiders had somehow followed them and invaded the Nest. Sheriti was eventually able to calm him enough to return him to bed. Only later did he realize his "spider" had been nothing more threatening than a leather-covered footstool.

Between such spells came moments of heightened, almost stiletto-sharp clarity, which only made the memories of his bizarre behavior and the anticipation of his eventual slide back into madness all the more painful. Equally troubling were the concerned and even fearful looks Sheriti and Teferi gave him, even in his most lucid moments. At least one of them remained at his side, day and night, during his recovery, and he could only imagine what terrors they must have witnessed during his more difficult moments. They spoke to him slowly and carefully, as a patient parent might speak to a slow and excitable child.

Finally, an entire day passed without Anok lapsing into his waking nightmares, and his patience with his caregivers grew thin. As Sheriti tried to feed him soup, he snatched the bowl and spoon from her and waved her away. "I'm not some helpless babe, woman! I can feed myself!"

The look of hurt on her face immediately made him regret his words. "Sheriti, I'm grateful for your care, but I'm starting to feel like my old self again. I could do with less care and more company. Please"—he gestured at the footstool next to his bed, which only days before had filled him with abject terror—"sit with me and talk with me as other than a child."

She tilted her head and smiled slightly. "Oh, Anok. I'm sorry as well. We're worried about you so much. I'm glad to see you feeling better, and in my heart, I knew you were. But we've seen improvement before only to be disappointed later. I'd barely dared to hope that your mind was clear again."

"As clear as it ever was, anyway. Please, Sheriti"—he patted the stool—"sit."

She looked doubtful. "You're sure you're feeling better?"

"Nothing is sure. I've been through a trial, and I'm not sure I'll ever be the same again."

"Then you found whatever you were looking for out in the desert?"

"I found . . . something. I'm not ready to speak about it." As he spoke the words his fingers unconsciously went to his chest. He realized that the medallion was gone, but somehow there was no concern. The medallion was nearby. It was as though he could sense it.

Sheriti noticed his gesture. She stood, walked to a nearby table, removed the lid from an earthenware jar, and extracted the medallion by its chain. "I kept it safe for you." She handed him the object and settled back on the stool. "I thought you were going to throw it into the desert."

Anok held it by its chain, examining it. He could feel something, something that hadn't been there before. Had the medallion changed? The Scale of Set that was within? Or had he himself changed during his journey into the desert? He could only be sure that he no longer feared the Scale, no longer wished to be rid of it.

"That's part of what I realized out in the sand. This thing is my legacy, and it cannot be denied. If I throw it away without uncovering its secrets, then it will torment me more surely than having it here."

She looked unhappy. "Are you sure that's the right decision? It's magic, Anok, and you don't like wizardry any more than I do. Any more than any sane person does."

How was he going to tell her what he must do? "A thing sometimes can't be taken at face value. Not just things, but actions as well. What may appear, at first, to be wrong, even insane, may have its purpose."

She seemed to roll the words around in her mind, like someone tasting an unfamiliar wine. "You mean that this trip into the desert, it's brought you some kind of peace?"

Seeing the hopeful look in her eyes, he faltered. How could he tell her what he must do? Right now, he couldn't. But perhaps he could tell another. "Yes, you could say that." He licked his half-healed lips. "Sheriti, I'd like to speak with Teferi and thank him for coming to find me. Where is he?"

"He's taken a room at the Green Lotus Tavern up the street. The way you've been crying out in your sleep, there was no way he could rest here."

"Then go find him for me, see if he's awake."

She looked doubtful.

He smiled at her. "I'm much better. I can fend for my-self for a handful of minutes. Go."

She smiled back. Reluctant though she was to leave him, the prospect actually seemed to please her. Whether it was on account of his improvement, or simply of being re-lieved of her burdens for a few minutes, he couldn't be sure. His illness must have been a terrible trial for her.

Finally, she nodded. "I'll go find him. I'm sure he'd want me to wake him."

Anok watched as she left, then waited a bit more to make sure that she wouldn't forget something and return. Only then did he remove the hidden stone from the wall be-hind his bed. He took off the medallion, studying it. Then he put it down on the blankets and painfully climbed to his feet. His legs were stiff from days of bed rest, and he leaned against the walls and furnishings for support as he moved.

His destination was a cabinet where odd items were kept, mostly smaller household goods cast off from the brothel above, stored in case they should someday become useful. He dug through them until he found what he was looking for, a small iron box with a hinged lid.

Anok returned to his bed and sat down heavily. He care-fully opened the medallion, and extracted the Scale of Set. He was surprised to feel it vibrating in his fingers, almost as though it was trying to ring, as it had previously, in the desert. That was strange. It had never done so before in the Nest, and there were no other magical objects here that he knew of. Had something been introduced in his absence?

There would be time to puzzle on that later. He carefully placed the Scale within the box and closed the lid, then slid the box into the hidden nook in the wall. He wondered, as he pushed the stone back into place, why he'd waited until Sheriti was gone to hide the Scale. Didn't he trust her? He pondered. *When it comes to the Scale, I trust no one.*

He pondered again. *I would trust her with my life. I have done so many times. Is this thing now more precious to me? Or is it the secrets that it may hold?* Perhaps he only sought to protect her from the secret and the dangers it entailed. That was a more honorable way of looking at it. He only hoped that it was true.

The sudden opening of the door startled him. He heard approaching footsteps and immediately leapt for his swords, draped across a nearby bench.

"Easy," said a deep, booming, voice.

"Teferi?" His hand was on the hilt of one of the swords, but he had not drawn it.

"It's me, brother," Teferi answer cautiously, peering around the curtain. "Don't you know me?"

Anok laughed and let go the sword. "Of course I know you, old friend." He wobbled to his feet, feeling at least a fraction of his old strength returning, and embraced Teferi. "Again, it seems, I owe you my life."

Sheriti looked around the curtain and smiled to see the two old friends together.

Teferi took a step back, his face turned serious. "You owe me only passage out of the desert. If it were not for the skilled care of fair Sheriti, I'd have been hauling only your corpse back from the Sea of Sand."

"And Rami," added Sheriti.

Teferi frowned slightly at the mention of the name. "It was the little rodent who spotted you, true. Of course, I had to bribe him to come search with us."

Anok smiled. "I'll pay you back."

Teferi returned the smile. "You certainly will." He glanced at Sheriti.

"I told you," she said.

"He does seem himself again."

"Who else would I be?"

"Who indeed?" Teferi raised an eyebrow at Anok. "You have often been someone these past few days. Someone I know not. Somebody whose acquaintance I have no desire to gain. We wondered if ever you would return."

Suddenly tired again, Anok sat on the edge of the bed. "Yet here I am, back in the Nest. Back where I was before."

Teferi looked concerned. "There was nothing for you in the desert then?"

Anok did not answer. He looked at Sheriti. "I would speak with Teferi alone."

She frowned but did not move.

"Please," he said, managing a smile. "It's man talk. It would neither amuse nor interest you. You've spent far too much time here these past days. Go find your mother. Inform her you're yet still alive. She may be wondering."

Sheriti smiled weakly and nodded. "I should do that. The master scribes may not forgive my absence for so long, but I am always welcome in my mother's arms." But she moved only hesitantly toward the stairs. He waited until he heard her climb the steps, then turned back to Teferi.

But it was Teferi who spoke. "I am sorry, brother, sending you on this fool's quest. Your gods are not my gods. I nearly sent you to your death, and all for nothing."

"No, old friend, not for nothing." He looked away, thinking. He wasn't sure how much of his experiences—be they fact, vision, or hallucination—he wanted to share. But he had to tell Teferi what he was about to do, and he had to make him believe there was a good reason for it. Moreover, his gut told him that he needed the aid of his old friend, even if he wasn't sure why. Somehow, he knew that he couldn't do this alone, and for that, he was going to have to ask his friend to make even more of a sacrifice than Teferi had already made.

Anok rubbed his forehead, searching for words. "There were gods in the wilderness, Teferi, just as you said, and they have set for me a destiny. But I warn you, you won't like it any more than I do." With a grunt, he pushed himself to his feet. This was no announcement to make sitting down. "I am going to join the Cult of Set as an acolyte."

Teferi looked at him, expression blank. He blinked. Then he turned to leave. "I will go fetch Sheriti. You are obviously still suffering madness."

"Come back!" The anger in Anok's voice surprised even him.

Teferi stopped, looked back over his shoulder.

"I say this to you with a clear mind, old friend. I have not spoken to you before of my father and his death—his murder—but it weighs on me every day. I have long ignored my past, pretending to be something—someone—I am not.

"But I am my father's son. I must know why he died, and I must avenge his death. The answers I seek can only be found within the forbidden walls of Set's temple. Only there can I extract my vengeance."

Teferi just looked at him, a pained expression on his face.

"That is how it must be done."

"You haven't told Sheriti this, or her mood would be even more dire than mine."

He hung his head. "No, I haven't told her. I don't know how I can."

"But you've told me."

"I need your help, Teferi. Once I join the temple I'll be watched, my movements will be limited. I need an accomplice who can act freely in my stead."

Teferi's face was grim. "You ask much."

"I do. I know you wished only to be free of Stygia. If you went and found another ship and left this place forever, I would not blame you. I might even be relieved. But for my own selfish reasons, I ask you to follow me closer to Stygia's dark heart. Refuse if you will, but I must ask."

Teferi stood silently. Anok could see his broad shoulders tense, his jaw muscles bunching beneath ebony skin. "I would do this for no other, Anok Wati. No other man, anyway. There is one other who we both hold as dear, for whom we would pay any price, do any deed."

Anok nodded.

"She should know."

"I realize that, but I tell you this only because I must, and because you can understand the meaning of Usafiri. It is bad enough I've dragged you to this dark place. She need not follow."

Teferi nodded. "It's better that at least one of us escape this slum to a finer life. If it is only one, let it be her."

"Agreed."

Teferi took a deep breath. "I know a way we can explain your joining the cult, one that will make it seem necessary without drawing her into the rest."

Anok blinked. "That would please me."

"There will be danger."

"There always is."

Teferi nodded. "I need to go then and spread rumors of your improving health. Until then, I leave it to you to make those rumors true. We'll speak of it again later."

Teferi turned to leave.

"Teferi."

"Yes?"

"Send word to Dejal. Tell him I wish to speak with him."

Teferi's face twitched, but he only nodded. He left quietly, latching the door behind him.

The wind of the closing door blew out the candles in the room, and Anok sat on the edge of the bed, lost in shadows.

He and Teferi, they had became coconspirators, planning a deception against their closest friend.

He'd always believed that no good ever came of sorcery. Now he was sure of it.

11

IT FELT GOOD to strap on his swords. It had been nearly two weeks since Anok had walked the streets of Odji. He'd felt like an invalid child the whole time, and it had grated on him constantly. Yet he knew he couldn't show himself at anything less than fighting strength. He had too many enemies on the street.

He knew that well. In fact, he was counting on it.

He heard the trapdoor to the upper floors squeak open and Sheriti's soft footsteps descend. He tightened his belt, squared his shoulders, and drew himself to his full height. Even the sandals felt unfamiliar on his feet. How long had it been since he'd been properly dressed?

Sheriti peered carefully around the curtains into his sleeping alcove. "Are you dressed?"

He grinned broadly. "Yes, in fact, I am."

She stepped into the archway. She was dressed in a flowing purple robe of iridescent silk. Belted around her narrow waist, it covered her from ankle to shoulders, baring only her arms, neck, and a tantalizing triangle of chest. A pink headcloth covered her hair, held in place by a thin ring of brass around her forehead. It was city attire, more appropriate to a scribe than a rogue of the streets.

She looked him up and down, smiling. "You look especially fine today. My strong warrior has returned."

He found that her compliment touched him more than he could have expected. But he was still transfixed by her appearance.

She noticed his stare and glanced down at her garments. "You don't approve?"

He rubbed his chin, glancing away in embarrassment. "That isn't it. I'm just surprised. I've never seen you dressed like this. You look like one of the noble class, not gutter trash like the rest of us."

"Anok—"

He silenced her with a wave. "You know what I mean. I knew this day would come, and yet nothing could have prepared me for it. You will be leaving these dark streets behind forever."

She looked suddenly uncertain, uneasy. "Only to trade them for dark towers and castles, peopled with full-blooded Stygians born to evil."

"Still, it's better than this."

She hung her head. "I'm not sure I should go, Anok. This is my mother's dream, not my own. She wishes for me a quiet life of safety, at any price. I'm not so sure I wish to pay the toll on this journey. I am expected, without fail, back at the Temple of Scribes in two days' time. The master scribes are already angry at my absence, and only lush bribes sent by my mother have earned this degree of forgiveness. Perhaps it's better that I not go at all."

Anok shook his head. "That's nonsense. It's for the best, Sheriti. There's nothing left in Odji for you. If you stay here, what will become of you? Will you be a wanted and despised rogue as I have become? Will you become a whore like your mother?"

Anger flashed across her face as her mother was mentioned. "And what if I did become a whore? Would it be so terrible?"

He stared at her for a long time. "Yes," he said finally. "It would be a terrible waste. Your mother knows that, and whatever else your mother is, she's a wise woman."

She avoided his eyes, frowning into the dark corner of the room. "A rogue then."

"You'll end up dead, or worse."

"And you?"

"Dead, probably. Just dead."

He jaw clinched. "It wasn't supposed to end like this, Anok."

"You're getting out of this slum." He paused, choosing his words carefully. "That's worth any price, any sacrifice."

She turned and glared at him. "Why, then, are you still here?"

As I had hoped.

At that opportune moment, Teferi rushed in, smiling. He couldn't have timed it better if he'd been listening from outside, which perhaps he had. He stopped and looked at both of them. "Am I intruding on something?"

"No," said Anok. "We were just talking." He patted his friend on the shoulder. "It's good to see you. This place has become my prison. I thirst for escape."

"Then away with us," he said cheerily, though Anok knew that most of it was an act.

The stated plan was simple, a trip to the Great Market-place, some shopping, some entertainment, a good meal, an evening drinking at their favorite tavern. That was what they'd told Sheriti anyhow. In fact, Anok and Teferi had quite a different scenario in mind.

It was a fine day outside. The sky was blue, striped with thin, lacy clouds like furrows in some celestial farmer's field. A cool breeze swept in from the Western Ocean, driving the heat back into the desert and sweeping away the cloud of smoke and stench that sometimes hung over Odji and replacing it with a tang of salt.

The mood on the streets reflected the weather. Odji was not a joyful place, but today people acted almost as though it was a holiday. Squealing children chased each other around parked donkey carts, and goats and geese rooted happily through the garbage heaps in the alleyways, looking for tasty morsels.

Sheriti's dark mood quickly passed, and as Anok studied her face, he felt growing unease with their actions. *It's a fine day for lying,* he thought. But he and Teferi were only trying to protect her the only way they knew how.

The market was busy, though the pace seemed less hectic than usual. Browsers took their time, watching the merchants. Some sellers stood on raised platforms hawking their merchandise, others sang or pounded drums or gongs to gain attention.

There were roving bands of performers—musicians, dancers, jugglers, acrobats, magicians—living off donations and bribes from merchants to stay near their shops, or to stay away, depending on the quality of their performance.

The Ravens stopped at a leathersmith's, where Anok purchased a set of scabbards that would allow him to wear his blades crossed over his back. He explained this to Sheriti by describing its advantages in allowing stealthy movement in confined spaces. In truth, he anticipated the arrangement would be more compatible with the robes of an acolyte.

Yet as he tried the scabbards on, even the thought of wearing those robes sickened him. *This will be the most difficult thing I've ever done. Even the Usafiri will seem a trifle by comparison.*

He was glad to move on.

Like most women, Sheriti was uncommonly attracted to shiny things, and as she had often done before, she dragged her male companions into a silversmith's shop. What was uncommon was that she was drawn to a tray of men's rings. She looked through them, found one she was taken with.

She showed it to Anok. It was ornately carved, as though circled by ancient vines, and was decorated by a strange two-faced creature.

The smith, a humpbacked man with long, black hair and

carefully manicured hands, scuttled over to see. "Yes," he said, his voice high and nasal, "the lovely maiden has made an interesting choice." He took the ring from her, slid it loosely over his extended pinky, and pointed at the faces. "This is Jani, an obscure demon worshiped by some of the nomads who wander the sea of sand. His cult is small, but he is said to be good luck for those facing peril. Two faces, he has, you see, and can watch for danger approaching from all sides."

Sheriti smiled. "That sounds right. How much?"

He named a price, and her smile turned into a pout. "It's just a little silver ring."

The smith pulled it closer to his chest. "I didn't make this one. Very old, very well crafted, and from very far away. I can show you other rings."

She reached out and grabbed his wrist as he started to turn away. "I like this one." She drew his hand closer and, while looking unflinchingly into his eyes, bent down and took his pinky into her mouth. She lifted her head slowly away from his hand, the pink tip of her tongue moving between her barely parted lips as she stood. "How much, again?"

The smith blinked, his mouth hanging open. He swallowed hard. He named a much lower price, barely more than the ring's weight in silver.

She nodded, removed the silver from her purse, and placed it in the smith's palm, allowing her fingers to stroke his as she withdrew her hand.

The smith seemed to choke on his own saliva and convulsed in a coughing fit. By the time he'd recovered, Sheriti had slipped the ring on Anok's right hand. "A gift," she said, patting his hand, "a remembrance." Before he could argue, she was headed for the door with Teferi a few steps behind.

Anok lingered, glancing first at the ring, then the silversmith.

The smith eyed him anxiously. "I meant no disrespect toward your woman, good sir. She was—very bold."

"She's nobody's woman but her own. This ring, it isn't cursed, is it?"

"Cursed? No, as I said, good luck."

Anok nodded and turned to leave.

"Except—"

Anok paused, glancing back over his shoulder.

"This Jani, because he can see all around, he travels only in circles. He can never leave the desert."

Anok glanced at the ring on his extended finger again. The two faces mocked him. He had half a mind to put it back.

But Sheriti had chosen it for him, and he didn't want to hurt her feelings. Finally, he clenched his hand into a fist. "Leaving the desert," he said to the smith, in parting, "is harder than it seems."

Anok stepped out of the shop and quickly caught up with his companions. He caught Sheriti's eye as they walked. "What did that mean?"

She tilted her head, obviously puzzled by his mood. "What? That I acted like a woman for once? I wanted to buy you a gift. I used all my powers of persuasion to get a good price."

"It's not like you."

"I'm not a child any longer, Anok. Or hadn't you noticed?"

"I'd noticed. You're usually just not so blatant about it."

She laughed harshly. "Perhaps you weren't paying attention."

Teferi was glancing back at them, eyebrow raised. He shook his head and turned away.

They walked silently for a while. A blind beggar sat on the edge of a fountain, shaking his beggar's rattle over a small leather cup with a few small pieces of silver in it. Sheriti paused to toss a gold coin into the cup.

Hearing the heavy thud of the coin against leather, the beggar's cloudy eyes opened wider. "Thanks to you, kind stranger. May Set smile upon you!"

Anok felt his face twitch at the mention of Set but said nothing.

Sheriti glanced at Anok. "You haven't got the sense of a beggar."

"What?"

"I bought you a gift, and you say nothing."

He glanced at the ring. Any other day it would have pleased him, but today it gave him no pleasure at all. In fact, it added to his sense of foreboding. Still, she was right. "Thank you. It's a fine gift. I'll wear it always."

"Or," added Teferi, "until he breaks it against someone's face in a brawl."

Anok almost smiled. "Until then, anyway."

"That will have to be enough," said Sheriti. A stall up ahead caught her attention, and she walked purposefully toward it, leaving her companions behind. "I need something from the poisoner."

In another land, that simple statement might have caused stares, or at least some sense of concern, but Anok just nodded, and Teferi, distracted by a nude Shemite slave girl being shown at a nearby stall, hardly seemed to notice.

Stygia was famed for its poisoners, who were treated as respected craftsmen and operated in plain sight. This one was typical, a stall lined with hundreds of small bottles and jars containing mixed, brewed, and distilled extracts of lotus, snake venom, the poison sacks of various crawling creatures, and various poisonous plants. They did not deal in magical potions, though those practicing sorcery sometimes bought their base ingredients at such shops.

Each container was carefully marked both for contents and its intended use, for any mistake could be fatal, and that was not *always* the intent. A poisoner did sell deadly poison, of course, to kill an enemy or simply rid a granary of rats. But they also sold poisons mixed and diluted to produce other effects. Their potions could calm a willful slave, break a fever, relieve a pox, or even, it was claimed, cure a body suffering from corruption. A bitter sip from the right bottle could rid a person of lice or fleas for weeks or clear a gut troubled by worms.

Poisoners also sold antidotes to poison, making money off both ends of the trade. Of course, each poisoner had his or her own special—and very expensive—poison for which they claimed there was no antidote, and of course the poisoner across the street always claimed to sell the antidote for *that*.

So Anok thought nothing of Sheriti going to make a purchase from the poisoner. At least, that is, until he saw that there was already another female customer in the stall. "Gods," he muttered, quickening his pace. Today's plan included an arranged "chance meeting," but this was not it.

Anok had almost caught up to Sheriti when the woman in the booth turned. Anok had recognized her from behind, but Sheriti only now realized who was standing there.

Sheriti stopped at the edge of the stall. "It's the barbarian," she said.

"So it is," said Anok, his heart sinking.

Fallon of Clan Murrogh recognized Anok and smiled broadly. To his embarrassment, she walked up between him and Sheriti, held his head in her hands, and kissed him hard on the lips. "Anok of Wati, I hoped I might see you again before I left this city!" She frowned slightly. "You look pale. Have you been ill?" She wiped her lips, as though having noticed something unpleasant.

Sheriti stood her ground, watching the two of them quizzically.

"I—" He looked from Fallon to Sheriti and wondered why this bothered him so. "I was lost in the desert for many days and nearly died."

Fallon's smile returned. "But you yet live! Perhaps there is a bit of Cimmerian blood in you then. We're harder to kill than Stygians"—she grinned—"or so has been my experience during my time here. Let's find a tavern and raise a glass. I'll tell you tales!"

Anok looked uncomfortably at Sheriti, whom Fallon seemed suddenly to notice for the first time.

Fallon looked Sheriti over. "I didn't know you, dressed thusly. You dressed like a fighter last we met. This"—she reached out and pinched a bit of fabric from Sheriti's dress between her fingers—"makes you look like some kind of whore."

"Fallon!" Anok glared at her.

Fallon frowned back at him. "I mean no offense. I'm not used to city finery. I suppose the local whores wear nothing at all, so that isn't it, anyway. I just meant that it doesn't look right on her."

"She's training to be a scribe."

"A scribe? How can someone who's tasted battle settle for life as a scribe?"

Sheriti stared back at her. "Some of us don't live to kill, barbarian. A quiet life would suit me fine."

Fallon laughed. "Well, you would know best." She glanced back at Anok. "You defer to this woman. Are you pledged, Anok, to this . . . scribe and her quiet life?"

Anok looked uneasily at Sheriti. After a long pause, he said, "No, I'm not pledged to her. Or anyone."

"Just as well, Anok. Your blood is too hot for a life of pens and parchment." She took a step closer and reached out to touch him, her fingertips gliding down the hairs on his arm, making his skin tingle.

Teferi stood back, watching the scene from a safe distance.

Sheriti seemed more bemused than angry. "What does she mean by that, Anok?"

Fallon ignored her. "I have a business proposition. Leave this stinking city with me."

Anok felt more trapped than he would have if he'd been surrounded by a dozen warriors. "You're leaving?" He tried to sound neither too interested nor too grateful.

"I've learned of certain goods, compact and easily transported, that can be obtained cheaply at the source and sold at a huge profit in the lands to the north."

Anok was surprised. "Trade?"

Fallon crossed her arms over her ample chest and

frowned. "I'm a proud Cimmerian. You think that, simply because I am a barbarian, I can find no better way to treasure than cutting throats and cracking heads?"

Anok blinked. "Well—yes, that *is* pretty much what I . . ."

"From what I've seen, cutting throats, usually from behind, and merely as a shortcut to riches—that's more the way of so-called *civilized* men. Take what you can and kill when you must is my code." She patted the hilt of her sword for emphasis. "I propose a trading expedition, true. But one more filled with peril than toil, for I have a thirst for the former and a distaste for the latter." She grinned.

"Trade," he repeated carefully, struggling to hide his skepticism.

"*Dangerous* trade," she insisted.

"Trade in what?"

The question seemed to stop her. She stared. Blinked. Stared once more. Finally, she said, "You're a man. I doubt you would understand."

Sheriti couldn't help herself. She started to laugh.

"What do you mean I wouldn't understand? You expect me to go with you on some expedition I can't even understand?" The day wasn't going at all as planned.

Fallon considered. "Well," she said, forming her word carefully, as though speaking with a child, "the poisoners here offer a potion, which when taken, will keep a woman from becoming great with child, no matter how many times she lies with a man."

Sheriti was laughing even harder.

Fallon shot her an annoyed glance but said nothing.

Even Anok had to smile. "I've lived half my life under a brothel, Fallon. I understand far more of 'women's business' than you'd think. I know the potion well. The Paradise buys it by the jugful."

Sheriti stepped past her into the poisoner's stall, placed a gold coin on the table, and pointed. The poisoner handed her a small, round bottle with a narrow neck. The stopper was sealed with red wax. She returned and showed the bottle to Fallon. "This is what you want." Then her voice turned mocking. "Oh, yes," she said, "the peril."

Fallon looked mightily annoyed. "I am a barbarian. Do not think me stupid. I have thought my plan through. You paid gold for that little bottle. The price here is too high. I have learned that this potion requires certain plants that grow along the borders of Darfar and Kush, and that it is distilled and mixed in Kheshatta."

"The city of wizards," said Teferi, edging a little closer. "A bad place."

It was Fallon's turn to laugh. "And *this* isn't?"

Anok nodded. "Yes, but Kheshatta is the center of much of the poisoners' trade. Many evil brews and extracts are made there in great secrecy and shipped all over Stygia and beyond."

"So it is said," continued Fallon. "In any case, I don't plan to stay long in this 'bad place.' The plant is distilled into a powerful poison, then mixed with extracts of lotus and other secret ingredients. Then it is diluted with a special tea, one part to a thousand. That bottle contains no more than a drop of the pure extract."

"How," said Teferi, incredulous, "do you know all this?"

She grinned. "There are many poisoners in Odji. It was not difficult to find one curious and eager to spend an hour alone with a barbarian woman. Eager enough to share certain information."

Sheriti smirked. "And you call me a whore."

Fallon did not flinch. "I said an hour. I didn't say what I did during that hour. He may have expected more than he received. What is it they say here? 'When a man with a goat on a rope offers you a deal, be sure he is selling the goat and not the rope.'"

Anok grinned, despite himself. "You learn the local ways quickly."

"I've heard most of this before," said Sheriti. "The potion is diluted before it leaves Kheshatta, and jealously guarded until then. Every brothel in the city has tried to buy directly from the source at one time or another, but it

isn't possible. The secret of its manufacture is too closely
kept, and the poisoners of Kheshatta always demand their
due."

"And this is Stygia," said Teferi. "The guardians of Set
tax poisons and frown on smugglers."

"Well," said Fallon, "the poisoners must be *persuaded*
personally, and for the guardians, there are always bribes,
should it come to that." She shrugged. "I did say there
would be peril. If it were easy, it would already be done."

Teferi nodded. "Suicide. This is what you call peril?"

Fallon glared at him. "I did not ask you to join me,
Kushite. I had considered doing so, yes, but now I must reconsider." She turned back to Anok. "So, what of you? Will
you join me on my journey?"

Why not indeed? Some part of him found it appealing,
yet Kheshatta might not be far enough to escape the White
Scorpions, and they would almost undoubtedly have to return through Khemi on their way north. That he might
strike out on his own, in such a profitable enterprise, was
exactly what Wosret most feared he would do. Such an enterprise, if it were even possible, might fund Anok's estab-
lishing another rival gang in Odji, and Wosret would never
allow that to happen.

"Going somewhere, Anok?"

The voice he least wanted to hear in all the world right
now. Lord Wosret's!

But of course it was Wosret. Anok had known he would
be about the market today, and he and Teferi had planned
for an eventual encounter. That had been the strategy, to
confront Wosret and present just enough provocation so he
would issue an ultimatum to join his gang. Then Anok could
credibly announce his plans to become an acolyte of Set.

Later he would claim to Sheriti that he had thought of
Dejal's earlier offer, and it had simply slipped out. Even
the White Scorpions would not dare to challenge the Cult
of Set, but having said it, he would have to go through the
motions—for a while. He hoped it would be enough to get

her back to the Temple of Scribes. By the time she realized his true intentions, it would be too late.

That had been the plan.

Had been.

He turned to face Lord Wosret, accompanied not only by his ever-present twin bodyguards, but also by two large Ophirean mercenaries wearing leather armor and broadswords.

Wosret stepped up to him, a little too close. "You have something you want to share with me, Anok? A profitable enterprise of some kind?"

"There's nothing, Lord Wosret. I don't know what you thought you heard, but—"

Wosret cut him off angrily. "I heard just enough to know you're plotting behind my back, Anok. I've been far too patient with you because I've known you since you were a boy. But I killed my own sons when they tried to cross me. I don't see why I should hesitate to kill you now." Wosret drew his sword. "Perhaps it would have been better for us all if you had died in the desert."

The older man stood far too close to Anok, but he didn't dare show fear or weakness in front of his men. Still, Anok knew the sword would be mainly for defense. Wosret would let his thugs do the bloody work.

He heard a sword slide out of its sheath, and someone stepped in at Anok's side. To his surprise, it was neither Sheriti nor Teferi, who was too far back to step in without causing alarm. It was Fallon.

"Hear me! Who would seek to take the blood of Anok of Wati, also faces Fallon, a Cimmerian of Clan Murrogh countryman of Conan, warrior-king of Aquilonia!"

The twins began to chuckle.

Fallon smiled a wolf's smile. "You think to yourself, 'no Conan is she,' and it is true. But come forward if you dare and learn how our hard land has made each of us— woman and child—swift, brutal, and dangerous! Come forward, and let it be your last lesson!"

The Ophireans, perhaps having previously encountered Cimmerians in their northern homeland, seemed to take the threat more seriously. They shuffled their feet nervously.

Wosret seemed to weigh both extremes of reaction, then snorted. "This isn't your concern, barbarian woman. Leave now, and no harm will befall you."

"A Cimmerian never backs down from battle, city-man!"

Anok glanced at her out of the corner of his eye, not letting his attention stray too far from Wosret's sword. *You aren't making things better, woman!* Yet he wasn't sure how it could get worse. The situation had gotten out of hand.

Now Wosret planned to fight, not talk, and he didn't intend to lose.

12

THE TWO GROUPS stood facing each other in the narrow market walkway, all swords drawn, sizing each other up. The Ravens seemed solidly outmatched, five men against two men and a barbarian woman. Sheriti had drawn her small scribe's dagger; but without the element of surprise, it was essentially useless in such a fight.

Anok briefly considered tossing her one of his blades. No. *This was all to protect her. I will fight for both of us, if it comes to that.*

Had it come to that? His mind raced, trying to think of a way to talk his way out of the situation. Wasn't that, after all, what the Ravens were famous for, not just as fighters, but as negotiators, ambassadors—talkers. On the street, since he was hardly more than a boy, everyone knew Anok was the one who could cool hot tempers, find middle ground where none was apparent, create compromise that benefited both sides of a dispute.

He knew how to tell people what they wanted to hear.

He knew how to make a bad situation better.

He was the one who could be trusted.

Even now, Sheriti and Teferi stood, weapons ready, but watching him, waiting for him to find another way.

Not today.

Talking was how he'd gotten here. Anok the trusted had become Anok the liar, Anok the deceiver.

To his best friend.

Making his other best friend his coconspirator.

Was that how Dejal had fallen?

At the thought of his lost friend, the glowing ember of rage that always seemed to be in his heart lately flared into flame.

Wosret, that oily vermin, wasn't deserving even of his lies! How long had he dogged Anok? Now to make demands—threats. How dare he!

"You seek the blood of Anok Wati? You seek the blades of Anok Wati? To have the former, you must first taste the latter!"

With that, he swung his right sword underhanded, up toward Wosret's heart.

With surprising speed, the older man swatted the blade up and away with his larger weapon.

But that was what Anok had been expecting.

His left blade stabbed, not for a mortal blow, or even a disabling one, but for Wosret's vulnerable legs, slicing a cut across his upper thigh like someone carving a roast. His goal was neither to kill nor disable.

He wanted pain. He wanted blood.

Wosret howled, staggering back, blood pouring down his left leg.

Anok might have been expected to follow up on the attack. Instead he stood back and assessed the situation around him. He knew that Wosret, the old coward, would withdraw and leave the fighting to stronger men.

Now it's four against three!

Sheriti stood behind Teferi, who faced off against the two mercenaries, while the twins, leering grins on their faces, surrounded Fallen. He considered helping his two friends, but though the mercenaries appeared formidable, they were being cautious, and Teferi could take care of himself.

Fallon, on the other hand, faced two skilled and enthusiastic fighters, each almost twice her weight and clearly out for sport.

Anok charged toward them, swords high, coming up on the nearer twin's blind side. He roared a challenge as he swung both swords together at the giant's neck.

The big man turned, parried, easily deflecting the swords with his broadsword.

Anok used the energy of that deflection, riding it like a swimmer riding a wave, leaping into the air and spinning past to land a step behind Fallon, his back to hers.

The barbarian took advantage of the other twin's distraction to attack. Her broadsword clanged against her opponent's steel, and Anok heard him grunt in surprise. He'd clearly underestimated his opponent.

Good!

A whistling of air from above caused Anok to raise his crossed swords above his head. He caught the blow of the descending sword with his flexed elbows, his muscles shrieking with the force of the impact.

The huge blade stopped less than a handbreadth from his nose, and his arms shuddered with the strain of holding it there.

For an eternity, it hovered. Then Anok screamed with effort, throwing the broadsword backward, stepping under the giant, left sword up for defense, while the right stabbed across to find the ribs exposed just past the edge of the giant's leather chest plate. He roared and staggered back, but Anok's aching arms warned him not to press the attack. Instead he put his back against Fallon, just to let her know where he was.

"This is familiar," she said, grunting as Anok heard the point of her sword deflecting off leather armor. "We've done this dance before."

"It's a broadsword," he said. "Swing it, don't stab with it."

"The man with eyes in the back of his head tries to tell me how to fight?"

"A sword piercing your heart right now might scratch my back."

"I could say the same. Let's finish these beasts."

"Aye. When you're ready."

He felt the muscles in her shoulders and back tense, and that was all the signal he needed. They sprang away from each other, furiously attacking their opponents.

Anok charged the wounded twin, ducking under his slicing broadsword, stepping to the giant's right, stabbing his sword deep into his exposed flank. Just as quickly Anok yanked the sword out, sweeping past him, using his superior speed to keep ahead of the giant's turn.

The weight of the broadsword was a momentary disadvantage that Anok used to full benefit. He stabbed the giant in the back of his lower calf, missing the tendon, but still drawing blood, then spun and sliced his forehead with the other sword. Neither wound was critical, but he had reduced his opponent's abilities to move and see.

The big man threw back his head and bellowed, swinging his broadsword wildly at the air, but already blood was beginning to flow down into his eyes. By showing his throat, he had displayed a weakness in his armor.

Anok had planned to try for a critical strike between his ribs, but now he had a new target. He moved in, crouched low, seemingly leaving himself open.

The twin swung his sword low, as though cutting grain, but Anok was ready. He sprang into the air, knees high, the blade passing harmlessly just under his feet, and as he did, he bought the pummel of his left sword up, smashing it into the other man's chin. His head went back, and the right sword plunged deep, striking bone at the back of the neck.

The twin fell backward, making a gurgling, inhuman cry of distress, blood spurting from his neck in a warm fountain.

A few yards away, the other twin turned in response.

Fallon's sword flashed down, slicing his sword hand off at the wrist.

He screamed.

She spun, her sword neatly slicing his throat. He gurgled and fell in a puddle of his own blood.

"Anok!"

It was Sheriti's voice. He turned to see Teferi finishing off one of the mercenaries, who was already down on one bleeding knee. His momentary distraction had let the other mercenary slip past him, to where Sheriti held up her dagger in vain defense.

The attacking mercenary was looking away from him, vulnerable, but there was no time to reach him. But somewhere in the fight, the man had lost or discarded his helmet. Anok swung his left sword over his shoulder with all his might, releasing it at just the right point in its arc.

The blade flashed through the air, spinning once.

There was a wet, cracking noise, as though someone had split the egg of an enormous bird, and the point of the blade buried itself in the back of the mercenary's skull.

He staggered backward off-balance, mouth open, his own sword falling as he tried to grab Anok's blade, now protruding from his head.

Sheriti dashed forward, the tiny knife in her hand a blur as she plunged it up into the roof of the mercenary's mouth. His brain twice-pierced, he fell and lay twitching on the ground just as Anok reached them.

He put his foot against the fallen man's neck and yanked his sword free with some effort. His intent had been to protect Sheriti, but she had already taken up the man's curved scimitar from where it lay on the street.

Besides, there was only one enemy left.

Wosret cowered against the back of a potter's stall a dozen steps away, his sword raised, his face pale.

Anok stepped toward him.

"Killing me will do you no good, Anok!" the old man

spat. "The White Scorpions will hunt you down and have vengeance. There will be no escape for you!"

Anok stepped closer still, bloody swords raised in display, enjoying the old man's fear. "Shall we find out?"

"Anok!" It was Teferi. "No!"

Part of him wanted to slice the old man up, slowly, make him suffer the way he'd made so many others suffer through the years. So what if he was one gang leader among many? So what if another would simply replace him? So what if the White Scorpions would come to kill him. *(Let them try!)* It would still be . . . *satisfying*.

"Anok." It was Teferi again. Anok was about to become annoyed, but then he recognized the tone of warning in the voice.

He heard something else. Footsteps, many of them, running toward them from both directions.

Wosret grinned. "I thought four good men would be enough to take you. I was wrong. But I had made allowances for error." Wosret faded back as half a dozen armed and armored men brushed past him. A like number appeared from the other direction. Doubtless Wosret had held them back for fear of spooking Anok before the trap closed.

The three Ravens and their new barbarian companion fell together in the middle, guarding each other's backs. There was only the briefest pause before the White Scorpions pressed their attack.

The market echoed with the clashing of swords and the shouts of battle. The only advantage the Ravens had was that there wasn't room for the entire dozen warriors to attack them all at once.

They were holding their own, but Anok knew it wouldn't last. They were already tiring, and their new attackers were fresh. Sooner or later they would start to fall. Probably sooner.

Between the attacking men, he caught a glimpse of Wosret's smiling face.

Anok growled. *It would not end like this!*

Anok felt his fear, his reason, his very humanity slipping off him like a snake shedding its skin. His swords flashed, again and again. He slogged forward into the attackers like a man wading into mud.

Swords clashed, mouths, faces contorted as the attackers shouted and screamed, but Anok heard only the pounding of his own heart in his ears. Time seemed to slow as one man fell, then two.

A sword sliced across his biceps, but he felt nothing but rage.

The Scorpions were falling back now, out of fear as much as any physical challenge.

Anok saw Wosret again, his smile gone. The gang lord's mouth hung open with concern. He began to back away.

I can't let him escape!

Anok slammed his right sword down on the nearest attacker's helmet, where it struck like a hammer on a bell. The White Scorpion fell forward, and as he did, Anok leapt over his head, landing on his back, using him as a human springboard.

Anok dived through the air, somersaulting over the next few attackers, until nothing stood between him and Wosret.

Wosret's eyes went wide with terror. He turned to run, but Anok caught him.

Wosret swung his sword weakly, and Anok knocked it aside with a mighty blow, then hooked the guard with his other sword and yanked the blade from Wosret's hand.

Wosret tried to run, but again, Anok was too fast. He found himself blocked by a blade at his throat. He tried to turn, but a second blade swung in front of him. The blades slid against each other, boxing in Wosret's neck, pulling him back against Anok's chest, until Wosret finally couldn't move at all.

He yelled, "Scorpions! Watch as I slice off your leader's head and feed it to his neck!"

Anok saw Teferi look over at him, a look of concern on his blood-spattered features.

Anok didn't care.

The old man had to die!

He saw Sheriti, her fine gown covered with blood and gore, the long, curved blade held in her two hands. The look in her eyes.

All this danger.

She was worried only for him.

Anok roared in rage, then sighed loudly.

"Drop your swords, back away, and he will live! I pledge my friends will not harm you."

"I am not your friend," yelled Fallon, still lusting for the fight.

"You'll leave them be, Fallon!"

Something in his tone of voice gave even the barbarian woman pause. She lowered her sword slightly, frowning.

Wosret grunted. "Do as he says. His word is usually good."

So you'd think! But Anok said nothing.

The men dropped their swords and began to back away.

"This isn't over," said Wosret.

"Yes," said Anok, "it is." The words hung in his throat, but he forced them out. "I'm going to join my old friend Dejal, as an acolyte in the Cult of Set."

Sheriti gasped.

Teferi looked grim but held his tongue.

"Even the White Scorpions wouldn't want to cross the Temple of Set, would they?"

"No," said Wosret, reluctantly, "we wouldn't. Assuming you're not bluffing."

"I'm not. But hear me now. You are through with me and mine. If you come after me again, there aren't enough strong arms in the White Scorpions, in all of Odji, to protect you from my wrath! Do you understand?" He tightened his blades across Wosret's throat until blood began to ooze from the contact points.

"I understand," Wosret gasped. "Now let me go!"

Anok uncrossed the swords and pushed Wosret away.

The old man bent to reach for his sword, but Anok barked at him, "Leave it!"

Wosret stood slowly, trying to maintain his dignity. He stepped over the body of one of his fallen men and walked away.

Anok watched him go.

Sheriti ran up, grabbing his arm, her fingers cutting into his aching flesh. "You didn't mean that, did you? You'd never join the cult!"

He couldn't look her in the eye. "I'm doing what has to be done for the safety of us all."

His friends were right there with him, Sheriti actually touching him, but Anok had never felt more alone.

13

THERE REMAINED, BEYOND Sheriti's distress, one
other problem with Anok's plan to join the cult. Dejal had
failed to respond to his messages.

Doubtless, Dejal was deeply involved in his initiation
into the cult. Perhaps the messages were not reaching him.
Perhaps he was too busy to respond, or did not take Anok's
intentions seriously. It didn't matter. Without Dejal's spon-
sorship, Anok, as one of mixed Stygian blood, he had little
chance of being taken into the temple as an acolyte.

Adding to his impatience was the fact that he was
largely confined to the Nest. He didn't dare let Lord Wosret or any of the White Scorpions see him on the street
without acolyte robes. He had even considered stealing
some, though that would likely lead to all the wrong kind
of attention from the cult. So he sent Teferi to do his er-
rands, and waited.

If ever there was a time when he could have used female
company, it was then. But Fallon had gone her own way
when it became clear he wasn't interested in her dubious

trade venture, and Sheriti had vanished upstairs and was apparently avoiding him.

Well, if so, good. Perhaps she was packing to return to the Temple of Scribes. That was what he wanted after all.

Wasn't it?

A knock came at the Nest's outside door, and Anok immediately took up his swords. Only after a series of other knocks—a code they'd worked out beforehand—was Anok sure it was Teferi. Anok opened the door cautiously, careful not to expose himself to the street, and allowed Teferi to slip inside. He carried a large basket, which he put down on the table in the middle of the room.

"I've sent another message to Dejal. This time I bribed a cook who works in the temple kitchens. If all goes well, Dejal will get the note you wrote with his noon meal."

Anok nodded. He wasn't hopeful. He was relatively sure at least one or two of the previous messages had gotten through, but there had been no response.

"You're sure he can read well enough to understand what you wrote?" Teferi was illiterate, at least in Stygian, and had shown little interest when Anok had offered to teach him to read and write along with Sheriti.

"A certain skill in reading is necessary for acolytes to the cult. Acolytes are required to study the books of Set, and those who would advance to the priesthood must study various books of magic."

Teferi grimaced. "Reading. It never leads to anything good. Anyway, you seem to know a lot about the cult."

"Dejal used to talk about it sometimes. He'd learned quite a bit about the cult from spying on his father."

"Spying. Probably a required activity of Stygian nobles."

"Careful, Teferi. I'm half-Stygian, too."

"That's what worries me, Anok. Your blood is—pardon, there's no better way to say it—tainted with corruption and dark magic. I've watched Dejal, seen what Stygian blood can do to a man. I've heard my grandfather tell stories of what happened to my own people, those who did not escape Kush before the Sikugiza—the dark time. For my ancestors, even coming to Stygia as slaves may have been better, for now we are free, and those whose blood is corrupted will never be free, until the end of time."

"Thanks, old friend," Anok said sarcastically, "I feel so much better."

Teferi removed a large bundle from the top of the basket. "I appeal to that part of you that is not Stygian. Turn your back on this insanity, brother. The Cult of Set will destroy you."

"Or I will destroy it."

Teferi laughed. "They say the Cult of Set has lasted since the first Stygians rose up and destroyed the Old Ones. And brave Anok will end it all in a day?"

Anok sat heavily on the bench next to the table and watched Teferi unwrapping the bundle. "Then perhaps I can wound it a little, or at least those responsible for the death of my father. Perhaps I can at least learn why he was killed."

"And that will help you how? He will be just as dead. Leave Stygia with me, or go to the Temple of Scribes with Sheriti. Or go adventuring with the barbarian woman if that is what you wish. But forget the cult."

"I can never forget them, Teferi. Not if I travel to the edge of the world, not if I live a thousand lifetimes. And I can't leave Stygia either. It's the only home I've ever known. It's in my blood."

"We're back to that again, then. Well, here—" He removed a jug of wine from the bundle, followed by bread, dried fruit, dried fish, nuts, a small jar of honey, and flaky pastries from the market. "At least you won't starve while waiting."

Teferi reached back into the basket and brought out a bundle of dark brown clothing made of coarse, foreign cloth. "I bought these from a caravan driver. This is what nomads from the Eastern Desert wear. The headcloth and face wraps will disguise you enough to travel the streets, if you're careful."

Anok reached for a piece of flatbread, ripped off a hunk, and put it in his mouth. "Thank you, brother. You are better to me than I deserve."

Teferi grinned just a little. "Of that I am certain."

As Anok chewed, he thought back to what Dejal had told him of the cult. There had been a time when he'd taken great pride in his forbidden knowledge and enjoyed the even greater sin of sharing it with an outsider like Anok. Unfortunately, Anok had shown only a little interest at the time. He'd been trying to forget about the cult and his father's death, and Dejal's gleeful stories had only been a painful reminder.

Anok stopped eating and looked up in surprise. "The things you forget," he said, tossing the rest of the bread on the table and rushing to an old trunk that sat in the corner of the room. The lid opened with a groan of its leather hinges, and Anok began to root around inside. It was full of clothing, trinkets, scrolls, and bits of parchment and papyrus. Finally, he found one of the latter, a piece of papyrus as long as his forearm, twisted into a cylinder and tied with a red piece of silk ribbon.

He brought the sheet to the table, pulled off the ribbon, and carefully unrolled the crackling papyrus.

Teferi glanced down at it. It was covered with crudely inked lines. "That's not writing. Is it a map?"

"Of a sort. This shows the layout of the Temple of Set. It's a copy Dejal long ago made of one he 'borrowed' from his father. He once plotted, not very seriously I think, to break into the temple and abscond with some of the cult's minor treasures. The map is old, but I doubt the temple has changed significantly in the last twenty generations. With this, assuming that it's accurate—and that Dejal copied it faithfully—I should be able to find my way to the quarters where the acolytes-in-training live."

Teferi looked alarmed. "You can't just walk into the Temple of Set, Anok, at least beyond the public areas."

Anok grinned. "I won't walk. I'll sneak." He ran his hand over the sheet. "In any case, that would be a last resort if Dejal doesn't respond to our latest message."

Teferi sighed. "Then it seems virtually a certainty."

Anok sighed and nodded. "I wish I could say otherwise. Still, there is a chance. This note is different. I thought perhaps Dejal was reluctant to return to the Nest alone. Perhaps he suspects there are hard feelings here—"

"Could be," said Teferi.

Anok gave him a disapproving frown, then continued, "—and suspects he might be walking into some kind of trap. Or perhaps at this stage of his initiation into the cult he is unable to travel freely. This one asks him only to scratch a cross mark into the curbstones in front of the temple, near the great statue of the snake. If you find such a mark, it will indicate that he has read my note and is willing to communicate. We can go from there."

Teferi sighed. "I suppose you want me, to go check for the mark now?"

"Yes, and tomorrow as well if you find nothing today." He produced another rolled piece of papyrus and handed it to Teferi. "This note has more specific instructions on how we can communicate indirectly. If you find the mark, bribe your contact to deliver it to him, then let me know at once."

Teferi plucked a dried date from the food bundle and took a bite before heading toward the door. "As you say, then." He paused at the door, looking at the assortment of tools and weapons leaning there. He reached out and took a long shaft of wood tipped with a stone head.

It was the spear Anok had found in the desert. He hadn't noticed it there before, but given the clutter, that was hardly surprising.

Teferi turned. "We found you with this in the Sea of Sand. I have been meaning to ask you; where did you get it?"

"I found it along the caravan road. It was probably dropped there by accident."

"Perhaps. But this is not just a spear, Anok. It is a Usafiri spear, like the one made by the young men of my tribe before going on their own journeys into the wilderness."

Anok shrugged. "You did say that—Jangwa, was it?— would provide what I needed? Perhaps he was watching out for me after all." Anok didn't seriously believe that for a moment, but he thought perhaps that it would humor Teferi.

Teferi only frowned and held the spear up, pointing at the band of carvings in the shaft, just below the bindings that held the stone point. "These are the traditional markings carved into every such spear. They invoke Jangwa, and are said to bring luck to the traveler." But then he flipped the spear around and pointed to another ring of carvings near the other end of the shaft.

Anok stared and blinked in surprise. "Those weren't there. Only the first ring of carvings was on the spear when I found it."

Teferi frowned. "I was afraid of that. No young man of my people would carve anything into the back of his spear. To do so would bring only bad luck. And these symbols represent Bovutupu, Jangwa's enemy, a trickster who leads travelers to their doom."

"Well then," said Anok smugly, "he failed."

"Do not scoff, Anok. You took off the face paint, didn't you? You were visited by other spirits in the desert."

"No," he said, lying, "of course not!"

Teferi just stared at him.

"Look, I was sweating, falling, and crawling through the sand for three days. After a time, it rubbed off."

"You did not consort with evil spirits?"

"No, of course not."

Teferi took a deep breath and let it out as a sign. "Very well then. But think carefully on what you may have seen out there, Anok. Visions, they are not always what they seem." He slipped out the door, and Anok bolted it behind him.

"And sometimes," Anok said to the empty room, "visions are exactly what they appear to be."

A sudden knocking startled him. It took Anok a moment to realize that it came not from the door he'd just locked but from the trapdoor leading upstairs. It was followed by a clattering of the latch and a squeak as the trapdoor was pulled back.

Sheriti padded softly down the stairs on bare feet. She wore a simple shift made of white silk, belted at the waist. The thin silk fluttered as she moved, the bottom of it fell just below her hips. It made her look younger and more innocent than she'd seemed in a long time. She was a woman now, and her appearance only made his heart ache for an earlier, simpler time.

She tilted her head, looking at him. "Do you mind company?"

Anok shrugged and sat on a padded reclining couch near the front wall. "I thought you were angry with me."

She chewed her lip. "I'm confused, Anok. I'm worried about you. I am not angry." She walked over and sat next to him on the couch, quite near, in fact. He was aware of the spicy perfume she wore in her hair. "This is our fault, Anok. I have been convinced it was so since you went to the desert. We, Teferi and I, made ready to move on to new lives, foolishly confident that Anok, who had always cared for us, would just as easily care for himself."

"I will care for myself," he said, trying not to let the annoyance he felt creep into his voice. "I *am* caring for myself."

"Really?" She put her hand softly on his shoulder. "You've nearly killed yourself in the desert. You've picked a fight with one of the most powerful gang lords on the streets of Odji. And now you've announced your intention to join a cult you have professed to hate as long as I've known you. How is that caring for yourself?"

He had no answer for that. Instead, he just looked away.

She was silent for a time as well. Then she said, "Anok, perhaps I shouldn't ask this, and you don't have to answer. But since the night Dejal left us, I've wondered. You spent the night hidden with the Cimmerian woman."

Anok glanced at her. She'd said quite a bit, none of which added up to a question. "Yes?"

"Did you lie with her that night?"

He considered. Should he answer? Or should he just

lie? What would one more falsehood be at that point, if it preserved her feelings?

But no, he felt he had to be honest. "I did." He couldn't bring himself to look into her eyes. "It wasn't my idea. She was *more* than willing, if you follow my meaning. But I confess that I did not resist her. Despite her strange nature, she is an attractive creature, and you must surely know that I'm hardly a virgin."

He glanced over to see if she was angry. She didn't appear to be. Rather she was looking at him, eyes wide, her face revealing some emotion he couldn't quite interpret. "I am," she said simply.

"What?"

"A virgin."

He blinked.

"You're surprised?"

"Well, yes. I knew you'd made certain promises to your mother and that you'd never been with one of the Ravens. But we were like family almost. And I've seen you with other men, flirting, embracing, kissing. I had assumed that there were other lovers you'd simply kept private."

"There have been other flirtations, liaisons, acquaintances, yes. But they were merely casual diversions. None has ever touched me in *that* way. That was the other promise that I made to my mother. Not just that I would never enter her profession, but also that I would remain chaste."

"Forever?" It slipped out before he could think the question through.

She smiled slightly. "Until I had found a man to whom I could freely offer my heart as well as my body."

He suddenly felt a catch in his throat. "You've been looking for such a person?"

She smiled coyly and nodded. "For a while, without success."

Relief, or disappointment?

"Little did I know," she continued, leaning toward him,

"that one was living under my very floor." She placed her other hand on his chest and leaned into him.

He realized that he wanted this—very badly, but still he found himself gently pushing her back. "Sheriti, this isn't right."

She gave that little bit of distance but did not withdraw. Her presence, the warmth of her body next to his, was intoxicating. "I've been thinking much about you lately, Anok. So long I've treated you as a brother, but that was a child's game. You are *not* my brother. You are no blood of mine. And we"—she lingered long on that last word, letting it hang in the air—"are no longer children." She leaned into him again.

Though his body censed at her touch, he tried to remain detached and aloof. It wasn't working. "Sheriti, this is—I don't *deserve* this."

She looked at him, her face close to his, her head cocked slightly to one side. "Anok, I've never known one who deserved it more." She kissed him hard, and he responded in kind, his tongue thrusting between her willing lips, his arms crushing her against him.

Still, part of him said he should stop. He pulled away from her lips, the taste of her still tingling in his mouth. "This will not change my plans."

She shook her head. "If I can change them, I will, but if we are parting, then it is even more important I give you this gift."

I'm not worthy. But he was too weak to say it, too overcome to do what should have been done. He pulled her down next to him on the couch, their arms and legs intertwined. His hand slid up the back of her thigh, under the hem of the shift, only to find nothing under it but soft flesh. She gasped, and it turned into a laugh of delight.

She began exploring him with her hands, her lips—soft, fluttering from place to place like eager butterflies, leaving delight everywhere they landed. He moaned. "Where did you—?"

She looked up and laughed. "I am the daughter of the

greatest whore in all of Stygia, Anok. I was raised in a brothel. I have been told, seen, and heard things you can scarcely imagine." She laughed again softly, as she returned to her attentions. "Inexperienced I may be, but I am not *ignorant*!"

It was a very long afternoon, which gave way to a very long night.

14

ANOK AWOKE TO see a beam of sunlight shining through the high window of his sleeping stall. Sheriti slept nestled under the crook of his arm, curled against his side, her leg hooked over his, her left hand resting on his heart. She snored softly, almost imperceptibly, like the purring of a cat, and he was careful not to wake her. He saw her lips curled up in a soft smile of contentment, and it made his heart swell to see it.

He felt as drained and exhausted as when he'd awakened from his trial in the desert, only this time pleasantly so. Yet even this pleasure was tainted by bitter thoughts of what he must do next. *Why did I let this happen? It just makes things more difficult. Sweet Sheriti, you deserve better than this. You deserve better than I.*

Yet some things, once done, could not be undone, and it was more true here than most. It was indeed a fine gift he'd been given, the best gift any man had possibly ever received. But it was not one he could keep, for more than a night anyhow.

There was a knocking at the door, and Sheriti's eyes shot open.

Teferi!

Anok looked into Sheriti's eyes, and she looked back at him. Both shared the same, unspoken, question. The situation was awkward to say the least.

Anok slid from his bed, finding a kilt to slip on. "I'll let him in," he whispered. "You dress."

He went to the door, paused, and tried to put on a sleepy face despite the pounding of his heart and the adrenaline that pumped through his veins.

He opened the door. "Teferi, come on in." He stepped back to let Teferi through the door, and as he did, he looked down to notice Sheriti's shift lying in a silken heap on the floor under the couch.

Teferi didn't appear to notice the discarded garment as he flopped down on the couch. "No word again from Dejal."

Anok just stood there, trying to decide how he could rescue Sheriti's clothing from just behind Teferi's feet and get them to her. Then he heard the curtain on his sleeping stall rustle. He turned just as Teferi looked up at the sound.

"Sheriti," said Teferi, "I didn't know you were here—" Then he noticed how she was dressed.

She wore one of Anok's kilts, cinched tight about her small waist, and one of his headcloths tied over her breasts like a halter.

Teferi blinked in surprise, looked at her, then at Anok, then back at her again. He licked his lips uncertainly. "Well," he finally said.

Anok said nothing.

Sheriti looked at Anok. "Our brother is no fool, Anok."

"No," said Anok, "he isn't."

Teferi managed an embarrassed grin. "Well, things keep changing around here."

Sheriti slipped in next to Anok, hooking her arm in his. "I hope you aren't offended, Teferi."

He looked up uncomfortably. "No, it isn't my business

what you two do." He looked away for a moment, then looked back directly at Anok. "Does this change—"

Anok shook his head. "We go ahead as planned." He saw Sheriti looking at him. She looked disappointed, but said nothing. *Better she should know now, before she builds false hopes.* "Go back and look for the sign from Dejal today. Failing that, I will have to consider going to him myself."

Sheriti stepped quietly past him, and as she walked away, he found himself missing her already. She casually bent over and plucked the fallen shift from under Teferi's feet, crumpled it into an unrecognizable wad, and tossed it into Anok's sleeping area.

Teferi watched, but said nothing. "I should go then," he said, rising. "I'll return later this afternoon, one way or the other." He glanced between the two lovers again. "I'll leave you to be alone."

"Please," said Sheriti, "you don't have to rush off, Teferi."

He shrugged. "I hadn't planned to stay long anyway. Anok is a prisoner here, not I, and I have business of my own to attend to." He slipped through the door. "I'll see you both later."

The door closed, and they were again alone.

Anok glanced at Sheriti, the sight of her wearing his cast-off clothing somehow as erotic as the most exotic silks. He tried to ignore the feelings that were stirring. "I'm sorry, Sheriti. I told you this would change nothing."

She hung her head. "It changes *everything,* Anok."

He nodded. "It does, as much as we would deny it." He stepped up and held her by the shoulders. "Sheriti—Lovely Sheriti. You've honored me more than I can say. But you must find another, one worthy of your heart. My own heart was poisoned long ago, by loss and hate that I can never forget, no matter how I try. You have to understand."

"I understand that you feel cheated by the loss of your father. But at least you knew him, Anok. You remember him—his voice, his teachings, his love. You don't know how lucky you are to have even that much, Anok." She shook her head slowly, sadly. "I will never know my father, Anok. He was just some *Mshai—a traveler,* what the whores call customers when no outsider is listening. Here, and then gone forever. I don't know if my mother even knows his name." She put her hand to her lips as though stifling her emotion. "You have so much more than I ever will, Anok. Why can't that be enough?"

He looked at her, every step of distance between them seeming like a league, making him ache with loneliness. "Sometimes, to have a thing once and never to have it again, is even worse than never having it at all. I wish things could be different, but they can't."

"I think—" She seemed to choke on her words. "I think I hear my mother calling. I have to go." She ran for the stairs and up the steps. He heard the trapdoor squeak open and fall heavily shut.

I have already lost more than most men could ever dream of having. How much more must I lose?

ANOK WAS SULKING at his table, and the sun was low enough to cast horizontal shafts of light across the room by the time Teferi next arrived at the door.

He'd set out some food earlier, but it sat in the middle of the table, untouched. All he could think about was Sheriti, and the shambles that his once simple (and he saw now only in retrospect, surprisingly happy) life had become.

He sought someone to blame for his pain and loss. Someone he could crush. Someone he could—*kill.* But no matter how many times he pawed through the facts, there was no simple answer.

Wosret? The gang lord was no different than a half dozen others in the city, or a thousand more who had ruled over the slums back into antiquity. In fact he was better than most, which is why Anok had often worked for him. Wosret was the fever, not the disease.

The men who killed his father? Truly, they were deserving of his wrath, if he could find them, if they were even still alive. But they were only the fingertips of a far greater evil.

It always came back to the Cult of Set itself. It, as well as the other cults that it had bested or incorporated into itself, was the root of all that was evil and wrong in Stygia. From the poverty, crime, and oppression of the slums, to the river of sacrificial blood that ran each Festival, to the festering rot of sorcery that plagued not only Stygia but also its neighbors to the south.

Without it, he was convinced, Stygia would be a green and peaceful land as legend said it had been when the world was young. Perhaps it could have been the seat of a great empire that united the known world. Instead it had become only a sandblasted, sun-bleached corpse of its former self, slowly turning to dust while the maggots within fought over every remaining scrap of meat. Even its once-great empire of evil had crumbled, nothing but a distant memory.

It was hopeless. How could one man bring down such an ancient and powerful evil? He couldn't. Perhaps he could kill the men responsible for murdering his father. Perhaps he could do some small, temporary damage to the cult. But in the end, it seemed hopeless. Even if Parath was real, and not a fevered dream, what help could dry bones in the desert be? He was alone on a short road, with no likely end save death.

So why did he leap to his feet when Teferi knocked at the door? Why was he so eager to hear of any word from Dejal? Why was he burning with curiosity about the inner workings of the cult, the secrets of its temples and shrines? Was some part of him *eager* to join the cult?

He pulled open the door, forgetting even to hide himself from passersby.

Teferi was slightly surprised by his sudden appearance. Then he seemed to read the question on Anok's face. "No," he said as he came in, "there is no word from Dejal." He brushed past Anok and sat himself on one of the benches next to the table. He spied the food sitting on the table, picked up a dried sardine, and bit the head off. He seemed to reconsider after taking the bite, chewed quickly, and swallowed. He tossed the rest of the little fish onto the table.

"I'm going to the temple, then," said Anok. "I'm going tonight."

Teferi looked up in surprise. "You can't be serious. It isn't some merchant's house that you can simply scale the walls and sneak inside. There will be guards, traps, and who-knows-what other horrors deeper inside. If it can be done at all, it will require preparation and planning."

"I don't intend to look for Dejal yet. If this map of the temple is correct, the acolytes' quarters are deep in the cat-acombs under the hall of Set, behind the altar. And I don't *know* if the map is even slightly correct. This will be a scouting trip, to see if I can penetrate the inner temple and determine if the map is at all trustworthy. I'll stay close to the outside and compare the map to what I see. I can also try to find—or make—an easier way into the building for my later return."

Teferi sighed. "That seems wise. I will come with you, and keep watch from outside."

Anok shook his head. "That won't do. No one without Stygian blood is allowed on the streets of the inner city after sunset. Even my mixed heritage may raise questions."

"Then I will go with you as far as the temple, then leave before sunset and wait for you outside the gates to the inner city. I will not let you face this completely alone."

Anok nodded. "You're a good friend, Teferi."

He looked past Anok. "Not good enough, perhaps. I should be more forgiving, more understanding. Perhaps."

"This is about Sheriti?"

"What else? How could you do it, Anok?"

"If you must know, it wasn't my idea."

"But you didn't resist very much, did you?"

He clinched his jaw. "Not enough, I admit. I am only a man."

"A weak excuse."

"Perhaps. She was—persuasive."

Teferi almost smiled. "Perhaps I expect too much of you." The smile vanished, and he shook his head as though to jog loose some troubling thought. "My feelings on this aren't clear, Anok. Part of me is happy that the two of you have seen between you what I have long known was there. Part of me is jealous, for I confess I have loved Sheriti from afar as long as I can remember. But I have long known her heart was never to be mine, and I have promised my ancestors I would find a Kushite bride, to keep our broken line strong. But mostly I am angry that you have taken her heart, only to betray it, starting this night."

"I never denied my intentions, Teferi. I warned her my path was set. I have lied to her about things, but never this."

"That makes it no less wrong."

His shoulders sagged slightly, and he sighed. "That is so, old friend. And that is all the more reason that I must do this thing quickly. The longer I stay, the harder it will be for her to return to the new life she's earned for herself. I have her heart, true, but I don't deserve it. She was meant for better than you or me, and in your deepest heart, you know that, too."

Teferi nodded sadly.

Anok turned his attention to getting ready. He found the bundle of nomad's clothing that Teferi had earlier brought him as a disguise. The cloth was some strange fabric, lighter and less coarse than the wool worn by most northern peoples, but scratchy to one used to even the poorest of Stygian silks. There were breeks, which again felt strange as he pulled them over his legs, since he was used to the kilts most often worn by the underclasses of Odji.

Before putting on the loose tunic and wide belt, he sought out the new scabbards he had purchased at the market and examined them. He'd intended them for stealth, and that was just what he would use them for. He inserted his two blades, then strapped the weapons to his bare back.

The leather straps crossed over his chest and fastened with metal hooks. Only then did he put on the loose tunic.

He reached back over his shoulder to feel the hidden blades. The hilts of the swords projected up slightly, as though he had wings hidden under his clothing, but he still had a thick headcloth and a cloak left in the bundle with which to hide the protrusions. It wouldn't pass close inspection at the city's gates, but that's what bribes were for.

Once he'd finished dressing in the unfamiliar clothing, he packed a leather shoulder bag. He included a set of his regular clothing he could change into, once he was inside the walls. He also added some other items he might need, flint and steel, a few candles, two coils of rope, and a folding grappling hook he'd won from Rami in a dice game years before (after taking Rami's infamous fixed dice out of play). The final item was a wooden bobbin wrapped with fine silk thread.

Finally, almost as an afterthought, he found a scimitar among the Ravens' trove of captured weapons and strapped it around his middle. "In case we run into trouble with the White Scorpions before we reach the walls. Besides, it will look suspicious if I don't check any weapons at all before going through the gates."

Teferi raised an eyebrow. "I don't suppose I get to take a hidden sword inside the city walls?"

Anok grinned and shook his head. "Too risky."

Teferi frowned.

Anok slapped his shoulder. "You did insist on coming, old friend."

DURING THE DAY, the various gates leading to the inner city always buzzed with activity and commerce. Just outside each gate was a small marketplace of stalls and street vendors selling foodstuffs, clothing, and other common goods. While the prices were far higher than in the Great Marketplace, in part because of the considerable bribes to the guardians of Set required to operate there, the quality of the goods was higher as well, and prices were still cheaper than at the few shops that operated within the walls themselves.

Other, more specialized businesses operated as well, including the weapon keeps. Only nobles of the upper class were allowed to wear weapons within the city, and since a constant flow of servants and workman were required to support those upper classes, the weapon keeps were necessary. For a small fee, they would safely store weapons just outside the city gates, then return them to their owners as they left the city. Of necessity, weapon keeps were among the most trusted and trustworthy merchants in all of Stygia. Any who were not usually ended their careers with a weapon checked across their throats.

Since the keeps were within easy sight of the guardians of Set watching the gates, Anok had elected to bring an extra sword and make a show of checking it while the guards were watching. Teferi left his sword, knife, and bow as well, though he grumbled to Anok throughout the entire process. As appeasement, Anok threw a few extra slivers of silver on the counter to have Teferi's blades honed and polished before he returned.

There were several arched gates at that portal to the city, one large one for tradesmen, where a constant line of wagons carrying goods waited for inspection, a second large gate where horses, chariots, wagons, and sedan chairs carrying ambassadors and members of the upper class were quickly ushered through, and a small pedestrian gate where servants, workers, and others of the lower class waited passage.

The line was short at the moment, as it was late in the day, and most of the traffic was moving out of the walls rather than in. Anok let Teferi go first and planned to let him, and the gold coins already hidden in Anok's palm, do the talking. Most of the people around them were non-Stygian, and had the well-groomed appearance of house servants. Many were probably night servants in some wealthy household and would spend the night safely locked within their masters' houses. There were also a few whores, dressed in colorful silk robes spun through with metal threads and headpieces festooned with colorful feathers. They, too, would be spending the night in the inner city, though under somewhat different circumstances.

In the midst of this grouping, Teferi and Anok stood out. While most of the others were quickly ushered through (though generous time was allowed to carefully search each whore for hidden weapons), the guards looked upon Teferi and Anok with obvious suspicion.

The guardians of Set were the enforcers of the Temple of Set, which in turn was effectively the government of Stygia. They served as guards, law enforcers, tax collectors, and captains of the slave armies.

Readily identified by their scarlet robes or sashes and ornate silver badges, most wore leather armor and were heavily armed. All were of the lower classes of Stygians, and most, like Anok, were of mixed Stygian blood. In some, that blood ran very thin.

Still, they were greatly feared in Odji, in part because they rarely ventured there, except to collect taxes or hunt down someone who had committed a crime in the inner city. In Anok's experience, they were downtrodden, treated poorly by their superiors and especially by the upper classes.

They were a cruel lot, and tended to take this abuse out on any lesser who got in their way. But while they were the sort of people you didn't want to make angry, they were ever eager to do as little work as possible and to subject themselves to danger even less.

They were eminently bribable.

The captain in charge, a tall man with a black beard, arms that bulged with muscles, and a belly that just bulged, sized up Teferi. He leaned on a thick walking stick, clearly intended to double as a club. "You there, Kush! What business do you have in the inner city?"

Teferi put on his best salesman's smile. "My friend and I are craftsmen, here to repair some broken roof tiles."

The guard poked at Anok's bag with his stick. "You don't carry many tools for such work."

"Most of the tools we need are already there," said Teferi. "The work was started by other fools who got drunk and didn't return from their noon meal. We were summoned to finish the job, and as part of our payment"—he flashed a grin—"we get to keep their tools. If they return to complain about it, I've been told they'll end up on a sacrificial altar. That will teach them to disappoint a High Priest of Set!"

The guard almost smiled.

He checked Teferi over carefully, but the big man simply wasn't wearing enough clothing to hide any major weapons. He waved him past, but put up a hand to stop Anok. As he reached out to pat Anok down, Anok pressed the coins into the man's hand. "We're in a hurry."

The guard glanced down at the coins glinting in his palm, careful not to show them to any of the other guards. "Tile work, it pays well, does it?"

"For those possessing skill," answered Anok.

The captain stared at his closed fist for a moment, his other hand clenching reflexively around the heavy stick he carried, as though comparing the weight of each.

Finally, he looked up at Anok. "If you're in an equal hurry to get out of the city, see me, and we'll have another talk about how well paid 'skilled' tile-workers are." He waved Anok past. "Go!"

The pair wasted no time in putting distance between themselves and the gate, and as they did, the crowds quickly thinned.

Anok had only rarely been to the inner city, and the place was still a wonder to him. The streets were wide and paved with cut stone. Though the buildings themselves were dark, there was plenty of sunlight here, and the tower on the Great Temple of Set was easily visible looming before them, the statue of the half-human, half-snake god staring ominously down at them.

Everything here was different from Odji. The streets

were clean, underground sewers serving all the buildings, garbage somehow disposed of out of sight, and servants standing by on street corners to clean up manure as fast as the horses could drop it. Rather than sweat, filth, and decay, the air was filled with perfume and exotic incense.

There was a serenity to it all, a quiet. There were no beggars, no street vendors announcing their wares, no brothels with whores displaying their naked bodies to passersby, no fights or arguments. The people on the street were mostly clean and well dressed, and they moved politely past one another on the street rather than pushing and shoving.

Yet under it all, there was something else, something that made Anok's skin crawl. Occasionally he would see a servant marked or bruised from a recent beating, and all of them wore an expression of subdued fear, a subtle tension that suggested punishment, or worse, was never far away for those not of high-Stygian blood.

The signs of Set were everywhere: the red-sashed guardians, robed acolytes and priests strolling the streets, statues, stone reliefs carved into building facades, serpent shapes in chariot fittings, railings, and door handles, and of course the ever-looming presence of the temple itself.

And under all the perfume and incense, it seemed to Anok that there was still a subtle but ever-present stench of death.

Teferi watched out of the corner of his eye as a group of acolytes passed them on the street. As they went by, he whispered, "Maybe we'll meet Dejal on the street, and you can forget this foolishness."

Anok shrugged. "Perhaps, but I'm not sure the novice acolytes can even leave the temple. That's the most likely reason we haven't heard from Dejal." He looked around. "I need a place to change clothes. Let's go up that alley."

They slipped into a narrow alley between two strangely subdued shops, one selling food, the other displaying clothing that seemed fit for an emperor. As with the streets there was no garbage or filth, though a slight odor from a large wooden bin behind the food shop provided a clue to part of the garbage mystery. The bin offered convenient cover, and Anok slipped behind it while Teferi kept watch. He changed into his best clean kilt and a loose tunic and cape that would help hide the swords strapped to his back under his clothing. Before putting on the tunic, he took out his knife and cut two slits in the silk just below the shoulders. That would allow him, with some difficulty, to draw the swords if necessary.

He stuffed the other clothing in his bag and rejoined Teferi. "Well," he said, "this will make me a little less conspicuous. The White Scorpions wouldn't dare show themselves inside the inner city."

They resumed their walk toward the Temple of Set.

"Anok," said Teferi, "have you, in all your days, heard of any thief successfully breaching the temple?"

He thought about it. "No, I don't think so."

"Yet everyone says the temple is full of treasure. Even in the public areas, there are said to be statues of silver and gold, encrusted with jewels. Everyone knows this is where the collected taxes and tribute from all of Khemi are taken, and that there are ancient objects of power hidden in its vaults. Even as protected as it is, even though it is within the walls of the inner city, it would be an almost irresistible target for thieves and adventurers."

"What of it? If I had stolen from the Temple of Set, I'd be on my way out of Stygia as fast as I could. I'd hardly be bragging about it in Odji."

Teferi nodded. "True, but have you ever heard of anyone who tried to penetrate the temple and failed? Even one?"

"No," admitted Anok, "I haven't."

"Yet some must have tried, probably many. That can only mean that they entered the temple and never left!" He stopped in the street. "Give up this foolishness, Anok! Dejal cannot be a new acolyte forever. Eventually he will emerge from the temple, and we can reach him then. You must wait!"

"Wait until Wosret and his men hunt me down and kill me in my sleep? No, I think not. If this is reckless, the alternative is suicide. No, I'm going in. If nothing else, it will without a doubt prove my sincerity to Dejal." He resumed his walk.

Teferi sighed and caught up with him. "I will make sure," he said, "that your funeral is grand."

THEY ARRIVED AT the great temple to find two snakes there, the great bronze statue of a serpent that coiled before the entrance, and a second one, smaller, but no less fearsome. One of the great constrictor snakes known as "Sons of Set" lay sunning itself on the flagstones. Its black scales flashed with iridescent highlights of color, and its blood-colored tongue, as long as a man's forearm, occasionally flicked out to taste the air. A lump in its middle, the size of a goat—or a child—suggested that it had recently fed and, therefore, was of little danger unless provoked.

Even so, the reaction of the passersby was much different than it would have been in Odji. There people would have kept their distance from the snake, giving it wide berth and moving away as quickly as possible. Here, the snake drew a crowd, all of whom were the worshipers of Set, all of at least mixed Stygian blood, some commoners, some nobles.

They gathered quite close to the snake, often less than an arm's length away. Some made a show of lying on the stones before the snake, offering themselves, knowing that there was little chance the languid and satiated snake would take interest, even allowing the flicking tongue to taste their skin. Others knelt and begged favors of Set, some for health, love, and safety, but more often for power, wealth, or harm to an enemy, requests Set was said to be most favorable to.

Anok's attention was especially drawn to three figures who watched the proceedings from a discreet distance: a high-ranking acolyte and a pair of guardians of Set, each

armed with a short sword and an ornate ceremonial spear.
To harm one of the greater sons of Set was a capital crime,
and the sentence would likely be carried out immediately,
without trial or delay.

The crowd actually served Anok's needs. He wanted to
scout around the temple discreetly, and having all eyes on
the great snake was quite convenient.

The temple was a huge and imposing building, set off
from the rest of the inner city by wide plazas and court-
yards scattered with low plantings, statues, and fountains.
Crossing those unseen would be the first challenge. That
night, however, the moon would not rise until late, giving
Anok ample darkness in which to enter the temple.

His next obstacle would be the temple walls themselves.
There were few doors, and the mica-glazed windows and
air shafts were located high enough in the smooth stone
that they would be difficult to reach, even with rope and
grapple.

The main entrance was of little interest. By night it
would be locked and heavily guarded, and there were surprisingly few other doors. Dejal's map suggested that the
lower levels of the building connected to a maze of tunnels,
many of which extended out under the courtyard and likely
connected to hidden entrances in other nearby buildings,
but it provided no details beyond the footprint of the building itself. While those tunnels might, in a pinch, be useful
for Anok's escape, it was doubtful that he would be able to
use any of them to get inside.

He needed a way up the side of the building.

They were almost to the rear when he found it. "Look
here!" He pointed out a vertical gap in the wall to Teferi.
The core of the temple was of ancient construction, and it
was unlikely that it was originally built as a temple to Set.
It was even possible it hadn't been a temple at all. At some
point, or points, long after its construction it had been modified, doors and windows sealed, a new facade built over
the original walls, towers and wings added. Here, judging

from the slightly different types of stone on either side of the gap, an extension had been added to the building.

After first looking around to see if they were being watched, Anok placed his hand into the opening and closed it into a fist, wedging it tightly into the narrow space. He leaned back, holding his weight with the wedged hand. "Perfect." Years earlier Rami had taught them a technique for climbing cliffs and inclines without special gear, by wedging the hands and feet into openings in the rock. They quickly discovered it worked just as well for climbing buildings and walls, a technique they had often used to their advantage.

Teferi had never really become good at it. He disliked heights, and his larger frame was less suited to the task. But Anok had become reasonably proficient, though Sheriti was the most nimble of them all.

Teferi looked skeptically up the wall. "You think you can climb that high?"

"See those metal grates? According to Dejal's map they cover air shafts. If I can just get close enough, I can hook a grapple over that decorative stonework above them and hang there long enough to pry the grate loose."

"You'll have no cover at all."

"It'll be dark, and with luck, if a guardian passes by, he won't be looking for trouble this far over his head."

Teferi frowned. "That's it then. The way in."

"You seem disappointed, old friend. You were hoping I'd decide it was impossible?"

He grimaced. "It was a pleasant enough hope, but there's a saying among my people. 'Hope may grow in Stygia, but it never bears fruit.'"

Anok gestured away from the building. "Let's go somewhere less conspicuous. I need to wait for dark, and you should be heading back to the gate soon."

Teferi nodded. "I'll wait for you outside the gate."

"The night is long, and I won't be able to get out until morning without arousing suspicion. If I emerge any sooner, it will be with guardians in pursuit. Go home, or back to the Nest if it suits you. This is my misadventure and my downfall if it fails."

"To the Nest then, but I'll be back at the gate at dawn."

"You don't—"

"Dawn," he insisted.

AFTER MAKING SURE that Teferi returned to the gate, Anok made a slow circuit of the inner city to kill time.

His pace was carefully chosen, not so fast to appear to be in a hurry, not so slow so as to appear to be dawdling. He kept his eyes ahead, not making eye contact with people he met, not looking around like a gawking sightseer. His goal was to appear to have legitimate business passing through wherever he went, but nothing so urgent or immediate as to draw attention.

It left him with little to do but think, and lately, that had been something he could do without.

He had confidence in his own abilities, yet he was placing himself at great risk. He might not survive, and he had to admit that, in some ways, that might be for the best. It would free not only Sheriti, but also Teferi, of any obligations to him. They could get on with their lives without him as a burden.

He didn't fear death, or so he told himself, but he didn't look forward to it either, especially in the form it would most likely take inside the temple. If he were captured, he would undoubtedly be sacrificed on the altar of Set, and for an intruder on this most sacred place, the sacrifice would undoubtedly be one by slow torture.

On the other hand, if he were to penetrate into one of the temple's more guarded areas, he could simply jump out into plain sight, call out a challenge, and be relatively sure of death by combat, probably with the satisfaction of taking many of Set's followers with him. A quick, glorious death. It was almost appealing.

Yet that wouldn't do either. Any option that might end

his miserable existence and set his friends free, would also leave his father's spirit unavenged and restless. He would die himself, without ever knowing the answers to the questions that tortured him. And what of this *sister,* whose very existence was now in question?

No. He had to make his plan work, whatever the cost, no matter how hard it would be.

But *could* he do it? Could he carry out the dark deeds he would doubtless be called upon to commit in the service of Set? If a few lies tortured him, could he live with his entire existence as one great lie?

"Let fate and skill decide it," he said to himself. "If I survive to join the temple, then I will do whatever must be done."

He noticed that the sun was now out of sight and the sky had turned red as blood. There were few pedestrians now, most of them in a hurry to get home or to the gates out of the inner city. He made his way back to the area of shops near the temple. He slipped down an alleyway behind a closed bakery.

There he found an unused doorway recessed into the wall behind one of the wooden garbage bins. He was able to push the bin away from the wall just enough to slip behind it and sit down in the narrow space hidden there. As he did, he heard mice scampering out of the way, but he paid them no mind.

He made himself as comfortable as possible, put his head down, and waited for full darkness.

To his surprise, he actually dozed off for a while, and when he awoke, it was dark as ink outside. It was time.

He'd memorized the route back to the temple. Years of practice navigating Odji in darkness or fog, without lamps or torches, had made him proficient at such movement, though the streets were unfamiliar to him.

He hesitated at the edge of the plaza surrounding the temple. At several points along the tops of the wall, in the towers, and around the front entrance, huge oil lamps burned. Even behind the eyes of the great statue of Set lanterns burned, so that the orbs shone with a terrible red glow that looked down on the entire city.

But the plaza was mostly dark, and, crouching low, he made his way across using the occasional statue or fountain for cover, waiting to listen for any sign of guardians. Finally, he reached the wall, but of course, the crack was not there. Such precise navigation was impossible under the circumstances. He would have to feel along the wall until he located the opening.

He looked around at the spires of the city, visible only as dark silhouettes against the stars, and judged that the crack should be to his left. He headed that way, keeping his hand against the stone. He'd traveled perhaps twenty paces before finding it.

Quickly he rigged his gear, tying the grappling hook to a short piece of rope, which he coiled over his left shoulder. He pulled his dagger from under his tunic and tucked it in his belt, then slung his bag over his right shoulder.

It was time to climb. He reached as high as he could, wedged his right hand into the opening, then clenched it to wedge it into place. He put his left sandal into the opening, twisting it to secure it in place, and pushed himself up.

He felt the unfinished edge of the stone dig into the skin of his hand and upper foot. He would be scraped and bleeding well before he reached the top, but the dark stone should hide any traces remaining by sunrise. Carefully he jammed his other hand into the crack, then his other foot.

Step by painful step he worked his way up the wall. It was so dark, he could only guess his height by looking out at the skyline. He was relatively sure he had gotten high enough to kill him if he fell. *Well, that's reassuring. Get it over quickly.*

Still he climbed, on and on. Then his fingers found a horizontal crack in the stone, one his sharp eyes had spotted earlier in the day and noted as a reference point. He should be high enough to use the grapple. He shifted his grip to free his left arm and carefully unfurled the rope. He couldn't see the projecting stonework or the grate at all. He'd have to throw by memory.

He let the hook out on an arm's length of rope, then swung it in a circle, cringing at the slight whistle it made as it flew through the air. *Now!*

He flinched as he heard the hook clatter against stonework, and his fist slipped slightly in the crack. The hook didn't fall back, but he couldn't be sure if it was secure. He tried to pull on the rope, but as he did, he felt his fist slip again, ripping the skin on his knuckles. Then his foot slipped completely out of the crack. His fist held for a moment, then ripped free as well.

He held on to the rope, still slack in his other hand, and struggled to squelch the cry of alarm trying to claw its way out of his throat.

The rope went tight, almost ripping itself from his hand. He flailed with his now-free right hand, and grabbed the rope with it as well. He slammed into the wall, hung there, spinning in the darkness.

It was a strain to hold on, but after a minute or so he caught his breath and was able to slip his toes through the loop he'd earlier tied into the end of the rope. He pushed himself up, supporting most of his weight with his foot, then was able to slip his other foot into the loop as well. Carefully, he reached out and found the grate, hooking his fingers through the opening and using it to stop his dizzy spinning.

That's better. Still, he could hear the hook grinding against the stonework above as he moved. He had no idea how well the hook was set. He wouldn't be even remotely happy until he was safely inside the air shaft.

Feeling along the bottom of the grate, he found something that might be a latch. He reached for his dagger. His hope was that the grates would be designed to hinge out for cleaning. He dug the point of his dagger into the opening and pried. The grate seemed to shift slightly upward in its frame, but it didn't open. Annoyed, he pried again, harder this time.

He was so occupied, he didn't hear the approaching footsteps until they were almost under him. He glanced down to see two guardians of Set, one carrying an oil lamp, walking patrol around the outside of the building. They talked quietly, clearly unaware of his presence.

I'll just hang here quietly until—

Suddenly, with a dry scraping noise, the grate began to fall out of its frame, not swinging out at the bottom as he'd expected, but falling freely out from the top! He tried to catch the falling grate, or at least slow it so that he could keep it from clattering down on the guardians below. As he did, the weight of the grating pushed him away from the wall.

There was a little scraping noise, the rope went slack, and he fell free, his fingers still hooked into the grating.

He only fell a few inches before the grating stopped, pointing straight out from the building, and he hung there by his fingers. He felt the wind of the grappling hook fall past his head as the rope slid across his face. Instinctively, he grabbed the rope with his teeth before it could get away and fall to the flagstones below.

"What was that?" It was one of the guardians.

"Just bats," said the other guard. "You'll get used to it. There are whole colonies of them living inside the air shafts. They're what the little snakes eat"—he chuckled—"most of the time."

Anok hung like a deadweight over their heads, trying to still his pounding heart and the whistle of breath in and out of his nose. The rope was clenched tightly in his teeth, but he couldn't tell how far the grappling hook was hanging. For all he knew, one of the guards was about to walk right into it.

But the men continued on their way without incident. He watched them, his fingers slowly going numb, until they disappeared around the end of the building.

The moment they were gone, he commanded his agonized muscles to pull him up. It was torture, but he was finally able to get one elbow over the edge of the grating, then the other.

He'd been completely wrong about the grates. They did hinge out for cleaning, but they were hinged at the bottom, not the top. He could only hope that both hinges and grating would be strong enough to continue holding his weight as he climbed on top.

He managed to swing up and hook his left foot onto he frame of the grating, then to push up and roll completely on top of it. He lay on his back, taking the rope from his teeth and reeling in the hook, careful not to make any more noise. He tucked the rope and hook back into his bag, then carefully climbed into the shaft.

As the guard had predicted, Anok found the floor of the shaft covered with a slippery layer of bat guano, which in turn was full of squirming insects that lived off the dung. He tried to ignore the nasty sensations as the stuff oozed around the edges of his sandals and between his toes, invisible crawling things scurrying across his feet. Fortunately, the shaft was just tall enough that he could move in a low, ducklike, crouch, and it wasn't necessary to crawl through the muck.

If it had been dark outside, it was darker still in the shaft. Only a little way into the tunnel, it made no difference if his eyes were open or closed. He traveled for some distance as the way slanted upward, until the wall, which he'd been following with his fingertips, vanished from under his left hand. As he'd been expecting from his study of Dejal's map, he'd come to a branch in the tunnel. He took the narrower path to the left, taking him toward the front of the building.

As he moved past the junction, he couldn't help but notice that the layer of guano and the insects that went with it vanished, to be replaced by dry, dusty stone. The way to the bat colony must lie down the other passage. He was happy about that. Not only did it make the going easier and less unpleasant, but stumbling into the colony and disturb-

ing any bats not out feeding would undoubtedly cause a
commotion, which in turn might summon the guardians.

Presently he became aware that there was—if not
light—then a pale absence of total darkness. But if there
were a source of illumination, he couldn't determine where
it was. He took one of his baby steps forward, and his foot
found only empty space.

He stumbled forward, off-balance, unable to catch himself. He dived forward into the unknown and found himself
slamming into the stone floor of the shaft, with only his
lower legs dangling over empty space.

He scrambled the rest of the way across the gap, got
onto hands and knees, and peered down the opening.
There, at the bottom of a shaft several times the length of
his body, he saw a dim rectangle of light and a glint of
gold. After his eyes adjusted, he realized that the shaft was
several times as long as he was tall and that it opened into
the ceiling of a room below, which was faintly illuminated
by the flickering light of some torch or lamp. Far down
near the floor of that room, he could see the edge of some
golden object. It was entirely possible, he guessed, that he
was looking down into the main chamber of the temple and
at a bit of the golden snake that formed the altar of Set.

He felt the edge of the opening. There was a ledge on
either side just deep enough that he could have gone
around, or the opening was narrow enough that he could
have easily bridged it with his prone body if he'd known it
was there. *But the map didn't show it.*

Or did it? He recalled now a number of markings that
he hadn't recognized on the map, each a box with a cross
mark through it. He hadn't understood what they were at
the time. Now he was relatively sure they marked a vertical
shaft.

He muttered a quiet curse. Not only could the map kill
him if it were inaccurate, it could also kill him if he simply
failed to understand it.

Reluctantly, he decided it was time to light a candle. He
reached into his bag and pulled out a beeswax candle,

along with a metal holder that he looped around his thumb to catch any telltale dripping of wax. Next he found his flint, steel, and a small wad of tender. Working only by touch, he lit the candle.

He saw two interesting things in rapid succession. The first was the snake.

It was a tiny thing, as long as his arm, but slender like a whip, thinner than his little finger even at its widest point. It was also milky white, almost transparent, its eyes, which seemed strangely to be studying him anyway, were sightless and pink. As he watched, the snake slithered into a loose coil, all the while keeping its eerie, blind eyes toward him.

He'd heard the guard say something about snakes eating the bats. Any bats that could get through the grating were doubtless tiny, but it still seemed surprising that such a slender snake could swallow one. Slowly he reached for the snake.

It waited as his hand grew closer.

Then, faster than the eye could follow, it struck, its tiny mouth clamping painfully onto the web of his thumb. As Anok yanked his hand back—too late—the snake's body whipped with surprising power. Then the snake dropped away, taking a tiny mouthful of his flesh with it.

He cursed—too loudly, he belatedly realized—and shook his wounded hand. He felt no burning or tingling that would suggest the snake was venomous, but the tiny wound bled profusely. He wiped his hand on the front of his tunic and immediately regretted it. It would be conspicuous later, if anyone noticed it while he was trying to leave the inner city.

He looked at the wound, a small but neat semicircle missing from the web of his thumb. By holding his thumb tight against his palm, he was able to stop the bleeding.

Anok had never heard of a snake devouring flesh before. Most serpents swallowed their prey whole. Some might strike with their fangs, but only to inject poison, not to strip away meat. Given his wound, though, he supposed

nothing he knew of snakes outside Set's temple might be
so certain therein.

Movement caught his eye, and he spotted the snake slithering away down the tunnel with surprising speed, its pale
head still smeared with a red sash of blood. *Good riddance!*

It was as he turned his head and moved the candle to
follow the fleeing snake that he noticed the other interesting thing. He was sitting next to a human skeleton.

He reflexively scrambled away from the thing, but
quickly realized that it was harmless, nothing but a collection of old dry bones with just enough desiccated tendon
left to keep it from falling completely apart. Except for
some thick pieces of leather and a few metal buttons and
hooks, even its clothing was gone. A short sword of poor
quality was still belted loosely around the spine, and a
shoulder bag lay spilled on the floor nearby, revealing a
few picklocks of metal and bone, a short saw with two
ivory handles, some rope, and a grappling hook not unlike
Anok's.

There was one other item as well, a golden ring in the
shape of a snake, with ruby eyes. He had seen priests of Set
wear similar rings, but this one had been in the bag, not on
the skeleton's finger.

A thief then.

But what killed him? The corpse lay with one cheek
against the wall, a skeletal arm still draped protectively
across the face. The stone underneath was discolored,
probably by the fluids of decay, but he saw no signs of
dried blood leading up to that point. No guard would have
killed him and left him there, and there was no sign he was
wounded elsewhere. There were no sword wounds on the
skeleton itself and no signs of a hidden trap that could have
killed the thief.

Anok's injured thumb throbbed, and he again rubbed
the hand against the front of his tunic. The blood had already soaked through, making the silk stick to his breastbone, in about the same spot where his father's medallion

SCION OF THE SERPENT

had so often hung. But it seemed as though he felt a curious itching there, as if he were allergic to his own blood.

That realization got his attention. Poison? But the itching was only on his chest. His hand, other than the bleeding and entirely expected pain, was fine. *I'm getting worked up over nothing. It's just some old bones and a little snake, while real danger is all around.* He chuckled quietly, and, as if to convince himself how little the bones bothered him, he picked up the golden ring and added it to his bag. Then he stepped carefully over the bones and continued on his way.

With the candle, the going was much quicker, and as he progressed, his trust of the map grew. He had a destination now, a hidden spot just out of sight of the entrance where he might be able to rig an easier access point for his next visit. Several times he encountered vertical shafts in the floor, but they were easily crossed, since he could see them. He had only to be careful not to reveal his candle flame to anyone below.

It was after he crossed one of the gaps that he heard the sound.

At first, he though he'd imagined it, but he stayed quiet, his ears straining against the silence. *There it was again.* A rustling noise, like someone running his fingers through dry grass. The source of the noise wasn't clear. It seemed to come from all around him.

But then it was gone. He remained motionless for several minutes but heard nothing. Finally, he began to move again.

He came to another tunnel junction and turned right. As he did, he heard the sound again, louder than before.

Something moved on the floor in front of him.

He reached for his sword, but stopped.

It's just one of those damned snakes!

It lay in the middle of the stone floor, its body forming an undulating curve along the stone, its head lifted as though watching him. Though the snake was motionless, still Anok heard the noise from ahead.

He stepped forward, and as the light of the candle advanced into the gloom, he saw another snake. And another. And another. Until finally the tunnel seemed, despite what the map had said, to terminate in a dead end.

He cursed. Then he cursed again.

The wall was moving!

Nor was it the sliding movement of some mechanical trap. The wall was throbbing, shifting, flowing, as though alive—

It was! Snakes! Those slender white snakes. Hundreds of them. Thousands. More than Anok could count. As many as stars in the sky.

All alive.

All moving as one.

The wall of living flesh began to advance toward him, not with any regular motion, but in a series of surging waves, as snakes seemed to fall off the front into a heap on the floor, which was almost instantly swallowed by the moving mass of serpents behind it.

As it moved, it swallowed up some of the lone snakes lying there. Two of the ones nearest him seemed agitated into action. They slithered forward rapidly, rearing up and striking at the exposed flesh of his legs.

He grabbed one out of midair, taking it between his hands and ripping it in two.

But even as he dropped the broken snake to the floor, its fellow sank its needle-sharp teeth into the flesh of his calf. The snake thrashed briefly, then fell away to crawl back toward the approaching mass.

He cursed Set and all his foul creations. A few of the snakes would barely hurt him, but if the mass of them set upon him all at once—

Long ago, Teferi had told him a tale passed down through his family, of a river in the dark jungles of Kush, where schools of tiny, sharp-toothed fish swam. No man dared enter that river, for it was said that those fish could strip a man, or even a cow, down to bare bone in just minutes.

Anok had laughed at such an absurd story.

He wasn't laughing now.

He backed way from the approaching mass. Its progress wasn't so rapid that it presented any real danger. There was ample time to escape.

Then the snake that had just bitten him, with its visibly bloody head, joined the mass and disappeared among its squirming fellows. There was a sudden agitation in the mass, radiating out from the point where the lone snake had entered, as though the snakes had just been given exciting news.

Anok's eyes widened.

His body tensed.

The wall seemed to collapse, like a block of mountain ice turning into water. It formed a squirming, surging wave of snakes that threatened to engulf Anok.

His duckwalk was too slow. He dropped down on all fours, the loop on the candleholder slipping over one thumb, and scrambled down the tunnel like an animal, fleeing the rustling horror that he could hear literally snapping at his heels.

He turned the corner and saw the first vertical air shaft ahead.

Maybe it would stop them. Maybe it would slow them down.

He bounded over the opening, but his hopes were dashed as he glanced back. The snakes' long bodies easily bridged the gap. It barely slowed them down.

There was only one thing to do. Retrace his steps as quickly as possible, without caution or concern for noise, and hope that the squirming horror wouldn't follow beyond the air shafts that were apparently their home.

He scrambled down the shaft, the sputtering candle attached to his hand continuously threatening to go out.

Then he heard the dry rustling noise—

Ahead!

He held the candle higher, to see a second wave of snakes approaching from both directions!

Just ahead was the opening to a vertical shaft. He straddled it, his back against the wall, watching the snakes rapidly closing in from either direction.

The smooth stone offered no place to attach his grapple, or tie the rope. There were only seconds left anyhow. No time!

The fall would definitely at least break both legs. More probably his neck, which would be infinitely preferable to the horrible death that swept in on him like ocean waves.

He braced himself, mentally preparing for the slight inward twist of his feet that would send him plunging down the shaft to his doom.

The terrible reality of his decision washed over him. *I'm going to die.*

Still, he couldn't make his feet move. Instead, he held out his hands, palms outward, and in a gesture of futility hissed, *"Stop!"*

A flash of light filled the tunnel.

—a flash of light that seemed to originate from—the palms of his hands?

Silence, but for the fading echo of his own voice.

Silence.

The snakes weren't moving.

Anok blinked.

A choking gasp of relief emerged from his throat.

From far below his feet, he heard a voice. "Did you hear that?"

"I heard something."

"You think the snakes got somebody?"

A silent pause. "There would be screaming if they did." Laughter. "It takes a while. Probably they just got a rat or something."

"I thought I heard someone say, 'stop.'"

Louder laughter. "As if that would deter the *Fingers of Set!* It's a rat, I tell you. Come. Perhaps we should check in on the virgins down in the sacrificial cells."

The voices grew fainter. "Well, they'd best *stay* virgins, or it'll be *us* on the altar next Festival . . ."

Anok crouched, motionless, trying to figure out what had just happened.

The snakes were still there, still alive. In each direction they lay, a motionless, knee-high carpet on the tunnel floor, regarding him with countless pairs of blind, pink eyes.

They weren't killing him, but they weren't going away either.

The palms of his hands tingled, and the blood-soaked spot on his skin burned.

What had just happened? *Sorcery?*

That wasn't possible. He was no sorcerer, no wizard, no cult priest. He was Anok, a simple warrior of the slums. *I don't do sorcery!*

Yet something had happened to save him. Something extraordinary.

Parath! The so-called lost god had promised that it would help him if it could. He'd almost forgotten that promise, perhaps never really believed it. Certainly, it had seemed a hollow promise at the time.

But it was the only explanation. He hadn't performed the sorcery; it was the old god acting on his behalf.

But the snakes were still here, and at the moment, his only way out was still the vertical shaft. He considered a plan to put one of his swords across the opening and hook the grappled to that. Would it support his weight without breaking?

Still the snakes didn't move. *What are they waiting for?* Well, perhaps there was another way. He stepped back across the air shaft, back toward his original destination. He held up his hand. "Back," he said quietly.

To his amazement, the snakes turned and began to slither away from him! He smiled, almost giggled. Even if he was just channeling the power of the old god, it was intoxicating. Was that what it was like to be a sorcerer?

He began to move back down the tunnel. The snakes moved away even faster, heading off in both directions from the branch in the passage. There seemed be fewer of

them as they traveled, and he occasionally began to notice
one slithering away into some tiny crack or gap in the
stone. As he neared the end of the shaft, the last of them
was gone, as though they'd never been there at all.

Ahead, he caught sight of a grating and reluctantly
doused the candle. He reached the grate and peered out
through the narrow holes at the night sky. He'd traveled
completely across the temple, and probably a third of its
length. Knowing how it worked, he had little trouble
swinging open the grate and finding a secure place outside
to attach the grapple.

As expected, he could just see a ledge below him in the
starlight. He'd climb down there, then rig a hidden coil of
rope that could later be pulled down to the plaza from below. On his next visit he would have but to pull down the
rope and shinny up. Easy.

Next time he would go much deeper into the temple.

Next time he would find Dejal.

As he prepared to climb down a second rope to the
plaza, he happened to glance at his hands. They still tingled, and as he moved them, he could see little pinpoints of
light in the skin, as though he'd ripped down a little frag-
ment of the night sky and held it in his hands.

Sorcery!

He still couldn't believe it.

15

TEFERI PACED THE length of the Nest, then turned to face Anok. "Sorcery," he announced firmly, "is never good fortune."

Anok sat at the table, contemplating the jeweled eyes of the serpent ring he had taken from the temple. The ring rested on top of an inverted drinking cup in the middle of the table, where a beam of light from one of the small, high windows illuminated it perfectly. The ring was heavy, solid gold, and would doubtless fetch a fair price at market, assuming the obvious connection to the cult didn't spook any buyer. *Perhaps we should melt it down ourselves and simply sell the gold and loose jewels.*

"Anok!" There was irritation in Teferi's voice. "Are you listening to me?"

He looked up. "Of course I am. You said something about sorcery and good fortune."

"I *said* that sorcery is *never* good fortune!"

"A few days ago I might have agreed with you. But without sorcery, I would never have lived though the night. We wouldn't be having this talk."

"Don't forget, it's sorcery at the root of your troubles in the first place. Did I not tell you what was passed down to me through my ancestors? Sorcery and magic corrupt the user's spirit, sometimes the body as well."

It was Anok's turn to sound annoyed. "The magic wasn't my doing, Teferi. It was the old god."

"This Parath you told me about. I am curious why you didn't choose to share this with me before."

"I said there were gods in the desert. I didn't hide that from you."

"If you believe his words, a fallen god. An exiled god. A god at war with both Ibis and Set. His enemies will become your enemies, Anok!"

"Set is already my enemy."

"You are enemy to Set. But until you harm Set, you could hope to be beneath the snake-god's notice. Now you may have marked yourself, and if the Cult of Set determines to crush you, it will."

"Parath will protect me. I see that now. I didn't believe it before, but I understand now that Parath will hide my intentions from Set until I can do what I must do."

"And Ibis. What of Ibis?"

"I don't care about Ibis."

"But this Parath does. If he is to aid you against Set, he will expect the same from you against Ibis. How many gods do you think you can kill?"

Anok leaned back, and couldn't resist a slight smile. "It seems a small enough worry. Really, what are the odds I'll survive my encounter with Set?"

Teferi frowned. "Don't joke!"

"What else is there to do, old friend? We always used to laugh at danger."

"Men and women who opposed us, made of flesh and blood, mortal as we, or even more so we believed. Rarely did we encounter sorcery, and when we did, we wisely headed the other way."

"Then perhaps I'm ready for greater challenges."

Teferi's tone turned grave. "I should leave you. I should abandon you to this fool's quest, Anok. I should find a ship out of this place and look for a better land. I should look for a fine woman with skin like polished mahogany, a strong mule that can pull a plow, and a few chickens. I should save my tales of adventure for my grandchildren."

Anok found the words made him feel both betrayed and relieved. "Go then!"

Teferi turned to look at him silently for a while. "No," he finally said, "I'll stay, for never have you needed me more. What kind of friend would I be to abandon you alone to this madness?"

Disappointment—and relief. "A wiser friend than I apparently have here now."

Teferi came and sat across the table from Anok. He looked once at the golden ring, then pushed it away. "When will you go back then?"

"Tomorrow night. I have a few things to prepare, but now that I know it can be done there is no sense in waiting. And the longer I wait, the more chance somebody will stumble on my return preparations."

"How do you know the same sorcery will protect you from those little snakes?"

Anok shrugged. "I don't. I just *feel* that it will work. I can't explain."

Teferi frowned but said nothing.

"We'll have to work out some way of exchanging messages in the short term. Hopefully we can work out a more successful method of getting notes out than we had in getting them in."

Teferi looked at him, eyebrow raised.

"That," said Anok, "would be much easier if you could read."

"It would also be easier if I could fly and breathe fire, but unless you impose some dark magics on me against my will, that will not happen."

"We'll devise something."

Just then they heard the trapdoor open, and both looked to see Sheriti descending the stairs. Anok and Teferi exchanged an uncomfortable glance.

Finally, Teferi began to rise. "I'll leave you to talk. We can settle the other matters before tomorrow night."

"Bring breakfast," said Anok. "Thick beer. We'll talk then."

Teferi glanced toward Sheriti and nodded. "I'll see you tomorrow," he said, letting himself out the door.

Sheriti strolled over on bare feet and took Teferi's seat at the table. She wore a simple shift of heavier, everyday silk. It was rather plainer and more functional, and certainly less revealing, than the one she'd worn a few night earlier.

Nevertheless, Anok thought she looked beautiful in it. The distance between them was painful, though she sat only an arm's reach away.

She licked her lips nervously. "You went to the temple then?"

He nodded.

"I'd ask how it went, but you're alive. That says quite a bit."

"Dejal's map seems accurate. I've rigged a quick way back inside. There's no reason not to carry through with my plan." *Well, only one.*

"I see."

There were silent for a while, not making eye contact.

Finally, Anok said, "I told you I was going. I told you nothing would change. You shouldn't even be here. Why haven't you gone back to the Temple of Scribes?"

"Because, despite everything you've told me, I still have hope. It may have no grounding, but if I give it up—I'll just die."

"And when I'm gone?"

"Then I'll hope for you to come back, later, if not sooner." She seemed lost in thought for a while. "Know this, Anok. Whatever happens, whatever you must do, whatever you must become—I will forgive you. I will forgive you, and I will wait for you."

"Don't—"

She raised her hand and cut him off. "I do this for me, not for you. I'm very angry at you right now—for you, not for me. You are about to do a terrible thing to my very best friend, and I don't know how I will find forgiveness. But I will."

Listening to her words was harder than he could have imagined. "I don't deserve you, Sheriti. I wish you could see that and move on."

"I wish you could see yourself as I see you. In this land of evil, you are a lamp in the darkness. You've kept Teferi and me going all these years. Even those you couldn't save from themselves—Dejal, Rami, the others—they are still better for having known you."

He wanted to tell her how weak he was, what a fraud he was, but he said nothing. If she didn't see it already, he didn't know what he could say.

There was a long silence. Then he said, "You should go. I have many things to do. As do you. You should go to the Temple of Scribes tomorrow."

She nodded tearfully and started to rise. He stood as well.

She took a step away, hesitated, then ran back into his arms. Their lips met, hot and desperate, their bodies pressed together, their limbs entwined. They fell onto the table and began throwing off their clothes. The ring was swept aside, clattering away somewhere in the darkness.

There were no words.

Words had already failed them.

This was all they had now.

16

ANOK AWOKE THE next morning to find Sheriti gone. It saddened him, but he was just as happy to avoid tearful farewells. It was strange, he reflected as he dressed, how it was as though he were preparing for death rather than a short journey within the same city. He was putting his affairs in order, saying most of his good-byes, and leaving the Nest as though he never intended to return.

Yet it was a short journey only in terms of physical distance. In other terms, it could hardly be a longer one. He was climbing from a high rung of the lowest class of Stygian society to the bottom rung of the very highest. Stygia's government was simply a puppet operated by the Cult of Set, and supposedly any acolyte was putting himself on a path that could lead to the office of the Speaker of Set, the true power behind King Ctesphon's court.

To mingle with commoners would be frowned upon, if not outright forbidden. He would have to bend to a new series of rules, different standards of dress and behavior. He would have to defer to authority in a way he'd never known. His old life, close as it would be, might as well be on the far shores of the Western Ocean.

But that was only the surface appearance of it. In truth, he was going into battle. In that way, he was like any young warrior headed off to some distant battleground, saying good-bye to loved ones with no assurance of return. Only he was not an army but a single warrior facing an adversary so great that victory, or even survival, seemed almost unimaginable.

Teferi knocked his special knock at the door, and Anok was quick to let him in. He peered around the room as he entered, looking for Sheriti, but not finding her, said nothing about it. As instructed, he brought thick beer, flatbread with honey, and some kind of beef sausage, beef of any kind being a rare treat in Odji.

They ate, drank, and discussed possible rendezvous points and illicit couriers. Most promising was their realization that low-ranking guardians of Set were easily bribable, and should be even more so where an insider to the cult was concerned.

Anok was confident that he could get messages out, as long as his money lasted, assuming he was allowed to keep any of his remaining wealth. He was sure that some sort of tribute would be required as the price of admission to the cult. He could only hope that less would be expected from the likes of him than from the son of a wealthy merchant. With that hope, he entrusted the few gems left from their last windfall to Teferi, keeping only his small stash of gold and silver coin.

They mutually decided that Teferi would move back into the Nest, taking Anok's place as the guardian of the Paradise. It would allow him to keep an eye on Sheriti if she returned from the Temple of Scribes for visits, and on one other very important item.

That was the last item to be taken care of. He went into his sleeping stall and pulled back the bed, making a point of showing Teferi the loose stone with its chipped corner.

He pulled it out and removed the hidden contents, the medallion and its hidden treasure within.

Only this time, it was different. As he removed the stone, the Scale began to ring, as it had in the desert. If it didn't stop, it was going to be much harder to hide and transport. "I don't know why it's doing this."

Teferi looked puzzled. "Doing what?"

"Don't you hear it?"

"Hear what?"

"The ringing sound from this." He held up the medallion.

"Anok, I hear nothing." He held his head closer, cocking his ear toward the object, then leaned back. "No," he said firmly.

That was very strange. Clearly he was "hearing" the sound with senses other than his ears. Perhaps that had been true in the desert as well. But why was it making the sound at all? Parath had said something about its having power over serpents. Perhaps some small fraction of its power had been transferred to him over long exposure. Perhaps that accounted for his ability to turn back the swarming snakes of the Great Temple.

He would have to figure it out another time. He had been staring at the thing too long, and it was feeding Teferi's suspicion about all things magical. No, best to get on with it.

This time, he showed Teferi everything, how to access the hidden compartment in the medallion, and what was hidden within. He also shared with him everything he knew about the Scale of Set.

"This is my one piece of leverage against the cult. I believe they want this very badly, and if Parath is right, it's a key to great power for them. It's possible I can use it against them, or maybe at the right time, I'll have to offer it to them to strike a bargain. But if the latter happens, I intend to be sure that they never are never allowed to have all three Scales."

Teferi looked skeptical. "If you choose not to withhold this Scale, then you may have no choice in the matter. They already have at least one. The Ravens provided it to them, by way of Dejal. For all you know, they already have the second one as well."

"I hope not. I'll deal with that when the time comes, if it ever does. I would prefer to learn to use the Scale as a weapon against them. Perhaps there is a way I can obtain the other two Scales and take their power for myself."

Teferi shuddered. "I do not approve of this, Anok. These Scales of Set are very bad magic, I fear. Powerful, yes, but with great power comes great corruption. This thing calls to your Stygian blood."

"Then all the more reason I should entrust it to you rather than keeping it myself. Your untainted Kushite blood will protect you from its influence, and in the presence of priests having full Stygian blood, it may be impossible to hide anyway."

Teferi was eventually won over and agreed to care for the objects so long as they could remain hidden. He wasn't really happy until they were back in their dark hiding place, and the chipped stone returned to its niche.

They finished their business by noon, and Anok found himself left with an awkward interval. He knew they shouldn't go to the inner city until late in the afternoon and that he couldn't enter the temple until after dark, and even with his disguise he didn't dare spend time wandering the streets of Odji, where he might be recognized.

After some uncomfortable silences, he and Teferi began to talk of old times, sharing stories that each of them knew by heart. They talked of Ravens long dead or departed, even of happier times when Dejal still called himself their brother, and they his. In time, they found themselves laughing themselves to tears.

But all the while, Anok was watching the shafts of light from the windows crawl across the floor and up the far wall. "It's time," he said.

Teferi's laughter faded, his mood turned somber. He nodded. They gathered their belongings and left, as though headed for a funeral.

TEFERI STAYED WITH him almost until nightfall, and had to rush to get back to the gates in time. If he arrived too late, even if he made it there without being arrested by the guardians of Set, there would be uncomfortable questions. Perhaps someone would ask about his companion in the strange dress of a desert nomad and what exactly had happened to him?

But he trusted that his friend would not let him down. That was the least of his worries. He found a hiding place on the other side of the plaza from his previous visit, closer to his exit point. He waited for total darkness, but no longer. He wanted to be safely inside the air shafts as soon as he could. It would be a long night.

While there were frequent patrols by guardians around the building, they all carried oil lamps, which made them easy to avoid in the darkness. He waited until the first patrol of the evening had rounded the far corner of the building, then made his way quietly across the plaza.

He was seeking a small statue, located beneath the air shaft from which he'd earlier exited the temple. Just below the opening, there was a small ledge where he'd hidden a coil of rope and his bag of burglar tools. He quickly found the statue. Looking up, he could not see the ledge though he knew it was there.

The problem was that the rope he needed to climb was coiled forty feet over his head. He'd prepared for that however. Carefully, he waved his hands between the statue and the wall, until he felt a gentle bushing, like a spider's web. It was a single strand of Stygian silk, fine almost to the point of invisibility in daylight, and incredibly strong— strong enough to pull down the end of the coiled rope far above him.

He took one last look around for guards, then slowly tugged until he heard the rope tumble down. He gave it a quick jerk to be sure that it was still secured at the top as he'd left it, and he rapidly began to climb. Very quickly he was at the top. He rolled over the lip of the overhang and lay on his back as he pulled up the rope and its attached strand of silk, with any luck leaving no clue to his passage.

Just in time as it turned out. A pair of guards rounded the front of the building. He watched them cautiously over the edge of the overhang until their light finally vanished at the back of the building.

He'd left the metal grate over the air shaft barely latched, and he had only to jiggle the grate slightly to pull it free. He tensed as the hinge squeaked some, but after several minutes of maintaining a tense silence, he decided none of the guards had heard it.

I always forget something. A better thief would have a vial of whale oil ready to quiet the rusty hinge. He'd been lucky.

He climbed inside and, after some deliberation, left the grate open rather than risk making more noise. If his business there was successful, it wouldn't matter. Otherwise, he'd likely either be gone by dawn, dead or captured. And once he escaped, it was unlikely he'd ever return there again. If he made things more difficult for the next temple raider, what of it? Of course, the next temple raider would still have to deal with the snakes.

With much greater confidence, as he was retracing his steps, he made his way deep enough into the tunnel to light a candle. As he did, there was a flicker of movement down where the roughly finished stone of tunnel wall met the dusty floor, a tiny white head appeared along with a curl of pallid body, gleaming in the candlelight. Blind eyes looked toward him, black tongue tasting his smell.

Anok felt a twinge of fear, but also of eagerness, as one felt when standing on the tall rocks south of the city, anticipating the long dive into the ocean waves. He felt the odd tingling over his heart, and now more clearly out through his arms, to his hands.

More heads appeared, from cracks in the wall, from out of the gloom, a few snakes slithering fully out into the open. He looked to the closest of those, knelt, and held out his open hand. "Come," he said.

The snake's tongue flicked.

"Come!"

The snake slithered forward a body length, its narrow body almost swimming through the dust, then stopped.

"Come!"

The snake advanced, the forward part of its body high, its head darting toward Anok's exposed hand.

He braced for the pain of the bite.

It did not come. The snake slithered its body across his palm, cool and smooth, its head diving low. The body arced under his arm, then wound itself around his wrist, firmly, but tightly. Almost with—*affection*.

He smiled, reached down, and stroked the head, smaller than a fingertip. The black tongue, moist and leathery, stroked his skin. Then he lowered his hand close to the floor. "Back," he said.

The snake calmly slithered off his arm and away across the floor.

"Back," he said more loudly. One by one, the snakes began to vanish back into their hiding places, until there was again at least the impression that he was alone in the cave, save for a small house scorpion, previously unnoticed, crawling across the floor toward him.

A lone snake head, along with a hand's length of body, shot from a crack in the wall, snatched the scorpion in its mouth, and dragged it—legs, claws, and stinging tail waving helplessly—back into the darkness.

Anok found himself rocking unsteadily on his feet. His head buzzed as though from strong drink, and his senses seemed detached and oddly out of sorts. His hand and arm tingled where the snake had touched him, as did his chest. He felt flushed and warm, despite the evening chill. He felt—*good! Powerful!*

Was this what it was like to become a sorcerer? If so, then it might not be as bad as he imagined.

He advanced, turning at the branch and passing the bones of the thief. He felt compelled to whisper a greeting as he passed, to quiet any spirits that might be lurking about. Then he crossed the bat corridor where he'd initially entered, and he moved into a passage he'd not yet explored.

As expected, the floor slanted down and ended abruptly in a large vertical shaft, far wider than he could reach across, and so deep that the candle's feeble light was swallowed in the gloom below. Air flowed upward, judging from its coolness possibly from some subterranean source. He had found his connection to the catacombs beneath the temple.

What the map hadn't told him was how he would get down. He was removing the coil of rope from his satchel when he noticed a small stone ledge extending from the wall to his right, and then below it, another one, and another. They projected just far enough to provide purchase for a hand or foot, and were wide enough to stand on with two feet. They formed a ladder of sorts and extended out of sight down into the dark.

He repacked the rope and carefully stepped out onto the nearest of the ledges. It held his weight, so he hooked the candleholder over his thumb, swung himself out into the shaft, and began to climb downward.

He counted the steps, trying to estimate the distance he had traveled. After sixty steps, he presumed himself to be at about ground level, but still the shaft plunged down into darkness. After another twenty steps, he spotted another side passage, similar to the one through which he'd entered the larger shaft.

He glanced downward and could see *something* that suggested the bottom of the shaft was below. It was lighter than the stone, and he held the glare of the candle away from his eyes, straining for a better look. The bottom of the shaft was just visible, and he thought for a moment that it was covered with sand, its surface somehow irregular with pits and lines.

Then his vision adjusted again, and he saw that the pit was filled to an even layer with human bones. Dozens, hundreds of scattered and cleaned skeletons, disassociated skulls staring up at him with empty sockets. There was no sense that they lay in a single layer upon a floor. Instead, he had the impression that the shaft extended down, and the bones filled it to some undetermined depth.

So startled was he, that he jerked the candle, sending a cascade of wax down his hand. He hissed in pain, shaking the stinging crust of hardening wax from his skin. He shifted the candle to a more secure grip and was so distracted that he didn't see the dark shape moving smoothly across the bones below him.

Instead, he first became aware of the sound, like the grinding of huge teeth. It took him a moment to realize what he was hearing was something of great weight moving across the compacted bones, grinding one against another as it passed.

He looked down to see a black S shape covering much of the floor below, having emerged from some unseen side passage, he imagined. Before he could understand what he was looking at, or even react, the head of the great snake reared up with both great speed and infinite smoothness, like the rising of an ocean swell. With no effort at all, the huge head was at eye level with him, close enough he could have reached out to touch the broad snout, contemplating him with copper-colored eyes the size of melons.

There was no time to reach for his sword, no time to duck to safety. Before he could move, he'd be no more than a mouthful for the great serpent.

He remained motionless.

As did the snake, bigger than any Anok had seen, at least twice as big as any of the sacred sons of Set that ranged the streets of the city to feed. It studied him with cold, merciless intelligence.

The tongue slid out, as long as his arm, as thick as his wrist, black, shiny, forked, it slid across his arm, leaving a sticky film, and he couldn't help but shudder.

Then the wide, lipless, slit of a mouth parted, wider and wider, revealing the black tongue, the puffy white interior of the mouth, the countless knife-sharp teeth the size of spearpoints.

Wider, until he could imagine his entire body being drawn down that terrible gullet.

Wider, until he was sure he was doomed.

The snake hissed, a long, high sound like wind escaping from a cave. He could feel its breath on his face, and the sound chilled him to his bones.

The coppery eyes glittered in the candlelight, regarding him with an evil intelligence.

Then the mouth closed and, with the same liquid grace, the head lowered. The great snake swiftly curled back upon itself, and with the rattling of countless bones, vanished into some hidden recess in the wall.

He hung there for a while, afraid to shift his grip, lest his weak knees and numbed fingers send him tumbling down into the pit, until strength returned to his limbs. He took one more step down and carefully swung himself into a side shaft, taking comfort that it was far too narrow to admit the great snake's head.

Once safely inside, he took a moment to catch his breath and collect himself. No magics had repelled the monster, nor was he sure even the most powerful wizard could. He had been caught, studied, *judged,* and spared, for reasons he could not imagine. This place, he was reminded again, was not a house of man. It belonged to Set, and all those who came here and lived did so at his whim.

He lit another candle, replacing the shrinking stub in the holder, and as he did, examined his surroundings. The shaft was nearly identical in size and layout to the horizontal shafts in the upper temple, but the stone here was far older and of a darker color than that of the building above.

There were more skeletons, so that he was nearly always in sight of at least one. Some were fresh enough that they still had tatters of clothing left, but none had flesh. They were all polished and picked clean, which made him wonder if the snakes were that thorough, or if other unpleasant scavengers hid in the cracks of the temple, perhaps also serving as food for the white snakes.

The light of his candle fell upon carvings in the walls.

Not the clean and ornate carvings of artisans but the kind of crude graffiti scratched into the stone by bored workers or resentful slaves. While he could imagine the purpose of it, the symbols were unlike anything he had ever, seen on any temple wall or ancient scroll. The catacombs might date back to the very dawn of time, when legendary giants ruled the land and supposedly kept Lemurians, the fabled ancestors of modern Stygians, as their slaves.

Or perhaps they were older than that, some civilization forgotten and lost to the dust of time. It seemed that such was the way of Stygia, one city built on the ruins of another, layer upon layer, like an onion, back to the beginning of the world.

Finally, he reached another shaft leading down and could see light below. The map told him that it was a large room of unknown function, which in turn would connect him to the acolyte living areas.

Better prepared this time, he removed a stout piece of wood that he'd tied alongside one of his swords. He tied the rope to the middle of it, then placed it across the opening. He could see little of the room below, so he put his head down into the opening and listened carefully for any sign of occupation. Hearing nothing, he tossed down the rope, lowered himself into the opening, and shinnied along the rope and through the room's painted arched ceiling.

The room was perhaps three times as tall as a man stood, half that distance wide, and three or four times that long. It seemed almost a hallway, though in the darkness at one end he could make out what seemed to be an altar, and at the other end was an open door. On the wall next to the door was a single oil lamp, the room's only illumination.

Perhaps the room was a shrine, though not of the sort common to Set. Another of the old gods? It was strange that even if, as it seemed was the case, the Great Temple was built on the foundations of older temples to other gods, all traces of those gods would not have been obliterated or modified to serve Set.

Perhaps the priests of Set were not so faithful to their

evil god as it seemed. Perhaps they kept congress with other, older gods, as another path to power.

The walls were lined, with carved columns or statues, dimly seen in the darkness, stretching from floor almost to ceiling and spaced an arm's width apart. He held up the candle and suddenly jumped back, convinced he'd been horribly wrong about his being alone.

From the top of the nearest "column" a metal helmet, horned and ornately carved, looked down at him, narrow eye slits giving the faceplate a sinister appearance. He had already thrown down his bag and drawn his swords when he realized that the wearer of the helmet was long dead, a skeletal giant dressed in helmet and plate armor, a sword as long as Anok was tall hanging from its belt. Or perhaps it wasn't a skeleton at all but the work of some macabre sculptor. In the dim light of the chamber it was impossible to be sure.

He heard footsteps—of mercifully human proportions— and slipped between two of the skeletal figures, his back against the cold wall, swords at ready. His ears told him there were two people in sandals walking toward the room. He heard male voices conversing calmly in whispers.

There was a moment of panic when he realized that his bag was still sitting on the tiled floor in plain sight, but it was too late to go back for it.

The sound of footsteps reached the door of the chamber and passed by without breaking step. He waited until the footsteps faded in the distance before sheathing one of his swords and emerging from his hiding place.

As he recovered his bag, he noticed the floor was clean-swept and free of dust. The room was used, or at least cared for. Once again he was in the world of men, where the greatest dangers walked on two legs. His task was complicated in that, since, he hoped to find favor in the House of Set, he didn't want to have to kill or even wound, anyone he encountered. Stealth was his friend, and violence a last resort.

The map, which he'd memorized, indicated that ahead

lay a rectangle of corridor lined with sleeping and study chambers used by the novice acolytes and high-ranking temple servants. He peered cautiously into the corridor, checking in both directions.

The corridor was narrow, illuminated by oil lamps set in wall sconces. The roof here was arched, though much lower than the shrine. It was covered with paintings of unreadable hieroglyphs and pictographs of strange animals and forgotten gods. He was relieved to discover that the side chambers were equipped with wooden doors, mostly closed, making it easier to slip past the sleeping acolytes. Finding the corridor empty, he slipped out of the shrine.

Then he realized he had another problem. He had to find the sleeping Dejal without having any idea which chamber was his and without waking anyone else.

He slipped up to one of the few open doors and peered inside. He carefully took one of the oil lamps off the wall and used it to see inside the dim room. He found an unused sleep chamber. A narrow wooden sleeping bench, little more than a trio of parallel planks pegged together, hung from the wall to his right. A crockery chamber pot was tucked underneath the foot of the bed. A small shrine to Set, a crude wooden table, and a small scribe's desk with bench were the room's only other furnishings.

He hoped it was typical of the sleeping rooms and, if so, Dejal would at least be alone. But how to find him? He replaced the lamp and took a few more steps down the corridor, standing near one of the doors. From inside, Anok heard a raspy snore, and a smile slowly spread across his face.

Knowing Dejal as long as he had, Anok knew many things about him. Dejal snored. And not just any snore, a nasal whistle that various Ravens had teased him about over the years. As far as Anok knew, Dejal had never grown out of it.

He slipped down the corridor, pausing at each door. From some there was silence, from others snoring lacking

Dejal's familiar whistle. From one he heard the sounds of a pen scratching across papyrus, punctuated by the tapping of the quill against the side of the inkpot. He was especially careful to move quietly past that door.

Finally, when he was beginning to wonder if Dejal was there at all, he heard it. He stood outside the door for several minutes, just to be sure. There was no doubt. It was Dejal.

He sheathed his sword, slipped the dagger from under his belt, and relit his candle from the wall lamp. It would likely be dark in the room, and he had to be sure Dejal would recognize him. Then, with one finger, he carefully lifted the latch on the door. He pulled slightly, testing the hinges. They moved quietly.

From somewhere around the corner to his right, he heard footsteps. There was no more time for hesitation. He slipped inside, closing the door behind him, hearing the latch bar click softly back into place. He could see Dejal curled on the bench, wrapped in a light blanket against the underground chill, his face toward the wall.

Anok placed the candleholder lightly on the table and knelt next to the bed. Fortunately Dejal was not a light sleeper. Unfortunately, he often awoke groggy and disoriented, and Anok couldn't leave to chance what would happen then, even if the former Raven looked favorably on his arrival.

With one motion he swept Dejal out of bed, hand clamped over his mouth, the edge of his dagger against his throat.

Dejal flailed, tangled in his blanket, then stopped struggling as he felt the blade tighten against his throat.

Anok felt Dejal's pounding pulse, the cold sweat of Dejal's face on his hand, but he seemed calm enough to listen. "Dejal," he whispered, "it's me. Anok Wati."

At the name Dejal twitched, and Anok could see his eyes harden over, trying to get a look at his attacker. Anok leaned over his shoulder slightly, face toward the candle so he could be seen.

Dejal's body seemed to relax slightly when he recognized Anok.

"I don't mean you harm, brother. I just want to talk. Can I trust you to uncover your mouth?"

Dejal nodded.

Anok withdrew his hand slightly, leaving it ready to snap back at the slightest sound.

"What's the meaning of this, Anok?"

"You didn't answer my messages. I changed my mind about joining the cult."

"And I gave you your chance. I took your message to Ramsa Aál, the Priest of Acolytes and asked for dispensation for you. But he refused, and even forbade me to send you a message in return."

Anok lowered the knife. "Why?"

"Why? I wasn't given a reason, though I suspect it is your impure blood. I had thought I might be able to use my family influence to overcome that. If you had entered with my class of acolytes, perhaps it would be different, but petitioning for late entry draws additional scrutiny."

"No, I mean why weren't you allowed to send me a message? Why should they even care?"

Dejal shrugged. Then he pointed at the sleeping bench. "Can I get up, or are you planning to slice my throat?"

Anok tucked the dagger back in his belt, while Dejal sat himself back on the edge of the simple bed. He moved the small bench over from the desk and sat on it.

"You're an outsider, Anok, and inferior, in the eyes of the cult. Likely they feel I will be contaminated by any contact with you. Set knows what they'd do if they found you here. How did you get in, anyway?"

Anok heard the click of the latch, but before he could reach for his weapons the door banged open. A man in the robes of a priest stood there, flanked by two guardians of Set brandishing long spears. The point of one of those weapons hovered in front of Anok's throat, the other over his heart.

Dejal half stood. "Ramsa Aál! Master, he came uninvited—"

"Uninvited by you, acolyte. This one is my guest." He turned to study Anok. "So, I, too, am curious. How exactly *did* you enter the Great Temple of Set and survive?"

17

RAMSA AÁL WAS tall, even for a Stygian, slender yet well muscled, his narrow face distinguished by the ivory-colored skin of the most ancient noble families. His eyes were pale blue and twinkled with the kind of delight one might see in someone greeting an old friend, or in an evil child about to torture a bug. "You should know," the priest said, "that there are many more guardians waiting outside. If you were to try escaping, you wouldn't get five paces alive, even with me as a hostage. But that's not what you came for, is it?"

Anok rose, slowly, keeping his hands away from his body and his weapons. "I came to beg acceptance into the Cult of Set as an acolyte."

"So I have heard. I have read your letters to your friend with great interest."

"And yet you forbid him to respond."

Dejal glared at him. "Anok! Show respect to the priest!"

"If I am made an acolyte, I will follow all customs of deference and respect to authority. But until then, I will stand and, if necessary, die as a man."

Ramsa Aál smiled slightly. "You're proud—spirited. I respect that. And so I will answer your question in my fashion. I wanted to see what you would do when your messages were not answered. Despite Dejal's endorsement, I wondered how strong your desire to join our cult was. Were you worthy of such an honor? Did you *want* it badly enough?"

Anok met his gaze without flinching. "And . . . ?"

"And you have proven not only your desire, but your resourcefulness. It is quite exceptional that you have penetrated this far into the temple." His tone turned cold. "It is more than exceptional. It is impossible for a simple thief, no matter how resourceful." He stepped closer to Anok, his hand extended, palm out, as though testing the heat of a flame. He waved it in front of Anok. "You have been near an artifact of mystic power." He waved his hand some more, finally leaving it hovering over Anok's heart. "Quite recently. Is that how you escaped our guardians of the darkness?"

Anok said nothing. Did he know about the Scale of Set? Was Anok's deception to be exposed this easily?

Ramsa Aál glanced down, noticing Anok's bag. He bent and waved his hand over it. Then he picked it up and began to dig around inside. The priest's eyes went wide, and he pulled out a small object that glinted in the lamplight.

It was the golden ring Anok had found in the air shafts! Anok realized it must have fallen into the bag when he and Sheriti swept it off the table back at the Nest.

Ramsa Aál turned it, examining the carving. "The Ring of Lies. One of our elder priests lost it over two years ago." He looked at Anok. "How did this come into your possession?"

"I found it in the air shafts high in the temple, among the bones of a thief picked clean by the little snakes."

Ramsa Aál laughed. "The Fingers of Set? Delightful. You saw them, and yet you survived?" He looked again at the ring. "This ring has no power that would save you there. How did you do it, Anok Wati?" Again, he waved his hand in front of Anok. "It was *you,* wasn't it?"

"I told them to go away," said Anok, matter-of-factly.

"You, an untrained novice, repelled the Fingers of Set by sorcery?" He laughed as though pleased.

"I told them to go away. They did. Call it what you will."

"Dejal said you had promise, but this is beyond that by far."

"Then you accept me as an acolyte?"

The priest smiled slightly. "Perhaps. Tell me, Anok Wati, why do you wish to join our cult? To honor the great god Set? To gain enlightenment?

Anok hesitated. What did Ramsa Aál expect to hear? He took a deep breath. "As a child, I knew wealth, comfort, and status. My family held power. All that was lost to me. I was orphaned, lost, and suffered the streets of Odji for many years. I wish to have it again."

"Comfort? Status?"

"Power!"

Ramsa Aál's smile widened. "Wise is the man who knows what he wants and is not afraid to say it. The Way of Set does indeed offer power, for those worthy, those strong enough, those who serve him well. For those who are not, for those who fail him, there is pain, suffering, and death. Do you understand?"

"I understand."

"Then kneel, Anok Wati, and accept the blessing of Set."

Anok dropped to one knee and bowed his head, as he had seen other acolytes kneel before priests.

Ramsa Aál's hand rested on his shoulder. "By the ancient texts and the great serpents that are his embodiment on Earth, you are pledged to serve Set. Say it!"

"I am pledged to serve Set."

The hand grew tighter on Anok's shoulder, the thin fingers digging painfully into his flesh. "You pledge your life and heart, even to willingly offer your blood as sacrifice on his altar?"

"I pledge my life, my heart, and my blood." *My lies.*

The fingers, inhumanly strong, grew still tighter, until Anok thought the bones of his shoulder might snap. "You are Set's instrument! You are Set's slave! You are Set's servant!"

"I am Set's instrument, his slave, his servant."

The priest abruptly yanked his hand back, holding it over his head dramatically. "You are honored, Anok Wati. You are one of us! You are of Set!"

AS HE WAS ushered away, the one thing that lingered in Anok's thoughts was the look on Dejal's face. Obviously this outcome wasn't what the former Raven had expected, nor even desired.

Nor was it what Anok had expected either. He'd thought he might have to beg for entry into the cult. In fact, his earlier bravado in facing Ramsa Aál had been intended mainly to make his later groveling seem even more humble. Anok had long ago learned that pride, especially false pride, was a poor negotiating tool. He had placed his life, for the time being, in the hands of the temple, and his posturing should reflect that.

He was led away by a pair of guardians of Set, but their weapons were not drawn, and they acted more as guides than guards. He was taken beyond the living area, through a large common area decorated with fountains, wall paintings, and statuary glorifying Set, and up a wide, curving stairway to the main level of the temple, then toward the back.

Anok had some vague idea of where they were from his study of the map, but as he had intended to avoid those areas he had not committed them to memory. They briefly crossed a broad corridor that Anok recognized as a public area of the temple, adjacent to the main ceremonial chamber, then headed toward the back of the building.

They entered a large room built around a huge rectangular bath set with blue tile. A layer of steam hovered over the water, and the smaller round cleansing pools that surrounded it. An island of rock in the middle of the pool, from which steaming water flowed in a continuous stream, suggested that the temple had been built over a natural hot spring.

One of the guardians began knocking on a series of doors as they passed. "Wake! Wake! By order of Lord Ramsa Aál, wake!"

The doors popped open one by one, and beautiful, wide-eyed female faces peered out.

"Out," barked the guardian.

The women filed out, all young and beautiful, and none, he noted, of pure Stygian blood. For a moment, he thought they wore tight-fitting garments of black lace or sheer, patterned, silk, but he quickly realized that they were completely nude. Their bodies, from ankle, to wrist, to neck, were covered in ornately patterned tattoos he had mistaken for clothing. *Temple whores.*

The guardian turned and addressed the women. "This outsider has been welcomed as a special servant of Set. Cleanse him and dress him in the robes of an acolyte. Then summon us."

The women nodded and bowed their heads, then silently led him into a side chamber, where he was stripped of his clothes, and more to his concern, his weapons and belongings. All were spirited away by one of the whores before he had a chance to object or even guess where they were being taken.

A woman stepped in on either side of him and each hooked her arms around his. Their skin was exceptionally soft, glossy with a sheen of some oil that smelled of exotic spice. He was led to one of the smaller cleansing pools, then he stepped into the water, warm, but cooled by passage through the larger pool on its way from the hot spring. The two women climbed into the pool on either side of him and began matter-of-factly to wash him.

Their manner was unashamed, as he would expect of whores, but also strangely practiced and detached. He tried to look into their faces, but they did not return his gaze, and their eyes seem strangely vacant. They moved like trained animals doing a complicated trick, and he came to suspect the women were drugged, enchanted, or both.

Though the women were attractive, he found their manner disturbing and decidedly unerotic. He settled back and let them do their work without protest—but without much enjoyment either.

His mind flashed back to his encounter with Ramsa Aál. Why did the priest show such interest in him? Surely it couldn't be only based on Dejal's description. And how had he known that Anok had entered the temple or could be found in Dejal's cell? Anok had left no trace that he was aware of, raised no alarm.

"Is this what you wished, acolyte?"

Anok was startled from his thoughts by Ramsa Aál's voice. He looked up to see the priest standing over him.

"Your desire for luxury, comfort"—he reached down to one of the whores, and curled a scarlet lock of her hair around his finger before letting it slide free—"the service of obedient slaves. Set offers this, and more, to his most loyal and useful servants. This is but a taste—if you prove worthy of such favor."

"I will do my best to serve Set. May I prove worthy."

"Let us pray that you will."

Anok dared not ask the question he most wanted to ask, why Ramsa Aál was interested in him. Instead, he moved to something less provocative. "How did you know I had entered the temple, or where to find me?"

Ramsa Aál smiled slyly. "I was summoned by the greater son of Set you encountered in the air shaft."

Anok blinked in surprise and disbelief. He had heard tales that the great snakes were intelligent, perhaps as smart as a man, but had never believed it. Still, if the snake had given warning, he might have been observed by unseen eyes as he emerged into the catacombs and followed to Dejal's cell. "The snake spared me. It wasn't like the small snakes. It was no doing of mine."

The priest tossed back his head and laughed. "It would

take a more powerful wizard than you, or even I, to command the great serpents. They speak directly to Set, and are his agents in the mortal world. You were spared because Set himself wills it. You are here because Set wills it. Know it or not"—his lips curled up into a cruel smile— "you have always been his servant."

18

THE FOLLOWING DAYS passed slowly for Anok. He was less than a prisoner but also less than a free man. He was not allowed to leave the temple, and his weapons and belongings had been taken from him.

He had not heard from Teferi and presumed his friend had been unable to find anyone to deliver messages. Anok had been observing the Temple guardians and had identified several he thought would be susceptible to bribes. But since his silver had been taken from him along with his other belongings, Anok had nothing to bribe them with.

Anok could only be patient and hope that increased freedom would eventually be granted. From his chamber, he'd observed that the more advanced acolytes seemed to come and go as they pleased when not performing duties for the priests. Most lived away from the temple, in their own homes or apartments, a situation that would be infinitely preferable to Anok. At most, it appeared that if he could hold on for just a few more months and maintain the favor of Ramsa Aál, the problem might correct itself.

There were a dozen other novice acolytes in Anok's

group, including Dejal. The others were cold to Anok.
They had already undergone weeks of training and initia-
tions that apparently had been so terrible that several of
their number had failed to survive. Although they knew of
his trial, it did little to allay the inevitable resentment.
Clearly, they did not feel it was right that Anok could simply walk in and be placed among them as an equal.

But he had the endorsement of Ramsa Aál, and their obvious fear of the priest kept their resentment in check. Instead, he was shunned. They would not speak with him
unless ordered or some aspect of their training required it.

Dejal was the sole exception, but he, too, was cool and
distant. Anok realized that Dejal had somehow hoped to
gather favor with Ramsa Aál by recruiting Anok to the cult.
By arriving at the temple on his own, Anok had thwarted
that hope. As a result, Dejal was not the ally Anok had
hoped for. Still, he was polite, possibly hoping to somehow
to exploit the relationship at a later date. Anok had observed that Dejal would do almost anything to advance his
status with Ramsa Aál and the other priests.

Yet favor rarely seemed to find Dejal. He was tolerated
because of his father's wealth and position and because he
had come bearing to Ramsa Aál the Scale of Set. But that,
it seemed, would only buy him so much.

With no one to talk to, Anok instead listened to others
talk and kept his eyes open to observe the going-on at the
temple. He quickly learned that Ramsa Aál, though not a
High Priest, clearly was a man of great importance in the
cult. Priests his senior in title and age approached him with
respect and reverence. Even the High Priests of the temple
seemed to treat him as an equal.

Along with the priests, another high-status group was
the elders. From what Anok could see, they gained their
position by virtue of their important families, wealth, po-
litical power, or often some combination of the three.

Acolytes were of a lower status, though technically still
outranking the guardians, servants, slaves, and temple
whores. In practice, most of these "lessers" answered only

to the priests and elders, or to orders relayed from them by the acolytes.

Acolytes of higher rank were allowed a certain familiarity with priests, but acolytes of all ranks were treated like dogs by the elders. Such encounters were so unpleasant that acolytes would go out of their way to avoid elders in the corridors and usually would approach them only when ordered by the priests.

As such, Anok was surprised one day to discover Dejal chatting causally with an elder in the priests' gallery, a large staging hall located just behind the main ceremonial chamber. Anok slipped behind a nearby column, before either of the men noticed him, and eavesdropped. It was not long before he realized that the Elder was Dejal's infamous father.

Anok had never seen the man though he'd listened for years to Dejal's bitter complaints about him. His name, Anok knew, was Seti Aasi. Like Anok's father, he was a merchant, though a local one, a caravan trader in spices and relics from the East, reportedly a man of some wealth and power.

Anok peeked around the corner for a better look, then quickly ducked back into hiding, reviewing in his mind what he had just seen.

Like most elders while at the temple, Dejal's father wore white robes trimmed with stripes of gold. They were worn only at the temple, the elders entering and leaving through a special cloakroom at the front of the building. On the street, they dressed as any other member of the higher classes, save for a golden necklace in the form of a snake holding its own tail in its mouth.

The man himself was far less impressive: round-faced, balding, a graying patch of neatly trimmed beard projecting from a weak chin. He was at least a hand shorter than Dejal or Anok and of average build. He had soft hands with neatly trimmed nails that reminded Anok of a woman's.

Anok stifled a chuckle. The man was hardly the fire-breathing monster whom Dejal had often described.

Unable to resist and overcome with curiosity, Anok slipped around the column and walked casually up, as though going about other business. He stopped and bowed his head formally. "Greetings to you, Dejal, and to you as well, elder." He looked at Dejal and smiled. "I thought perhaps you might introduce me to your father." Then he smiled at Dejal's father. "I have heard many things about you from Dejal, lord."

The expression on Seti Aasi's face shocked him. The Elder looked at Anok with undisguised disgust. "You are Anok Wati then? The Odji trash who led my son astray all these years and who now seeks to steal favor from him in the Cult of Set? You have nerve approaching me, scum! You should be on your knees before me, begging forgiveness for all the trouble you've caused me and my son!"

Anok glanced at Dejal, whose face was dead and neutral as a statue. "For what trouble I have caused him, I recall also times when I saved his life on the streets of Odji. I recall also that it was not I who drove him from his fine home to seek comfort among"—he let the word drip off his tongue—"scum."

Seti Aasi's face turned red with anger, and he was about to speak when he was stopped by Ramsa Aál's voice. The priest stepped through the doorway from the inner temple and though he looked at all of them, it was Anok to whom he spoke. "Is there a problem, Anok Wati?"

"No problem, master. I was paying my respects to Elder Seti Aasi, father of Dejal. Long I have heard of his great deeds, and I wished to meet him in person."

Ramsa Aál glanced at Seti Aasi with something between indifference and contempt. "I am not surprised his deeds are known to you. They are known to me as well." There seemed to be some hidden meaning to the words that was lost on Anok, but he let it go by. Clearly there was history between the two men. Perhaps even, Anok noted with interest, *rivalry.*

Dejal's father looked uncomfortable but said nothing. Then, finally, "I have other business to attend to. Three caravans arrive today. There is," he said, with a sideways glance at Ramsa Aál, "a world beyond this temple, and I am quite powerful there." He turned and headed toward the front of the temple.

"I'm sure you are," said Ramsa Aál to the departing Elder. Then he added more quietly, "There."

Dejal gave Anok an angry glance, then spun and headed away himself.

Anok just stood there, and Ramsa Aál glanced at him, eyebrow raised. "Don't you have duties to occupy you, acolyte? I could find more."

Anok bowed his head. "Of course, master. I shall be off to my studies."

"See that you are."

Indeed, Anok did have things to do. As a novice acolyte, not only was his freedom of movement limited, the hours of his days were all planned as well.

While the daily routine varied somewhat, it followed the same general pattern. The morning began with bathing, without the aid of whores. Despite that first time, their services were generally reserved for the priests and elders of the cult, or used as a special reward for the acolytes. In fact, it seemed that word had gotten out about Anok's special welcome to the cult, and that had become yet one more thing for his fellow novices to hold against him.

Next came breakfast. The food and accompanying wine were always excellent. This was followed by an hour or so of chanting to Set in the main ceremonial chamber. Then they were gathered for instruction by one of the priests, usually a talk on sorcery or service to Set.

There was a light midday meal, after which they returned to their cells for several hours to study the Scrolls of Set. Anok took advantage of the study time to look for some reference in the writings to Parath and his downfall, but thus far he had found no mention of the lost god. Perhaps he was well and truly lost, and if so, that, too, might be part of Set's plan. The power of any cult, even of Set's itself, came from the prayer and devotion of its followers. There could be no followers for a god unknown.

The latter part of the day was filled with a variety of exercises, chants, group rituals granting power to the priests, and, most interesting to Anok, demonstrations of sorcery, usually by the more advanced acolytes rather than the priests, who seemed content to supervise.

Over a period of time, he was witness to a spell that made an opponent's bones as flexible as rope, various spells of hypnotic control, the casting of illusions, the apparent transformation of a walking staff into a cobra, and the transformation of a feral street dog into a huge and vicious monster.

He was uncertain as to the true purpose of these demonstrations, for they were only taught the most basic of the spells. He knew that the use of powerful magic was said to lead to corruption, and if so, the actual purpose of these revelations might be aimed more at those performing the spell than those observing. Anok noted that each priest had his own personal circle of followers, and it seemed that from within those followers each priest sought to cultivate the greatest degree of dark power possible. He wondered if Dejal had made similar observations.

Anok's aversion to sorcery was quickly fading. It was apparent that some of the novices had already received individual training in the casting of more advanced spells. He was actually eager for his turn and rationalized that only through sorcery could he stand any chance against the cult. It would be a fine flavor of justice, he thought, if he could subvert their own sorcery and use it against them.

And so he worked, and studied, and observed. He swallowed his pride and groveled to the priests where it seemed necessary. He endured the shunning of his fellow novices and the lonely hours that resulted. In time it all became almost routine.

Yet there were other cycles of routine in the Temple of Set, and some were timed not by the turning of the sun but by the cycles of the moon. It would soon be time for Festi-

val again, and if it was a time for terror among the people
of Odji, it was a time of great anticipation for the denizens
of the temple.

For Anok, it was a subject of dread. He feared he would
be required to join the hunting parties roaming the streets
of Odji for sacrificial victims, or even worse, to spill their
blood on the altar of Set. He didn't know if he could maintain his deception under those circumstances. He tried to
tell himself that those unlucky enough to become sacrifices
would die with or without him, but that didn't seem to
make the idea any more bearable. As it happened, he was
soon to learn that Ramsa Aál had other plans for him the
night of Festival.

The priest approached him one evening as he was leaving the dining hall headed for his cell. Several other
novices, including Dejal, contrived to pause within earshot
and listen in on the conversation.

"The diligence with which you pursue your studies
pleases me, Anok Wati."

Anok bowed his head in respect. "I live to serve Set,
master."

The priest twisted his mouth into a half smile. "A lie!
You seek power, acolyte, and you serve that desire over all
else. But that pleases me, and it serves the needs of our lord
Set as well. Through power you will make yourself useful
to him. Through power you shall become his fist and his
sword."

"Then grant me power, master, that I may serve you better. I desire to be taught the ways of sorcery, as some of the
others have been."

"The others have been instructed in response to their
own needs and talents. You have not because you are different than they. Answer me this, novice, and we shall see
how well your studies have taken. What are the methods of
sorcery?"

Anok's mind raced. Doubtless this was one of the basic
lessons the novices had been given in their first days of
training, but Anok had touched on the subject only through

his reading and his eavesdropping on the conversations of others. He formulated the best answer he could based on what he knew. "First there is the false sorcery, consisting of natural illusion, deception, and device."

"Useful skills for even the most powerful of sorcerers. Go on."

"Then there is sorcery through the use of talismans, totems, charms, sacred gems, mystic weapons, and other objects of power."

"Which some call 'fool's sorcery,' based on the idea that any fool can wield such an object. Yet only the most powerful and skilled sorcerers in all of history have successfully created such objects, and they often grow more powerful in their antiquity. Only a fool would underestimate the power inherent in such an object. Next?"

"Then there is learned sorcery. The utterance of spells, the performance of ceremonies, the mixing of potions, alchemy, the methods of which must be learned from other sorcerers and the ancient texts, then refined through practice and study."

"Solid, basic sorcery, the mainstay of most acolytes' training. It is this learning that I suspect you desire. But there are yet more kinds of sorcery are there not?"

Anok struggled to assemble the scraps of knowledge he had gained and put them into words. "There is also the sorcery of summoning. That is to say, calling forth the power of gods, demons, and spirits."

"One of the most powerful forms of sorcery, and one of most dangerous. To summon such beings is often to put yourself in their thrall, and their powers can overwhelm even the strongest-willed sorcerer." He looked Anok in the eye. "There is one other form of sorcery. Do you know it?"

Anok thought furiously but came up with nothing. "I am sorry master, I do not."

Ramsa Aál nodded. "This isn't your failing, acolyte. Few have knowledge of it, and it is rare that it is even discussed. There are those with a special talent, through some accident of birth or early history, to tap directly into the well of power that serves all supernatural entities, gods and demons alike. This talent is rare, and dangerous, for the powers these seekers harness are almost too great for a man to comprehend, and they can destroy the wielder as easily as his enemies. It is like trying to chain the lightning, or put harness to storm waves, and, talent or not, many have perished in the attempt." His eyes met Anok's, his lips pressed together in a narrow line. "You are such a talent, Anok Wati, and we shall soon see if you are worthy of your gifts."

"What do you mean master?"

"Until now, your stay here has been an easy one. As you've doubtless heard, the other acolytes were subjected to many harsh trials, and you have until now avoided them. But it is near time for your own . . . *examination*. On the night of Festival, you shall be tested."

"How will I be tested, master?"

"Deep in the catacombs under the temple, there is a place called the Maze of Set. There you will face your trial. I can say no more. Know only that you will be tested to the depths of your soul and that you may well not survive."

Anok surprised himself with his reaction to this news. He was neither fearful nor concerned. He was eager to meet the coming challenge.

Ramsa Aál studied his face, then nodded. "On the night of Festival I will come for you. Make yourself ready."

"Yes master." He watched as the Priest of Acolytes turned and walked away down the corridor.

Dejal and the other acolytes looked at him and whispered among themselves, laughing all the while. Anok found himself growing weary of the treatment. He walked purposely toward the group. The other acolytes, seeing him coming, scattered, until only Dejal remained when he arrived. "You heard?"

Dejal smiled knowingly. "I heard, brother. You are to be taken to the Maze of Set on Festival night."

"You know something of this?"

"Of what your trial might be? No. I've never heard of such a thing. But I have heard of the Maze of Set. It's the place where the priests take failed acolytes. Very simply, brother, they enter the Maze and never return. Never."

19

THE DAY OF Festival came to the temple, and with it, all routine was broken. The morning meal was large and festive, with fresh-boiled lobster from the reefs beyond the harbor, loins of beef, a rich stew made from oysters and chunks of swordfish, and mounds of spicy cakes and bread sprinkled with pungent herbs.

The temple itself was busy all day, with a constant stream of elders and lesser followers of Set coming to the great ceremonial chamber to lay offerings of gold, silver, jewels, fine silks, and other goods before the altar. Then they would bow down and chant to their evil god, asking him to favor them with power and wealth.

Several middle-ranking acolytes did nothing all day but collect offerings and carry them away to the temple's hidden vaults for safekeeping. Anok had always known the Cult of Set was wealthy, but he saw now that he'd never really known *how* wealthy. Though the merchants of Odji strained under the burden of taxes, an entire year's collection for the slum could hardly match what he saw willingly handed over at a single Festival day.

Tribute to the temple seemingly granted returns that made it worthwhile for the rich to be generous. The Cult of Set and the puppet government of Stygia controlled all aspects of trade and industry, the ports, the caravan routes, travel on the rivers, the poison trade, mining, and even the recovery of mystical artifacts from the vast inland deserts. Without the aid and permission of the cult, the rich would not long stay that way, and those most favored by the cult were richest of all.

Most of the temple acolytes went about various appointed duties, herding worshipers in and out of the temple, sharpening and polishing ceremonial knives, supervising the arrival from the jails of chained prisoners doomed to give their lives to Set, and performing rituals to prepare the altar for blood sacrifice.

The servants were also busy, and Anok took note of two in particular who seemed to be a focus of attention, despite their lack of any obvious activity. They wore red robes of the yoked sleeveless style often worn by servants with ceremonial duties. They were exceptionally dark-skinned, south-sea islanders perhaps, their skin so deeply toned that it almost seemed to have a bluish-purple cast. But the most unusual thing about them was their hands.

Like many of the dark-skinned races, the palms of their hands were a different, lighter color than the rest of their skin. But while it was common for that skin to be pinkish white, the skin on their hands was red as blood. As he came closer, he saw that the same reddish tinge showed around the edges of their eyes, and when they spoke, their inner lips, tongue, and even their teeth, were startlingly red. He could only guess what dire function these strange men might serve in the night's ceremonies.

Anok felt somewhat at loose ends, having entirely too much time to think about the trial to come. Did Ramsa Aál truly intend to dispose of him? Anok didn't think so, though the priest's true intentions toward him remained a mystery. He was certain, though, that it would be a trial in every sense of the word, and the price of failure would doubtless be a horrible death.

Yet however dread his trials might be, he preferred them to staying in the upper realms of the temple and seeing what horrors would pass there tonight, even more so if he were required to participate in them. In the Maze of Set only his blood could be spilled, and he was no innocent.

After the morning feast, there was no noon meal at all, only tables of food set up in various locations around the temple, designed to be taken in hand and eaten while doing other tasks.

Anok found himself wishing he had his swords for the night's trial, but despite repeated searches since arriving at the temple, he had never determined where they had been taken, or if they were even still there. With that alternative out, he decided it was time to improvise.

He wandered over to the table where the sacrificial knives were being prepared. Already, a line of the polished blades stretched across the front of the table. Two acolytes worked busily at the other end of the table, sharpening blades with a hand stone until they could cut a hair. So intent were they on their task, it required little effort for Anok to pick up one of the blades and secrete it under his robe.

He walked hurriedly back to his cell, certain that at any moment he would be stopped and challenged, but it never happened. Once behind closed doors, he removed the blade and examined it. It was sheathed in ornately carved leather, and the handle was made of something like black ivory or horn. The pommel was heavy silver, formed in the shape of a viper's head. The blade was curved and as long as his forearm.

As he drew it, he saw that the steel was very fine, marbled in the fashion of the finest swords he had ever seen. The blade itself was ornately engraved as well, with the image of a nude maiden, arms overhead, eyes downcast, as though waiting calmly to be sacrificed. Both edges of the

wide blade were sharpened, and it tapered like a serpent's
tooth to a fine point.

It wasn't a sword, and it was better suited to slicing than
stabbing, but it was far better than no weapon at all. He removed the leather ties from a spare set of sandals and tied
the sheath around his middle, so that it hung, invisibly he
hoped, along his spine. Once in the maze, he could take it
out and strap it properly around his waist.

He spent the rest of the afternoon studying the scrolls
and left his cell only when the sounding of the temple gong
told him it was dusk. He encountered Ramsa Aál as he
climbed the stairs to the main level of the temple. The
priest was accompanied by four muscular guardians armed
with swords.

Did he think Anok would try to escape? That he would
refuse the trial? That had never been Anok's intention, but
now he saw that it was not even a possibility.

The priest smiled to see him though. "You seem almost
fervent to begin your trial, acolyte." He continued down the
stairs, and Anok walked with him. The four guardians
marched along close behind.

"I want to prove myself, master, if that is truly the intent."

"What other intent would there be, acolyte?"

"Dejal told me that the Maze of Set is where failed
acolytes are taken for . . . disposal."

The priest smiled slightly. "Acolyte Dejal is correct."
His statement hung in the air, and Anok waited for clarifi-
cation. It did not come.

Anok heard running water ahead and smelled the stench
of sewage. They emerged into a large chamber with a stone
channel in the floor. A sluggish flow of clean water ran
through the channel, and a stone bridge passed over the
channel to a door on the far side of the room.

The priest stopped to watch two men working near
where the water disappeared into an opening in the wall.
Anok realized that they were the two dark-skinned servants
he had seen earlier. The men worked near a stack of black
pottery jars, each the size of a man's torso, tightly sealed

with cork and red wax. As they watched, the men used
knives to pierce the wax on one of the jars and pry the cork
out of the wide mouth. As they did, a dark fluid sloshed out
on the man's hands, and dripped to the floor already
stained—with blood.

Anok's eyes widened. Ramsa Aál glanced at him and
smiled in amusement.

Anok watched as the servants slowly poured the contents
of the jar into the running water. The fluid quickly mixed
with the clear water, turning it immediately to the dark red
color of blood. He glanced at the priest questioningly.

Ramsa Aál motioned for the guardians to give him and
Anok some space, and the four feel farther behind. Then
the priest leaned in and spoke lowly to Anok, his words for
no one else's ears.

"It isn't blood, if that's what you're thinking. It's a special dye, potent, extracted from the crushed bodies of a
beetle found only on an island far across the Southern Sea.
One jar would turn a small pond to blood. It is brought here
in great secrecy and at great expense. It can only be han-
dled by those with dark skin, as it would turn such as you
or I red as blood, and that might give away our deception.
As it is, we try to keep our friends here within the walls of
the temple."

"The blood that runs into the sea."

He laughed. "Now you see. Much *real* blood will be
spilled here tonight in Set's name, yes, but there is not
enough blood in all of Stygia to account for that legendary
outflow. The dye is mixed with water here, then collected
in a cistern beyond this wall. Later, just before dawn, a
floodgate will be lifted, and it will spill into the sewers for
all to see."

"But why?"

He laughed. "Power is often best gained by the terror of
lesser men. Blood is spilled, not merely to serve Set. Because of it, our enemies fear us. Our slaves fear us. Our
servants fear us. Our *followers* fear us." He watched the
bloodred water flowing into the wall, then proceeded

across the bridge and out the door on the other side. Anok walked with him.

The priest continued, "Lesser men, Anok Wati. It would seem that I send you to your doom. But as you have seen, things here are not always what they seem. Terrible death is the inevitable fate of lesser men who enter the maze. It need not be yours."

"How is my trial different then?"

"It isn't. *You* are different, or so I hope."

"And what will I find in the maze? What am I to do there?"

The priest said nothing but quickened his pace. They turned away from the acolytes' cells down another corridor, one that Anok had never seen before. They traveled some distance until they reached a point where the corridor continued, but the illuminated torches did not.

The guardians each took torches from an alcove in the wall, and lit them from the nearest lamp. Then they continued their journey into darkness. The floor slanted downward, and the walls changed as well. The way was narrower, and the damp walls seemed to be carved from solid stone.

Anok could not tell how far they had traveled, though he was sure they were no longer under the temple or even the plaza that surrounded it. Finally, after another series of twists and turns, they reached a chamber with two large doors set into the wall. The doors were made of heavy oak and iron, and locked with heavy iron bars.

"This," announced Ramsa Aál, "is the Maze of Set. This door"—he pointed to the one on the left—"is the way in. This other door"—he pointed to the one on the right—"is the only passage out. All you need do is find your way from one door to the other. Knock, and these men will open the door to allow you to escape. I warn you that it will not be as easy as it seems. Remember, too, that as an acolyte, there are certain rules that must be followed, even within the maze."

Despite the last, cryptic, comment, it seemed somehow too simple. "Is that all?"

The priest smiled slightly. "Perhaps not. The Maze of Set is used for the safekeeping of many objects of mystic power. These are not the trinkets of so-called 'fool's magic.' These are objects so ancient and powerful that they *choose* who may wield them. They are scattered deep in the maze. You may not recognize them for what they are, but if you are worthy, one of those objects will show itself to you. You will be allowed to take it from the maze if you escape. If you fail, the object will be returned to its hiding place to await the next seeker. Reward, or death. Those are your choices."

Anok stared at the door, heart pounding, trying to imagine what dangers might await him there.

Ramsa Aál reached inside his robe and removed an object. Round, shiny, it fit in the palm of his hand like a duck egg. He held it out for Anok to see. "To aid you in your task, I offer you one additional boon. It is only a small thing, but survive, and you may keep it as well. It is called a Jewel of the Moon." He handed it to Anok.

Anok looked at the jewel, rolling it between his fingers. It was oval, flattened, translucent, and polished to a high shine. It looked like nothing more than an especially nice river rock. "What is it?"

The priest only chuckled. "It is useful, if you can learn its secret." He gestured at one of the guardians, removed the bolt from the entrance door. "Now," said Ramsa Aál, holding out his hand, "give me the knife."

Anok feigned ignorance, but it clearly wasn't working. Reluctantly, he reached under his robes, untied the leather straps, and pulled out the sheathed knife. "How did you know?"

"The blade is sacred, blessed, and touched by the power that is blood. A sorcerer can sense such objects. You will learn that."

Anok handed the knife to Ramsa Aál, who drew the

blade and made a show of examining it. "A fine blade," he said, swinging the knife through an arc that nicked the palm of Anok's right hand. "Oh," he said, "sorry."

Cursing, Anok shook his wounded hand. The cut was not deep, hardly more than a scratch really, but it stung, and he could feel the warm, sticky blood welling up freely.

The priest slid the knife back into its sheath. "You seek weapons, Anok, yet you already have everything you need." Then he stepped aside to allow Anok through the door.

Inside was only darkness. He had a sense that he was entering a much larger chamber. He stopped inside the door and turned, expecting one of the guardians would hand him a torch. Instead, he saw the door slam shut, forming a perfect seal that let not even a sliver of light through. Standing in complete darkness, he heard the bolt being placed, then silence.

No, not silence. First he heard dripping water, echoing as though through a vast cave. Then something else, a sliding noise, like leather against stone.

Then a hiss. *Snake!*

Something touched his foot, just a brushing contact, but he sensed something moving past him on the floor. Another sound, farther away. And another. Not one snake. *Many.*

They were all around him, but how many, how large, he couldn't be sure. If only he could see!

Another hiss.

Loud. Close. *Threatening.*

The jewel felt cold against his sweaty palm. Jewel of the Moon? What he wouldn't do for some moonlight right then. *Wait! Could that be it?*

He held the jewel up closer to his face. He wished he could see it, examine it for some clue. He rubbed it between his fingers, realizing for the first time the characteristic tingle of magical power.

"Light!"

Nothing happened.

"Illuminate!"

Again nothing.

"Summon moonlight!"

Nothing still.

Yet all around him he could hear things. Sense movement.

The cut on his right hand stung from the sweat of fear, and the blood ran down his fingers, making them sticky.

Why, he wondered, had Ramsa Aál cut his hand? There could be no doubt the act was intentional, but the wound was too small to disable or especially hinder him. The threat here seemed to be snakes, and snakes weren't drawn to blood.

Yet it was a night of blood sacrifice, and blood was power.

Blood was power.

He took the jewel, and pressed it into his bloody palm. As he did, he heard the familiar ringing of magic. The jewel began to glow with a cool blue light that seemed to spread strangely through the air as the red dye had through water, until it illuminated the entire room as though by a full moon.

He was in a cave.

A cave full of snakes. Hundreds of snakes.

Around him, columns of stone hung from the ceiling over his head, and more still rose from the floor around him. Water collected in shallow pools in the stone.

And everywhere snakes.

They were sons of Set, sacred snakes, the smallest as big around as his wrist, others, the greater sons of Set, as large as any he'd seen on the streets of Odji. Yet even those snakes generally took smaller prey, they were generally too languid, too well fed, to endanger a wary adult. The snakes around him were active, crawling rapidly across the floor, swimming in the pools,

They seemed hungry.

A moderate-sized snake, its middle as thick as his thigh,

its head as large as a coconut, suddenly surged toward him, head held high, mouth open to strike.

He instinctively held up his hand. "Stop!" He felt the familiar power surge through him, and the snake slowed, then stopped. It contemplated him, seemingly confused, tongue tasting the air.

"Back!"

There was a hesitation. Then the snake turned and crawled away.

Anok walked farther into the cave. As he did, he was alarmed to see snakes following him. They watched him with their slitted eyes as he passed, then they joined the parade.

He stopped and turned, holding up his hands as he had in the air shafts. "Back!"

And back the small ones went. But the larger ones, ones as large at the snake that had first tried to attack him, did not. They waited until he had continued down the tunnel a ways. Then they began to follow again.

His power over serpents was obviously very limited. He could command the larger snakes barely, and the greater sons of Set not at all.

With the light of the jewel to guide him, he quickly advanced into the caverns, hoping to outpace the snakes. It wasn't working. It took time to pick his way around the many stone columns that sprouted from the floor—and the seemingly bottomless pits that sometimes split the floor—but the snakes were relentless. More, ever more, joined the growing throng.

If only I had my swords! Yet there were too many. He might have killed a few, but he would quickly be overrun. And one more thing. The greater sons of Set were sacred to the temple. To kill or harm them was forbidden, under penalty of death. Ramsa Aál had warned him the rules must be followed, even in the maze. Which meant that he couldn't harm the snakes no matter what.

On he went. The passages branched again and again, and

he could only guess which way to go. There was no time to ponder, no time to look for clues to the way out. Instinct was all he had. He felt hopelessly lost, and after a while, he was sure he was passing a spot he'd passed before.

Ramsa Aál had told him a sorcerer could sense mystic objects, and there were mystic objects in the center of the maze. Certainly he would have to locate the center before finding his way back out of the maze.

Pausing, with a wary glance back at the rapidly approaching wave of snakes, he held up his left hand as he had seen Ramsa Aál do, turning it slowly, trying to feel for the tingle of magic.

There!

Keeping just ahead of the snakes, he took a wide passage to the left, on a ways, then down the center of three passages. The tingling was stronger.

He was closer, but there were more snakes there, many of which blocked his path in such a way that he had warily to go around. The followers had drawn closer.

He emerged into a wide chamber that went on as far as he could see. It was full of huge and spectacular formations, columns frosted with crystalline needles, frozen rock waterfalls, delicate sheets of pink stone that grew from the wall like leaves on a tree. Every turn revealed some new wonder. Yet there was no time to admire their beauty. Ahead was something unlike anything else he'd seen since entering the door, an object made by man. An altar. Surely that was it, the place he would find the promised object of power. *And may it be a weapon I can use against the Cult of Set itself!*

So focused was he on his goal that he stopped focusing on the ground ahead. He stepped over a stone and put his foot down right next to the head of one of the great constrictors.

It struck, the needle-sharp teeth digging into his ankle, the powerful jaws clamping down relentlessly.

He staggered and fell, landing in a shallow puddle of water. Still holding on to his ankle, the snake began to swing its coils over his body, winding itself around him, again and again, from knees to chest. He struggled to push them away, but the great snake was far too powerful to resist.

"Back," he said desperately. "Release me!"

But the snake was too large, too intelligent, to succumb to his feeble sorcery. It shifted, and he felt the coils tighten around him, pinning his arms. He struggled to hold on to the gem, lest he be plunged into darkness as well.

By then, the rest of the snakes had arrived, but they did not join in the feast. Instead they gathered around him on all sides, to watch their brother crush the life out of him.

Tighter! The bones of his arms seemed to creak with the strain. He struggled to breathe. Yet with each exhalation the coils pulled tighter, and each intake of air in turn became smaller.

He felt his rib cage bending, threatening to crack like an eggshell.

Around him, hundreds of cold, merciless, eyes watched.

Then something loomed over him. Something huge.

A great black tongue flicked out, just touching his cheek. Great copper-colored eyes contemplated him from above.

Tighter! His head throbbed as though it would explode. The room grew dark, but he knew it wasn't the jewel that was failing, it was his eyes.

Still the great snake looked down. Familiar.

It was the same great snake he'd seen in the air shaft.

The snake that had spared him.

"Agent of Set," he said to the snake, struggling to find the air to gasp out the words. "You spared me . . . once before . . . Spare me again . . . that I may serve . . . in Set's . . . plan. I beg . . ."

Tighter. No more words. No more air. The jewel slid from his numb fingers, its light dimming as it sank into the shallow water and clicked against the stone floor.

Blackness swallowed him like a snake.

HIS EYES OPENED. He gasped for air, and it came freely. His bones, his body ached, but the constrictor that had been killing him was gone. They were all gone.

Save one. In the dim light, he could see the greatest of the great sons of Set coiled but a few yards away, neck rising up in a graceful arch, head held high.

Watching him.

It could strike at any moment, crush him in its great jaws, swallow him whole.

It did not.

It watched him.

The water was cold as he pushed himself upright. He reached into the water and grabbed the fading blue orb that was the Jewel of the Moon. As it touched the watery blood on his palm, it immediately flared to full brightness.

He struggled to his feet.

He wanted to lie down.

He wanted to die.

He wanted to offer himself to the great snake and have done with it.

Instead he stepped toward the altar. One step.

Then another.

And another.

Inch by painful inch, he advanced on the ancient stone slab.

It was a simple thing, hardly more than a rectangle of stone, except for the inlaid gold symbol of a snake on its side. The symbol of Set.

How ancient was it? Was this the first altar of Set? Was this the very place where the evil cult was born?

Closer. He saw that there was something on the flat top of the altar, small and dark, like a piece of thin rope. He held out his palm, feeling the electric tingling. That was what he had come for. Closer. He held up the jewel to better see what it was.

It moved, just a slight stirring.

A snake. It was just another snake. It was tiny, darkly greenish, like tarnished brass. Such a tiny snake, even smaller than the blind, white serpents that Ramsa Aál had called the Fingers of Set. Yet his senses told him that it held great power.

But how? It was just a little snake, all alone in a cave of its most gigantic brethren.

It seemed harmless, stretched out there. It seemed asleep. He reached down toward it with his left hand.

With blinding speed the tiny snake struck, fangs like fine needles sinking deep into the blue vein on the back of his wrist. He howled with pain as poison, like red-hot metal, was injected into his veins. He jerked his hand back, trying to shake off the snake, but it held fast.

The body of the snake whipped around, circling his wrist, once, twice, three times. It pulled tight, the scales burning like hot metal where they touched his skin.

The snake's body became rigid, as though turning to iron, and it began to glow with red heat. Flames danced around the snake, emanating from his charred flesh.

The coils seemed to tighten, the snake's body sinking into his flesh like a hot coal into a bank of fresh snow. The pain was unbearable, his wrist searing away, poison burning its way up his arm as though seeking his heart. He dropped to his knees.

Tighter! He could see the bones of his arm through the ring of charred flesh, the metallic coils of the tiny snake curling tightly around them. He cried out in agony.

Then the glow around the snake began to fade. The flames vanished. Charred edges of flesh turned pink, then red, melting and flowing over snake and bone. Before his amazed eyes, his wrist began to heal itself, liquid flesh turning solid, skin stretching and knitting to cover the gaping wound.

A gasp of relief escaped Anok's lips. The agony faded. His arm was whole.

But the snake was still there. He could feel its power

burning within him. Mystic power, dark and potent. Power with the potential for . . . He wasn't sure yet. And there was one other thing.

The image of the snake was burned into his skin, like a tattoo, its head on top of his hand, its body coiled around his wrist, its tail trailing up his forearm. *What did it mean?*

The great snake stared down on him, looking somehow satisfied.

He staggered onward, past the altar. He had to find his way out of the maze. He struggled on down the tunnel, until he found snakes.

Hundreds of snakes, coiled, heads raised respectfully, in two rows, forming a path into the tunnel. Cautiously, he stepped between them, expecting that, at any moment, they might attack.

Still he could feel the little snake's power burning within his veins. He felt his pains fade, his strength return. He strode forward, faster, more purposeful.

As he passed them, the snakes bowed their heads. *Servants of Set! Then what am I that they bow before me?*

Onward he marched, until ahead, in the blue glow of the jewel, he saw the arched shape of a large wooden door.

As he passed them, the last of the snakes slithered away, fading back into the darkness.

He walked up to the door, paused, then slammed his fist against the thick wood three times.

There was a short delay. Then he heard the guardians fumbling with the bolt. With a creak and a parting of cobwebs, the ancient door opened. Torchlight glared through the opening, drowning out the soft light of the Jewel of the Moon.

The guardians peered in at him, curious, and perhaps a little amazed.

He stepped through the door, heard it swing shut behind him. "Is it dawn yet? I must speak with Ramsa Aál."

AS ANOK ENTERED the upper temple, he discovered that it was, indeed, dawn. Light the color of blood spilled through every window and door. If the mood the night before had been festive, now it could more accurately described as torpid.

Refuse, human and otherwise, lay scattered about the ordinarily spotless floor. While before, the temple had hummed with activity, now it was nearly deserted, save for a few bedraggled servants and acolytes who, blood-spattered and weary, headed for their sleeping chambers. Only the guardians of Set remained alert, more so than usual, vigilant in the task of guarding the spent and vulnerable family of the temple.

Anok was led up several flights of stairs to an area above the temple entrance, where the high-ranking priests kept their private chambers. Ramsa Aál's chambers were near the middle, quite near to those of the temple's High Priest, a position reflecting his growing power and status.

Anok was ushered directly in, a runner having been sent ahead to announce his coming. He found the Priest of Acolytes sprawled in an armchair in front of a great expanse of windows looking out over the black walls of the inner city, to the Western Ocean beyond.

The ocean was dark, rippled with wind-driven white-caps, but no wind reached them here, a fact that Anok could only account for through the use of magic. It struck him. Who would use sorcery, risk corruption, just for such a casual matter of comfort? He also found himself wondering how the spell was done.

The temple faced the setting sun; therefore, the sky was deep indigo, almost black, against which the buildings of the city stood, pink in the first light of morning. The priest stared out at the horizon, his arm casually draped over the arm of his chair. He held a curved sacrificial knife, perhaps even the same one he had taken from Anok, now dripping with blood. On a small table next to him, a large incense burner emitted curls of smoke, and Anok recognized the pungent odor of black lotus power. He kept his distance and tried not to inhale the mystical and intoxicating fumes.

Perhaps it was intoxication by the lotus that prevented the priest from noticing Anok's arrival for a time. Finally, he glanced up with a start, as though Anok had suddenly materialized in the room with him. He blinked with surprise. "Anok Wati! Acolyte, you live!"

"You act surprised, master. Indeed, for a time I had my own doubts, but Set has delivered me from the maze with his blessings."

Ramsa Aál pushed himself from his chair and walked, with just the slightest unsteadiness, over to Anok. He smiled and nodded. "Yes! I knew you would succeed. The High Priest and I had a wager. There will a ceremony of empowering in my name next full moon!"

"How happy for you, master." Anok was too weary to hide the sarcasm in his voice, but the priest either failed to notice or did not take offense.

"You live!" Again, his amazement.

"I live, master."

"And you have brought with you from the maze a gift of Set?"

"I have."

"Let me see it!"

Anok hesitated, then held forward his hand. "It is not something truly that can be shown."

Ramsa Aál's eyes widened, and he reached out to take Anok's hand and examine it. He first looked at the back of his hand with the small serpent's head, then pulled back the sleeve to see the coils circling it, the tail pointed back up the arm toward his heart.

"The son of Set! I had hopes, but I never dreamed—" His fingers traced the outline of the snake. "This is a very powerful mark, acolyte, one never before granted in my lifetime."

"What does it mean?" Anok asked. Yet he already had a sense of it.

"It means power. A direct connection to the power of Set." He rubbed his wrist, as though some of the power might rub off onto him. "It is power—raw, ancient, and primal. Power that few mortals have ever wielded. But only if you can learn how to tap it, and only if you can survive standing so close to the fire." He looked into Anok's eyes. "I will help you, acolyte. If you are worthy, we will wield this power together!"

Anok's eye twitched at the last statement, but he said nothing aloud. *I will wield this power myself, and I will strangle Set in his own coils!*

20

INTERLUDE

MORNING CAME, AND to Teferi, the Nest seemed like a tomb.

It was the first Festival in living memory that he had spent alone. It was, he had to admit, by choice. The beautiful girl from the fruit vendor down the street, the one with the cinnamon-colored skin, big eyes, and full, tantalizing lips, had invited him to a small party with some of her friends. There had been, he was almost sure, more to the invitation that remained unspoken.

Yet he had refused, told her he had other plans, when he had none. He was in no mood for partying with beautiful strangers, for smiling and laughing and pretending that all was right with the world, while blood was spilled right outside the bolted door.

So he came back to the Nest at sunset, threw the bolt, and opened a cask of wine.

He had hoped, perhaps, that Sheriti would come down the stairs and join him, but while he heard the sounds of passion and revelry from the brothel the night through, he remained alone. Indeed, he had not seen her for many days, since shortly after Anok had gone to the Temple of Set. Perhaps she had returned to the Temple of Scribes as Anok had hoped. Teferi hoped so as well.

He had heard nothing from Anok, and his attempts at getting a message into the temple had been unsuccessful. When he finally bribed a temple servant and learned that Anok lived, that he had been accepted as a novice acolyte along side Dejal, Teferi did not know if he should celebrate or despair. His friend was both found and lost.

He sat at the table, watching the morning sun turn from red to burning white as he finished the last of the wine. His thoughts turned to lands unseen by him, known only through stories passed down from generation to generation. He dreamed of vast plains of grass broken by stands of gigantic trees, where herds of great animals, like houses with legs, wandered and grazed.

In his mind's eye, he saw among these great beasts a band of hunters, tall, muscular, nearly naked, skin as dark as his own. The men, armed only with long spears and stone knives, stalked the great beasts with skill and confidence, mighty hunters who, with one kill, could feed their village for a week.

This imagined land was fertile, vigorous with life, untouched with the corruption of magic or the twisted passions of so-called civilized men. How he longed to be there. How he longed to stand shoulder to shoulder with those hunters, knowing that he faced danger to feed his own.

A dream. Only a dream. That land had long ago been corrupted by sorcery and greed, his perfect garden lost to him forever.

And in his troubled world, he had found few things worth having, few treasures worth keeping, save friendship. So why, now, did it trouble him so?

He knew Sheriti had been right. With friendship came responsibility. He was his brother's guardian, his shepherd, his keeper. If Anok had wandered down the wrong path, had fallen into darkness, never more had he needed his brother Teferi. Anok was his responsibility and his burden.

If he could, he would aid him in his quest. If he must, he would put him down like a mad dog. Only the future would tell.

He was shaken from his malaise by a frantic pounding at the door. Teferi stared at the door without moving, wondering who it could be. Despite the promise Anok had extracted, he was concerned it might be Lord Wosret or one of his assassins. He did not trust the man, and was sure they had not heard the last of him.

Again the pounding, followed by yelling. "Teferi! It's Rami! I know you're in there! Open the door!"

His initial annoyance was washed away by something in the tone of Rami's voice. The thief was desperate, and more than a little afraid.

Teferi stood, walked over, and unbolted the door.

Rami bounced in, his eyes wide, his face sweating. He grabbed Teferi by the arm and pulled. "Come with me!"

"Where!"

Rami's mouth opened, but nothing came out. Finally, he said, "I can't say. I won't say. It's too terrible. You have to see yourself!"

Teferi was used to the little Shemite's nervous temperament, his excitability, his tendency to exaggeration, all high on the traits that annoyed him about the man. Yet none of that explained his current behavior.

"I'll get my weapons." He strapped on his sword and dagger. He considered his bow and quiver for a moment, then decided it was better to travel light.

"Let's go."

He followed Rami at a trot, his longer legs ensuring he had no trouble keeping up with the smaller man as they ran north from the brothel, winding through the narrow streets. As was usual the morning after Festival, it was quiet. Hungover shopkeepers unshuttered their stores late, and even the beggars, those who had survived the night, sat quietly in doorways watching passersby with haunted eyes.

They did not go far, a few streets over, a short run north,

before Rami stopped at the entrance to a narrow alley. He pointed, his hand shaking as he did so. "In there."

Teferi looked at him. "What?"

Rami shook his head. "This is it. I brought you here for old time's sake, but I wash my hands of this business. Some children found it, who knew the Ravens from the street. They saw me walking home from my party, and they told me. I told you." He turned. "My part is done. This is too dangerous. I'm going into hiding. Don't look for me."

Teferi looked after him. His palms sweating, his heart pounded with growing dread. He laughed nervously, telling himself how foolish he would feel later when this was nothing.

He walked slowly into the alley, measuring each short step, like an old man. Step pause, step pause, step-pause.

He smelled rotting garbage. Flies buzzed noisily from mounded piles of filth and rubbish. Then he saw a wall, spattered with blood, smeared with bloody handprints, recording some terrible struggle he could not imagine. Ahead, he saw something on one of the garbage piles, a rumpled something wrapped in white silk, soaked through with black blood.

He took another step forward, his knees nearly buckling. His face froze as a mask of despair. He saw a shock of honey hair, a great, black fly perching on it, rubbing its front legs together, watching him with bulbous, green eyes.

He ran forward, stumbling, falling on his knees in the rotting filth, sending swarms of flies scattering. He took her head in his arms, her skin cold and lifeless, and clutched it to his breast.

"No!" He screamed up at the sky. "By all the gods, please, no!"

21

EXHAUSTED FROM HIS trial, Anok returned to his cell, falling immediately into a deep sleep full of disturbing dreams.

He walked the halls of the Great Temple in golden daylight. The building was clean and pristine. The people, priests, acolytes, elders, followers, all seemed calm and happy, smiling and greeting each other as they passed.

But from the ceiling, everywhere, the snakes hung, heads down, waiting. And as people would pass beneath, the snakes would fall, like descending arrows, the small ones filling their victims with poison, the large ones crushing them in their coils. Yet nobody seemed to see but Anok. He tried to warn them, cried out, but no sound came from his lips, and the people only looked and smiled, oblivious to their fate.

Then, suddenly, he was standing outside the Maze of Set. His father was there, alive and well. Like the others he seemed happy. He smiled at Anok as he took the bolt from the door and swung it open. "I'm going inside," he said.

Anok tried to plead with him, but his words came out as

gibberish. He tried to go to his father and stop him, but his feet would not move. The image of the snake on the back of his hand came to life, rearing up, biting his hand again and again with its tiny, sharp teeth, filling him with its stinging venom.

His father took a step toward the door.

With all his might, Anok willed his voice to work. *"Father!"*

His father stopped and turned back to him, a look of dawning recognition on his face. "Sekhemar?"

Then the greatest son of Set, the mighty snake of the catacombs, struck him out of the darkness, its huge jaws clamping down on his father.

He heard bones crunch. Hot blood spattered across his chest, and the snake pulled his father into the darkness, the door slamming shut behind them, the bar falling back into place.

Suddenly Anok could move. He ran to the door, pulled at the bar, only to find it immovable. Behind the door, he could hear his father's screams.

He pounded on the door with his fists. "Father!" He pounded and pounded until his fists were bloody. Father!

He awoke with a start, the sound of fists pounding on wood echoing in his ears. He did not realize the sound was real until the door smashed open, the latch hanging in splinters.

A guardian stood there, looking somewhat sheepish. "Pardons, acolyte, but you did not answer, and I bring a summons from Lord Ramsa Aál. The matter is urgent."

He sat up in his sleeping bench and nodded. "Let me get a clean robe."

He dressed quickly and followed the guardians. He expected to be led to Ramsa Aál's chambers, but they went instead through the main ceremonial chamber and into the priests' gallery behind the chamber. He saw Ramsa Aál there surrounded by guardians, their weapons drawn against some unseen threat. The priest's hood was thrown back, showing his white hair rumpled and uncombed, his eyes red-tinged and wild.

Then he saw the object of their attention and gasped. Teferi was on the floor, forced to his knees by five guardians who pinned his arms and held him despite his struggles. His face was bruised, and blood tricked from his mouth.

Ramsa Aál glanced up at him. "Acolyte! This foolish savage invaded our temple in broad daylight and was quickly captured. I thought you should see him die, since he kept calling your name." The priest studied Anok's face with interest. "You know this . . . Kushite."

Anok looked at Teferi desperately. Then he nodded to Ramsa Aál. "He is my friend, master. I beg you spare him."

The priest looked at Anok, his head tilting oddly. "An acolyte of Set has no friends, Anok Wati. He has only those masters he obeys, lessers that he commands, and enemies that he crushes." He made a signal to the captain of the guard, who raised his sword and started toward Teferi.

Anok leapt in front of him. "Stop!"

Ramsa Aál looked at him with curiosity. "You have something to say, acolyte?"

Anok thought furiously. How could he save Teferi's life? "I've deceived you, master. I was ashamed. I told you once I desired wealth, power—servants. I was a poor orphan in the slum, but I came into a sum of wealth through my adventures, and in my false pride, I hired this Kushite as a servant. He is even now in my employ. He only comes to bring me a message. He means well, but as you can see"—he glanced sadly at Teferi—"he is stupid."

The priest considered. "A message? You should have left your old life behind when you came here, Anok Wati. An acolyte of Set should be past such concerns."

Anok bowed his head. "You are right, my master. I have acted incorrectly."

"But I am curious now"—he looked at Teferi again—"what matter was important enough for this invasion. Let us at least hear that before we kill him."

Anok started when heard this last, but said nothing. He couldn't give up hope if something could still be salvaged. He stepped up in front of Teferi. They looked at each other for a moment. Then Anok slapped him hard in the face with the back of his hand. "Moron! Idiot! You come here and embarrass me! You are not worth the sliver of silver I pay you each month! Better I should let them take your head and be rid of you!

The anger and rage in Teferi's eyes as he looked up at Anok was real, and it stung him deeply.

Teferi spat a mouthful of blood on the floor at his feet, then looked up again. "Sheriti is dead."

Anok's body and mind froze. It was as though he had been turned into a statue, Teferi's words frozen at the entrance to his mind, where he refused to let them in. Then, finally, his burning lungs reminded him to breathe. He gasped and coughed. "Sheriti?"

Ramsa Aál looked at him with cold interest. "A woman, Anok Wati? Love for a woman weakens the sorcerer's focus. It is well to taste of the flesh. That is why we have whores here. But congress of the heart is for lesser men. You are better off without her."

Anok ignored him, his attention focused on Teferi. "How?"

"Murdered."

"Who? Who did this?"

Teferi shook his head.

Anok took a deep breath. He knew already. "Wosret. It has to be." He felt the rage welling up in him, washing away all other emotion. "The dog must die!"

Ramsa Aál took a step closer. "Rage?" He stepped in front of Anok, studying his face. "Anger is the friend of sorcery. In rage we tap power. In rage we find out who we truly are." He walked around Anok, studying him. "Perhaps something useful can come of this. Do you wish revenge, Anok Wati?"

He nodded. "Yes, master."

Ramsa Aál nodded slowly. "Then go find it, with my

blessing. When you have had your fill, return to us, and we will see what you have learned."

"My servant, master. He is stupid, but he fights well. I may need his help."

The priest glanced down at Teferi, as though he had forgotten him. "Very well. Release him."

The guardians holding Teferi stepped back, throwing him to the floor as they did. He lay sprawled there for a moment before pulling himself slowly to his feet.

Another of the guardians put Teferi's captured swords and dagger on the smooth floor, and kicked them across to him.

"I will need my swords as well, master."

He raised an eyebrow. "Will you? You may be surprised. But if you think so . . ." He looked at the captain of the guardians. "Go to my chambers. In the cupboard near the window, in the bottom, you will find a leather shoulder bag and two swords. Bring them here."

The guardian nodded respectfully. "Yes, lord."

Anok gestured at Teferi to follow, then went after the guardian.

"Anok."

Anok turned back to the priest. "Yes, master?"

"Come back to us, acolyte. To have a talent such as yours extinguished by some street thug . . . It would be . . . unbecoming."

22

ANOK AND TEFERI jogged through the streets of Odji, headed back for the Nest. For a long time, nothing was said. Anok was numb, from shock, from lack of sleep. He should have been physically exhausted as well, but he wasn't. He felt charged, physically invigorated, his wounds practically healed, and he couldn't help but think that the throbbing tingle at his left wrist had much to do with it.

"I'm sorry," said Anok, finally, "about what happened in the temple."

"If you ever touch me like that again, I will beat you until but a spark of life remains in your body."

A voice within him said, *I'd like to see you try,* and it frightened even Anok. *Where had that come from?* He tried to brush past it. "In case you didn't notice, I was saving your life back there. Only by making you seem beneath his notice, could I shake Ramsa Aál of the idea of executing you. I didn't." He choked on his own words. "I didn't want to lose my two best friends in one day."

"The day is young," said Teferi, grimly. "What will we do now?"

"Kill Wosret, painfully, if at all possible."

"That will not be easy."

"I think it can be done," said Anok. "The real trick is staying alive afterwards."

"How will we go in?"

"The front door. They won't be expecting that, especially in broad daylight."

"I've tried that plan once already today. It didn't go well."

"You were one. Now we are two."

"Against a small army of thugs and bodyguards. And none, save us, in all of Odji would be foolish enough to stand against Wosret, no matter how they hate him. Perhaps we should find the barbarian woman. For enough gold, she might aid us."

"There's no time," he said. "We will have to be enough."

"We'll need more weapons then."

"That," said Anok, trotting up to the door of the Nest, "is why we're here."

They unlatched the door, went inside, and headed immediately for their weapons cache.

Anok strapped on an arming sword, to supplement the two shorter ones he already wore on his back. He slipped a pair of good throwing knives and a dagger into his belt. Then, after a moment's thought, he removed the dagger, wrapped it with a piece of papyrus, and tied it with a bit of leather cord. This package he tucked back into his belt with the knives.

Teferi added a backup sword and picked up his powerful Stygian bow and a quiver of arrows.

It was then he heard a muffled sob from somewhere behind him. He turned, and saw that the trapdoor to the brothel was open. He looked at Teferi. "You brought her here?"

Teferi nodded sadly. "Where else?"

Anok licked his dry lips. "I'll be a minute. Wait here."

He climbed the narrow steps up through the trapdoor, and followed the sound back into the living quarters.

Whores watched him from several doorways, their appearance strange to him because they were all fully dressed. He looked back and saw that the front of the brothel was shuttered tight, closed for the mourning he surmised.

He followed the sobs to an open door near the rear of the building. He was passed in the doorway by a young Kushite whore, tears streaming down her face, who ran into another room and slammed the door behind her.

He stepped into the room. Two sturdy chairs had been set up in the middle of the room, a pair of bed rails slipped between them, and blankets draped across the top to form a kind of high bed. On it, a body, so surprisingly small, lay wrapped in silk. The room was heavily perfumed, and incense burners smoked in every corner. But none of it could completely hide the unmistakable smell of death.

A single high-backed chair crouched next to the makeshift bed. On it sat a tall woman, dark-haired, slender, and graceful, that Anok immediately recognized as Kifi, Sheriti's mother. Her long neck arched gracefully, and she carried her head high, as though posing for a portrait. Her features were, as he remembered them, beautiful in a fragile way. He could see a bit of Sheriti's beauty there in her face. She wore a dress of golden-orange silk that covered her from neck to feet, and the light from the windows behind her turned her hair into kind of a halo.

She did not look at him or acknowledge his arrival. She simply stared straight ahead.

Anok stepped up to Sheriti's body, placing his hand gently on her head, stroking her hair. Her skin was ghostly white, save for a purple bruise across one cheek. A silk scarf wrapped around her neck showed traces of soaked-through blood.

He bent down and kissed her cold and lifeless lips.

He was startled when Kifi suddenly spoke. "We live in a world of men," she said, "cruel and violent. It is not a world that is kind to those unfortunate enough to be born women. This place, this brothel, is a kind of fortress of women, under eternal siege by the world of men. Yet they find us useful, and so we survive each assault and live another day."

She looked, Anok noticed for the first time, much older than she had only weeks before. Her eyes were puffy and lined, her lips narrow and drawn.

She continued, "Some say I was wrong to bring a daughter into such a place, and it could be that they were right. But I loved her, and did what I could for her, and looked for a way to give her a better life than I myself have lived. For all my years of struggle, I have achieved some measure now of property and wealth, rare for a woman in Stygia. But of happiness, Sheriti was all I had, all I ever will have.

"So for her, too, I sought some kind of happiness, without success. Until that day when you rescued her from those bandits. I will never forget when you returned her to me in the market. You were filthy and thin, and yet you carried yourself proudly. And I remember the way she clung to your arm, the way she smiled when she described the rescue. She begged me to let you live in the stables under the brothel. Truth be told, she did not have to beg very hard." She turned and looked at him for the first time. "She was proud of what you taught her, the reading and writing, and it brought her great joy. As for the rest, even though I knew her adventures with you were dangerous, you made her happy, something I could never do. For that, I will forever be grateful."

"I know who killed her," he said. "Lord Wosret of the White Scorpions. He killed her because of me."

"He killed her because he is an animal, and that is what animals do. What will you do, Anok Wati?"

"Teferi and I go to find Wosret to extract our revenge. I promise you that he will be dead by nightfall. I will not allow him to live another night with her blood on his hands. That is my pledge to you."

She shook her head sadly. "I ask no such pledge of you,

Anok. No vengeance will bring our Sheriti back to us. No vengeance will make the short days of her life any sweeter or her memories more dear. You cannot save her."

He hung his head. *I couldn't save her. I went away and let her die.* "I do what I must." He turned to leave.

"I don't know why you joined that foul cult, Anok. I know you must have your reasons for that as well. But you cannot save Sheriti, Anok.

"Why don't you see if you can instead save yourself."

THE WHITE SCORPION compound was located on the eastern edge of Odji, at the foot of the hills above the city. It was a large, two-story villa surrounded by gardens and a low wall. In some ways it resembled a newer, shoddier, somewhat-less-secure version of the house where Anok had lived as a child.

Teferi and Anok observed the front of the compound from an alley a short distance away.

The front gates were open, and half a dozen tough-looking men stood just inside those gates. More men patrolled the gardens around the house or stood vigilant on its balconies. He noted that many of them still seemed to be shaking off the effects of their Festival revelries. Some looked asleep on their feet. Others rubbed their heads constantly, as though suffering from throbbing pain. Considering how completely Anok and Teferi were outnumbered, it was a small advantage, but better than none at all.

Anok noted a flat-roofed building across the street from the compound, with a large pile of hay piled up against one wall. Around the corner, a rickety-looking wooden ladder leaned against the wall, just out of sight of the compound. "There," he said, "is your position. You will station yourself there with your bow and pick off the guards as they come out."

"And what will you be doing?"

"I," he said, "will be bait."

"That will be cutting things close."

"You're a good shot. I hope you're not still too angry about my hitting you."

Teferi smiled humorlessly. "We will see."

"I'll move as soon as you're in position."

Teferi nodded and started to leave, then hesitated and turned back. He put out his hand. "Brother."

Anok hesitated a moment, then clasped his arm. "Brother. If I fall, you must finish the task."

He nodded. "If we do not meet again, may our spirits hunt together in the eternal forest." Then he turned and, crouching low so as not to be seen, trotted toward the ladder.

Anok crouched behind a cart across the street, where he could see both Teferi and the gate. The black giant tested the ladder carefully before climbing slowly up, trying each rung before climbing to the next, keeping his feet near the outside so as to put the least strain on the dry-rotted wood. The ladder did not quite reach the top of the wall, but it got him close enough to reach the clay tiles surrounding the edge, and pull himself up and over.

Finally, he was lost to Anok's sight. Anok could only imagine his friend crawling across the rooftop to his position, taking out his bow, nocking the arrow, and while keeping it parallel to the roof so as not to be seen, drawing the mighty Stygian bow, muscles glistening with strain, waiting for the moment.

Anok stood and walked across the dusty street, calm and purposeful in his gait, a smile on his face. His marked wrist itched and burned, and he found himself unconsciously rubbing it. *Give me strength,* he thought. *Give me speed.*

The guards watched as he approached the gate, but there was no sign of recognition. They put their hands on their swords but did not draw. They would be used to seeing a man wearing his swords on his belt. Unless they were sharp, they might not notice the hilts of the two swords peeking occasionally over his shoulders, and he had moved his other knives to the back of his belt. Their eyes were on the arming sword he wore at his waist, and that suited him fine.

"Greetings," he said while he was still well out of sword range. "I've come to have audience with Lord Wosret. I have a proposal that will gain you all much gold."

The men looked at him skeptically. They wore light leather armor on their chests, shoulders, and shins, and dome-shaped helmets that left their faces and ears exposed. They also wore arming swords, though poorly made blades considerably inferior to his own. The man on his left, he noted with interest, leaned with his hand against a stout wooden post that supported the iron gate.

Anok reached casually behind his back. Before leaving the Nest, he had wrapped one of his daggers in a piece of rolled papyrus and tied it with a piece of leather cord. "Let me show you this map." He causally pulled out the disguised dagger and held it over his head. If they had been smarter, they might have noticed the curious, overhand way that he held it.

Another man, wearing a mail shirt, a small chest plate, and a broadsword, appeared a few steps behind the other men. He looked at Anok, and his eyes widened. "Wait," he said. "I know you! You killed—"

Two more steps.

One.

Now!

He slammed the dagger down through the bones of the first man's hand and deep into the wood, pinning him in place. The man screamed and tried to pull it out. He succeeded only in removing the blood-spattered papyrus wrapping so that the blade gleamed in the sun.

Anok stepped back, spinning out of the way just as something buzzed past him like an angry hornet. The arrow appeared buried deep in the second guard's chest, and he staggered back.

He could hear shouts from across the compound as the alarm sounded, and the third man drew his broadsword.

Anok answered with his arming sword in time to deflect a flailing roundhouse by the armored man. An arrow flashed past and rebounded off the chest plate with a loud *thunk,* followed by another that pierced the mail and buried itself in the guard's left arm.

Anok took advantage of the distraction, slashing the side of the man's leg just above the shin armor, then knocking the sword out of his hands as he toppled.

Another dozen men, swords drawn, charged in from either side. But even before they reached him, their numbers were thinned. The arrows fell with uncanny accuracy. To his right a man fell, then to his left, then to his right, then the leading man to his left, slowing the others behind him.

Anok turned to his right. Grabbing the hilt and swinging the sword over his head, he brought it down two-handed into the chest of the first attacker, sidestepping past the man's oncoming blade. His arming sword pierced the first man's leather armor like silk, catching only against the back side of his doublet. He pushed the man away into his followers, letting the large sword fall with him.

Out of the corner of his eye, he saw Teferi leap from the rooftop to the hay pile below. He bounced to his feet and again raised the bow.

Anok drew his two smaller swords just in time to fend off attacks from both directions at once.

Another arrow felled the man to his right.

Someone else slipped past, running for the gate carrying a spear. Three steps past the gate, the spear-carrier fell dead, an arrow in his eye.

Anok dived between the two bodies of attackers into the garden, rolling down a gravel path and coming up next to a waist-high rock that offered him some cover.

He could see Teferi, closer now, walking slowly across the street, pulling off shot after shot, a towering engine of death, though Anok could see his quiver was almost empty.

Anok smiled as he deflected one sword while ducking under the arc of another. *Wosret never thought archers were any good in the city. Perhaps I'll remind him of that before I kill him!*

The rock offered Anok a brief advantage, as he could keep his defenses high and limit the arc of his opponents' swings. But it hindered him as well, and the longer he stood there, the more attackers arrived to challenge him.

Enough!

"For Sheriti!" He stepped from his cover and began to advance toward the house, where he knew Wosret hid.

Anok's blades danced through the air so rapidly they were almost invisible, flashing like the wings of a dragonfly. Outnumbered six to one, he drove them back, taught them fear.

He knew he had never fought better or harder. *Grant me this one battle.*

He pushed the men back. Beyond them, he saw Teferi, surrounded by three armored men, holding his own, but barely. The big Kushite had never been as skilled with the sword as the bow, yet he answered the call. "For Sheriti!"

The big man's strength seemed to double. One attacker's broadsword was knocked from his hands, another's sword hand was crushed against a garden statue by the heavy pommel of Teferi's sword.

But then he misstepped, only a tiny stumble, but it put him off-balance. The remaining attacker swatted his sword aside.

One of Anok's attackers fell, his throat sliced open, and Anok charged over him as he fell, changing his direction to rush to Teferi's aid.

Again the attacker's broadsword swung, knocking the sword from Teferi's hand.

Anok felt a glancing slice across his rib, felt the hot blood running down his side.

The attacker swung his sword around, over his head, plunging it down point first into Teferi's chest.

Anok saw Teferi looking up. He knew what was coming. There was no fear in his eyes.

Anok ran, knowing he would be too slow. The sword fell from his left hand and he stretched out toward Teferi, as though he could somehow reach out and stop the blade.

Desperately, Anok yelled, but instead of a warning, something totally unexpected, even to him, escaped his lips.

As the sword, came down, time seemed to slow for Anok. He saw the point pierce effortlessly into Teferi's ebony breast, set on a clear course for his heart.

And the word came:

"Water!"

The blade, still plunging turned transparent as glass.

Transparent as—*water!*

The sword held its shape for an incalculable moment, then broke into a cascade, a splash that spilled against Teferi's chest and momentarily washed away the blood from his now-open wound.

For a moment, attacker and attacked stared at each other, transfixed with wonder. Then Teferi pulled a long dagger from his belt. It flashed up, plunging hard and deep under the man's armpit.

In little more time than it took for them to beat, one heart was traded for another.

Anok's attention returned to his own situation. He was down to a single, short sword, and still his attackers came.

Teferi was down.

Anok's advantage was gone, his dance of death ended.

And somehow he knew that the spell of water was spent and could not be used again so soon.

They were lost, Sheriti's vengeance undone, unless—

He felt in his heart for the cold fire of rage that still burned there, and he threw open the floodgates that kept it in check.

Vengeance! The snake branded into his arm seemed to burn like a smith's forge.

He plunged the remaining sword into the gut of an attacker and stepped back, leaving it there. He raised his hands.

The nearest guard charged at him, sword high, ready to slice him in half.

"Melt!"

As he'd seen in the temple that day, the man's bones lost all substance. He fell like a loose tapestry, falling helplessly on his own sword. He lay there like a beached jellyfish pierced by a stick.

The other men hesitated, their eyes wide.

He raised his hands.

They bolted and ran.

The way was clear to the house. Teferi forgotten, he marched forward relentlessly.

He marched into the entry hall. Another guard charged at him with a spear.

"Burn!"

The wooden shaft of the spear burst into flame, and the man threw it down. His eyes went wide with horror, then seemed ready to bulge out of his head. His skin began to bubble as the blood boiled in his veins. He fell screaming, a torrent of steam shooting from his mouth.

Onward, Anok marched. Down the hall from which the spearman had come.

A manservant stood at the entrance to the cellar and watched him with alarm. As Anok approached, the man took down a mace from where it hung on the wall and stepped toward him.

He held up his hand. "Bleed!"

The servant stared in horror as blood oozed from under his fingernails, then popped out of his arms and chest like sweat. It ran in rivers from his nose, like tears from his eyes, and he gasped a liquid gasp of blood and fell on the floor dead.

Anok turned slowly.

From a doorway, Wosret looked at him, his eyes wide with terror.

"Anok Wati," he said desperately, "I have no quarrel with you!"

"It wasn't me you killed, was it, Wosret?"

Wosret stepped backward through the door, into a wine cellar, a wall torch revealing rows of wine jars stacked on their sides to the low ceiling.

"I don't know what you're talking about! I killed no one!"

Anok laughed. "Liar! You kill every day! Do you even notice it anymore, or is it like the swatting of a fly?"

"You dare say this? You, who are soaked to the skin with the blood of my guards."

"They attacked me, Wosret. Unlike you, I have a code of honor. I told you to leave me and mine alone, and if you had but honored that pledge—"

"I don't know—"

Anok cut him off with a wave of his hand. *Lies!* He felt the power surging in him, the anger like a roaring flame in his heart. *Wosret had to die.*

As if in answer to his silent request, a tiny white head popped from between two of the jars behind Wosret. Unseen by him, it looked out with blind eyes, tasting the air with its flickering black tongue.

Then another appeared, on the other side of Wosret, nearer the floor, a bit of its body emerging and hanging down in a curl.

Then another.

Then two more.

Then a dozen.

Anok noticed a metal grate near Wosret's left foot that probably led to the sewers. As he did, a wave of squirming white bodies boiled up through it.

Wosret saw them and screamed like a woman, falling back against the stack of wine. In response, dozens of tiny snakes struck, their teeth setting into his flesh like hooks into a fish, their outstretched bodies pulling him tight against the wall of jars, while their fellows rolled up over his feet and up his legs like a wave.

He screamed.

Up they came, waist high, tiny white heads plunging in, emerging streaked with blood, falling away to be replaced by a dozen more squirming fellows.

Out from behind the jars they came by the hundreds, covering his hands, his arms.

Wosret screamed and howled. With a mighty effort, he pulled one arm from the squirming mass behind him, only to hold it before his face and see naked bone as the snakes fell free of his fingers.

Up they came, until they covered his face and plunged into his screaming mouth like water closing over a drowning man.

A line of bloodied white bodies flowed back into the drain.

"What a terrible death," said Anok to himself. Then he threw back his head and laughed.

Still he felt the power in him. It ran through his veins like poison, and he liked it. Still the rage burned for—*what was her name?*

It didn't matter.

He looked up at the stairs and wondered who else was left to kill. Please let there be someone else to kill!

Then—*happy day!*—he heard heavy footsteps coming down the stairs, the scrape of a drawn sword accidentally touching stone.

His lips curled up in a smile. He held up his hands, fingers curled, feeling the power rushing up in him like a mighty tide, building to—*something.*

Oh. This would be very good.

Outside there was thunder, though the sky had been cloudless when he'd entered the house.

He heard someone outside, saw the point of a broadsword slip through the door.

The sky rumbled.

The enemy stepped through—tall—menacing. He had no chance.

Anok opened his mouth and prepared to bring down the fire—

"Anok!"

He took a deep breath, and on the exhale—*"Ligh—"*

"Brother!"

He blinked. *"Teferi?"* He blinked again, at last recognizing his friend, who stood leaning against the doorway, eyes wide, sword hanging from his hand, a blood-soaked wad of yellow silk clutched to his chest.

Teferi's voice had stopped him, but the power still raged, demanded release. He thought of the man whose blood had boiled. That would be nothing compared to the rage that boiled within him.

The snakes were gone. As Teferi watched, Wosret's skeleton, picked clean, fell forward and clattered to the floor.

"Brother, what have you done?"

Anok's body writhed in pain, his fists clenched, his nerves burned. He had called forth the fist of Set, and it would have to fall.

It wanted its target.

It wanted Teferi.

"No!" He gasped. "No!"

But the fist must fall.

He looked at Teferi, who looked back.

To Anok's eternal regret, as he looked into Teferi's eyes, this time there was fear—

He brought down his fists, throwing his hands open, as though trying to shake the blood off onto the ground.

Lightning!

In a blue flash, the world exploded.

FOR GENERATIONS TO come, they would tell of the day.

Of the day when the black cloud appeared out of the empty sky, hovering over the White Scorpions' stronghold, its surface boiling like a cook pot, flashes of lightning playing over its surface, until, in one great stroke, the lightning fell.

Some said there were ten bolts. Some said a hundred. Mostly it was Odji, and lacking the skills to count, they just said "many."

Many onlookers were blind for days, and when sight did return to those stunned witnesses who could still see, nothing remained of the stronghold but a pile of rubble the height of a man's knees. No stick of wood, no rock, no shaft of iron bigger than a man's fist was left.

Of the White Scorpions who defended the place, nothing remained but shards of bone and hunks of blackened meat that the dogs fought over long into the night.

23

RAMI ARRIVED BACK in Odji shortly after dawn the next day. He'd been gambling in a village an hour's walk south of the city, stealing the farmers blind with a little sleight of hand and some loaded dice. He'd managed to slip back to the waterfront before they'd figured him out, stolen a boat, and rowed his way back to the harbor.

Even where he'd been, they'd heard the thunder. The farmers, who were attuned to matters of weather, had been mystified by it, given the clear skies, but Rami had thought only about the take.

It was only after he tied up at the harbor, sold the boat for a handful of silver, and walked up the hill to his old haunts that he heard the whispers. Lord Wosret was dead, they said, the White Scorpions mostly dead, those that survived were scattered, often seeking the mercy of other gang lords.

It was all so strange, so unbelievable. Who could have done such a thing?

He wound his way through the Great Marketplace, overhearing bits of conversation. He was passing a poisoner's booth when he heard something that made him linger. He heard someone say, "—saw it with his own eyes."

He slipped in, pretending to examine a rack of potions, and listened as an old woman talked to the poisoner.

"—his brother was one of the Scorpions assigned to Lord Wosret's guard, and he was wounded early in the battle. He fled across the street, and thus survived to tell the tale. It was Anok Wati!"

The poisoner looked incredulous. "The Raven boy?"

"A grown man now, and from his robe, joined the cult, he did. Brought down the sky on them all, he did." She leaned closer. "Sorcery," she said in a too-loud whisper.

Rami grunted and slipped out of the booth, redoubling his pace, as he headed toward the White Scorpion compound. He knew the way well. It wasn't far beyond the market, at the foot of the closest hills.

He arrived to find crowds of people circling the site. But where the house had once stood, there was nothing. He pushed his way through. Many came to stare and gawk, but nobody seemed brave enough to stand upon the site itself.

Rami pushed on through. It certainly wasn't courage. It was the absolute certainty that whatever horrors had been unleashed there, they had played themselves out. As for the rest, he had to see it for himself.

He marched past the circle of onlookers, across the debris-scattered street and onto the low mound of rubble. Here and there he saw a recognizable object, a broken cup, a spearhead, half of a comb carved from shell. He spotted something glinting in the dirt and reached down to pull out a jeweled stickpin made from silver. Looking around to see if anyone was paying attention, he slipped it into his shoulder bag.

But mostly, he saw pulverized stone and splintered wood, pounded down to almost nothing. He wandered around, kicking his way through the stone, looking for other treasures, and thinking.

First Sheriti—what a waste!—and now this. He'd warned Teferi that no good would come of it. He'd said the same thing when he heard Anok was joining the cult. He knew it was all going bad, which was why he'd contrived an excuse to leave Khemi completely for a while. He'd had no idea *how* bad it could be. Well, his older brother had warned him to stop hanging around with people who had scruples. "Honor is for fools and weaklings," he'd said. Now it was just for the dead.

He reached into his bag, fingering the stickpin. That was a pretty good-sized stone. He wondered if it was an emerald, or just crystal? Perhaps he should be satisfied with his prize, whatever it was, and be on his way from this cursed place.

He wondered what was left at the Nest that might be worth stealing.

He turned around and was about to leave when he heard the noise.

He turned back and listened.

Nothing.

Perhaps he'd just imagined it.

Then he heard it again. A tapping, scraping noise. It was coming from under the rubble!

He wondered if there were rats down there, digging for buried corpses. He knelt trying to hear better.

Then a stone rolled back, and Rami yelped as a large bone poked out of the ground, almost hitting him in the nose, then vanished back into a hole in the ground. Rami fell backward sprawled in the rubble.

He stared at the hole, wondering how far he should run, and how fast, when he heard a voice, muffled by the earth. "Rami! Is that you? It sounded like you."

Oh, gods, the place was haunted.

"Is anybody there?"

It was Anok's restless spirit, come back to haunt him!

"Rami, you ass, get help!"

Cautiously, timidly, Rami crawled over to the hole on hands and knees and, with greatest reluctance, peered inside. The hole was narrow for a foot or so, and then seemed to widen out below. He was startled to see Anok's face looking back at him, illuminated by an eerie bluish glow. "Anok, is it really you?"

Anok glared at him. "Get help! Do you know how hard it is to dig your way out of a cellar using only a gang lord's hipbone?"

24

IT TOOK TWO hours to dig them out.

While they were still digging, Anok sent Rami to find a healer, who was waiting to tend Teferi's wounds as soon as they pulled him from the hole. He'd lost quite a bit of blood, but he was in good spirits, considering there had been plenty of wine to help deaden his pain.

Anok had made them take Teferi out first, then he'd climbed out on his own. As he emerged into the sun, he wiped the blood off the back of the Jewel of the Moon and slipped it into his bag.

While they bandaged Teferi, Rami took advantage of the delay to set up an instant business, selling jugs of wine from the cellar for two gold pieces each, more than twice what they were worth at market.

Anok looked at him counting the coins and shook his head. "Is there anything you won't try to turn a profit on?"

He grinned. "I'd sell tickets to my grandmother's funeral if there was some silver in it."

Yet when Anok took a step closer, Rami suddenly jumped back like a scared rabbit. "Whoa! No! I don't want any of that bad magic rubbing off on me. I did my part here today, but that's it. I'm taking my coin and leaving. I don't want anything else to do with you or the Ravens, which I guess now just means you two, ever again!"

Anok nodded. "I understand."

Rami swept up the last of the coins and threw them into his bag. "See that you do." Then he was gone.

Anok watched him walk away with mixed feelings. They had been more allies than friends. Still, the Ravens were all but gone. If things had gone just a little differently, Rami could have been the last. "At least," he whispered, "you got out of it alive."

He hired two strong men to rig a litter and carry Teferi back to the Nest. They put Teferi into Anok's bed, and he immediately fell asleep.

Anok paid the men. He fell down oh the couch, exhausted. He sat there for a moment, then remembered something. He went to a cupboard, reached into a cup, and took out the ring he'd hidden there. It was the little ring Sheriti had bought him at market. He'd been afraid to take it with him to the temple, afraid the cult would take it from him. But now that seemed unlikely, as long at he never told Ramsa Aál the ring's true significance. He slipped it on his right hand, closed it into a fist, and decided he never wanted to take it off.

He sat back down on the couch. The Mark of Set on his wrist throbbed and was warm to the touch. He pulled back his sleeve and found the skin around it raw and red. Touching it was like touching the rage that still seethed in his heart. Even the death of Wosret, the destruction of the White Scorpions, had not eased it, and he couldn't say why.

He could barely remember what had happened after the guard's sword had struck at Teferi's heart. He had no idea how he had known to do the things he had done, or how, if ever, he could do them again. Was it instinct, some hidden memory, or the promised aid of the lost god Parath?

He didn't know, but for the moment, the mystical energies seemed spent, as was he. He slumped down on the couch and was instantly asleep.

HE AWOKE TO someone moving in the room. He found several of the whores there, cleaning, tending to Teferi. Kifi, Sheriti's mother, sat on the table bench looking at him. "So," she said, "you've had your vengeance?"

He sat up and nodded. "The men who killed Sheriti are dead."

"And how was it?"

He considered the dark powers unleashed, the look of fear on Teferi's face when he'd looked into Anok's eyes. "Bitter," he said. "Bitter, like spoiled wine."

She nodded. "This I have learned from experience," she said. "It is never as sweet as in the imagining." She looked at his acolyte robe, folded on the end of the couch. "You will return to that place?"

He nodded. "I must."

"Then go," she said. "We will nurse Teferi back to health."

He blinked. "Sheriti. Won't there be . . . ?"

She shook her head sadly. "We did not think you would return. She is ashes now. She lives in our memories."

He stood, looked around the Nest one last time. "I may never return to this place."

She nodded. "Your road leads elsewhere. Only Sheriti bound you to this place, and now she is gone."

ANOK RETURNED TO the temple, this time through the front door. The guardians took one look at his robes, no matter how tattered and filthy, and waved him through. A few people took note of his appearance and turned to stare as he passed, but nobody waited to greet him. He wondered if word of the strange events in Odji had even reached the temple, if anyone there even cared?

He had expected that Ramsa Aál would want to talk with him, but the priest was in his chambers, recovering from Festival, Anok was told, and could not be disturbed.

And so, Anok had wound his way down the stairs to his cell. He would sleep a little more, then resume his studies and try to fathom what had happened to him and the meaning of the Mark of Set on his arm.

Somewhere in the hall outside his cell, he passed Dejal, who was headed in the other direction. To his surprise, Dejal smiled at him. "Brother, let me see!" He grabbed Anok's arm, lifted up the sleeve, and examined the snake burned into his wrist. "So, it's true! You've been gifted with the son of Set!" He looked at Anok. "Ramsa Aál is very pleased. But the best part is, he came to me today and thanked me for leading you to the cult! As your star rises, brother, so does mine, and a good thing, too." He grinned. "It is well that you pleased our master at Festival, for I failed him. I had promised him a virgin for his personal sacrifice." He started to walk away, laughing as he did. "It turns out," he said, "she wasn't a virgin at all."

Anok's blood turned to ice, and suddenly he knew why the anger in his heart still burned. Some part of him knew. Some part had always known.

Wosret had not killed Sheriti. Anok had killed the wrong man. It had been Dejal. Only Dejal could have lured Sheriti out onto the streets on Festival night.

How had he done it? he wondered. Had he invoked Anok's name? Had he perhaps told her that Anok had summoned her? Had he told her that he was ill? That he needed her? Wanted her?

He wanted to run after Dejal, make him tell how he had done it, tell every horrible detail so that Anok could make him pay for each one in blood and pain. Make him pay ten times over. A hundred. A thousand.

Kill him! A voice in his head said. *Kill him, kill him, kill him!*

He watched as Dejal reached the end of the corridor, turned, and vanished.

Not yet.

He still had to find his father's killers. He still had to make the Cult of Set pay for all it had done. In fact, now he had one more reason the cult must be destroyed.

He would learn the answers to the questions that tormented him. What secrets did the Scales of Set hold? Where was the third Scale? Did he have a sister, and if so, what had happened to her?

Most importantly, Dejal would pay for what he had done.

But not now.

Not today.

The rage burned in his heart, stronger than ever, and he could feel the mystical energies rebuilding within him as well. He would learn to harness that power, control it, use it. He would make the Cult of Set show him how.

Then he would destroy them, no matter the cost.

Be it his life.

Be it his soul.

Somewhere in the desert, Parath was laughing.

AGE OF CONAN:

ANOK,
HERETIC OF STYGIA

Don't miss the rest of the trilogy:

Coming November 2005
Volume 2:
HERETIC OF SET

Coming December 2005
Volume 3:
THE VENOM OF LUXUR

penguin.com

a285

In the land of Cimmeria, in the time when
Conan was King, a lone warrior battles
his own legacy—and a new legend is born.

AGE OF CONAN:
LEGENDS OF KERN

Volume 1:
BLOOD OF WOLVES
0-441-01292-2

Volume 2:
CIMMERIAN RAGE
0-441-01295-7

Volume 3:
SONGS OF VICTORY
0-441-01310-4

**Available wherever books are sold or at
penguin.com**

a284